THREE STONES OF DESTINY

Paul Vander Loos

Paul Vander Loos

Three Stones of Destiny Copyright © 2018 by Paul Vander Loos. All Rights Reserved.

Cover designed by Michael Lenehan

Paul Vander Loos
Visit my website at https://wizardsword.wordpress.com/

ACKNOWLEDGEMENTS

Thanks to friends and those who have invested in encouraging me in my writing efforts, and those who have bought and read my first book of the *Nine Worlds of Mirrortac* series – *The Wizard's Sword*.

The cover art design is thanks to the talented Michael Lenehan whose work can be found on the DeviantArt site http://mick2006.deviantart.com/ and can be contacted by email on micklenehan2002@yahoo.co.uk

Paul Vander Loos

YIDROGH

The stench was unbearable. Mirrortac's paws were tied behind his back and he was up to his neck in a muddy cold green slime. What a way to treat a distant cousin, although there was the small matter of the theft of these people's most treasured and sacred object – the Werdstone. But he blamed Phantac for that. It was he who set him on another mission without fully explaining the consequences of such an action. It had all seemed an easy matter from the First Heaven where the hard realities of life in the physical plane were mere abstractions. In the here and now, hardly able to move in a bog hole, and nauseous from inhaling the smell of putrid plant matter, the First Heaven was fast fading into dreamland.

The First Heaven – the gateway of the river of light. Mirrortac thought he was dead when he saw Phantac amid the mists and changing rainbow of colours that surrounded him. He had just arrived after leading many souls across from Hopocus where he had triumphed over the sorceress Helok and her partner the sorcerer Krak. Hopocus was a lower astral realm – closest to all physical worlds. Mirrortac's people, the erfins – a furry race of cat-like people – knew Hopocus as the Netherworld where demons and all creatures and beings of darkness dwelt. The erfins had believed that this world was beyond the great mountain that guarded their valley. But it took the courage and curiosity of one erfin to prove they were wrong. Mirrortac never knew then that the journey would eventually lead him through many worlds where he would encounter various races of people and encounter beings of both darkness and light. And all the while, he was inevitably drawn towards Hopocus where he completed the prophesy of an ancient legend wherein it said: *A great warrior will return from the outer world, bringing with him his sacred silver staff – the Staff of Thaum – which he will use to conquer the dark rulers of Hopocus and lead many out of slavery into a new life.*

Phantac had seemed like something out of a dream – his fur was a dazzling white, and yet he was clearly an erfin. His eyes were like brilliant emeralds, glistening. There was an immense air of calm about him as one came to expect of such spiritual beings, but it was no longer just a sense, but a palpable feeling. When he smiled, it lit up his whole being, and his voice was gentle and strangely familiar. Then there was the First Heaven itself.

Mirrortac struggled with the memories of what he had seen. How does anyone describe something that is always changing? Landscapes were in a constant state of flux – transforming themselves from vast fields of yellow flowers to deep valleys dotted with fir trees and populated with herds of strange animals. Feeding into this was an immense river of golden light, glistening with millions of tiny flecks as it tumbled out in a curtain from a gateway above. The river broke up into hundreds of streams that in turn split into hundreds and thousands more. And each one of the streams was tendered by god-like beings who shone with the brilliance of suns, dipping their hands into the golden soup and directing threads of it into the vast reaches of the Greater Sky where suns and worlds bathed in the void.

It was during their discussions surrounded by all this beauty that Phantac revealed this new mission. 'What? Can I naught stay here?' Mirrortac had pleaded.

Then Phantac smiled with that peaceful, patient expression. 'An incarnate being can naught remain in a spiritual domain. This is naught your time to give up the body,' he explained.

'I wish to return then to my kin in the Faug Forest. Have I naught done with my mission? Send another!' he retorted.

'You will have help on this mission, but you are the only one who can begin …' Phantac cut short what he was about to say. 'It is your tasking.'

Mirrortac sighed with resignation as he acknowledged the responsibility.

'Then what task must I do?'

Phantac waved his paws in the air and opened them, revealing three strangely marked stones.

'These three stones are in the likeness of three stones of great power – one for each of the Greater worlds that are linked in energies and empowered from a fourth stone – the crystal.'

Mirrortac's brows lifted. 'Werdstone? The Werd has a stone named for it?'

'Yea, the name of the Werd is lost in your erfin past. You shall soon re-discover this lost past and the great controlling power of this crystal stone. It is filled with the Werd – the secret knowledge of the Ancients. You must take this stone, but you shall face a great enemy who assumes the mask of god to your ancestors. It will be your task to protect the stone and find the other three Stones of Destiny and destroy them with the controlling Werdstone. The three stones are each named Oashu – the keeper stone of the Greater world of Mareos; Einuk – keeper of Nerthule; and Darm – keeper of Thenigmas. Only when you have all three and the Werdstone can they be destroyed, and the task completed.'

'And why must these stones be destroyed? What matter to the worlds are such stones?' Mirrortac queried.

Phantac struggled with the burden of explaining. 'The secret knowledge of the Ancients includes much of the lesser and higher magics that are dangerous in the hands of the unwise. When the stones are destroyed all the spells shall be broken, and all who be enslaved shall be set free. If the spells are not broken, then a great darkness will turn all life into something akin to the Netherworld.'

It was not long after that Mirrortac found himself back in the physical world in a freezing wasteland of bogs and strange moving lights in the sky. He was searching one such bog for any semblance of food when he met the first of this land's inhabitants. It emerged out of the centre of the bog like some slimy monster, carrying on its back a heap of stinking weed. As the creature materialised out of the pond, Mirrortac was struck by its likeness to the tall seeker-erfins of Eol. The male being was large and covered in a thick coarse black fur, with shorter ears than an erfin. A tuft of dark beard fell over his face and his large eyes protruded under a bushy brow. He was particularly muscular and thickset. The two stood facing each other for some time as the being adjusted the weight of the column of weed upon his back, which was half bent over to accommodate it. What happened next was even more startling – the being spoke in his head!

'*The noise of your thinking is confusing, strange one. Who are you and from what clan do you drag yourself here?*' came the gruff remark.

'Wha ... did you speak in my head? How ...? Mirrortac said aloud.

The being grimaced at him as though the question was plain silliness. Then with a sigh he spoke. 'You must hail from an ancient clan. I have naught seen such as you in all my seasons of the veil.'

'*He speaks the tongue of Eol!*' The erfin observed with surprise.

'Eol ... is that your clan, strange one?'

Another surprise. 'I said naught, yet you knew what I thought. Only the spirits do such things!'

The being shrugged. '*Why should it be otherwise? All have the same tongue here. You vex me with your talk of spirits. Go back to your clan. I must return to Erga before the White Veil has claimed Yidrogh.*' At that he turned and began to move away.

'Wait!' Mirrortac shouted. 'My clan is too far from here. I wish to meet your clan. My name is Mirrortac. And yours?'

'*I am a hyfnuk and all our people are roznoghs. Follow if you will, but expect no welcome in Erga.*'

'Perhaps I can help you carry some of that weed. You are bent over with the weight of it,' the erfin suggested.

The hyfnuk halted and swung around, his face suddenly contorted with near rage. '*Help ME carry the hyfnu!*' boomed the voice in the erfin's head. '*You will naught take any of my hyfnu. I will naught be deceived into giving up my task. I would carry more hyfnu for Yidu if there were need. I would crawl upon my belly with the heaviness of it.'*

'You can have your task then, and I mine,' Mirrortac thought back.

The roznogh snorted and sent his thoughts as he started to walk ahead, rolling under the weight of the hyfnu weed. *'It is my task under Yidu to collect the hyfnu. This is every hyfnuk's task. You are not a hyfnuk. What is your task, short one?'*

'My task is sacred. I can say nothing more about it.'

'Sacred. You are a holy one? I don't know of such a holy one.'

The hyfnuk said nothing more and continued to trudge across the icy wastes, his large furry feet scrunching on the cold wet ground. The mud on his body froze quickly, crystallising into lumps that dislodged and fell off as he walked. Mirrortac followed a short distance behind, shivering now despite his thick cover of fur. A burning cold wind stirred up from out of the darkest part of the horizon, hinting strongly of snow. The roznogh weaved his way through the maze of bogs, keeping the stream in close sight to the east. The damp surface of the ground frosted up into shards of ice that crackled under foot while the air blew past with a hollow eerie sound. A swirling darkness gathered and spread out towards them and the air grew colder by the moment. Mirrortac could hear a soft tinkling as the roznogh walked; the sound issuing from pebble anklets that he wore. The roznogh revealed them as protective devices, protected under special invocations.

The roznogh grumbled under his breath as they marched onwards until they came to a junction between the stream and another joining it from the east. They had walked some thousands of erfin-lengths by this time, and the wind had become uncomfortably cold. The roznogh stepped confidently onto the frozen surface of the stream, biting the claws of his feet into the ice as he traversed the narrow section. Mirrortac's passage was less sure, as he wavered on the slippery ice and finally fell with a slap on his buttocks. The hyfnuk continued with no regard for the fate of the clumsy erfin. Mirrortac threw up a mocking glance at the sky: *'What netherworld have you sent me to now, oh calm one!'* and the answer was immediate. *'In the valley you behold the mountain and say, 'I wish to be there upon its summit' but when you reach the summit, you see another mountain, higher than the one you are on, and say, 'I wish to be there', but in order to reach the higher summit you must first walk through the valley again.'*

The erfin scowled as he imagined Phantac's serene smile and the frustrating truth in what he said. He clambered awkwardly across the ice and limped towards the diminishing figure of the roznogh, cursing as he went.

The storm had covered the entire sky by the time Mirrortac had caught up to the roznogh, and the scent of snow lay heavy in the brooding darkness. He squinted anxiously around him, trying to spy any sign of the village or shelter but there were none. He asked if there was much further to go but the roznogh's answer was not so reassuring. '*You are foolish to be here without protection, empty one. You shall have to suffer the white breath of the wind atime. If Yidu looks kindly upon you, you may live long enough to reach clan-place.*'

The erfin groaned. A snowflake, propelled by the strengthening wind, struck him on the cheek, followed by another and another. He shielded his face with his paws as the blizzard began, bombarding them with a barrage of stinging whiteness. The air whistled around them, blanketing the way ahead in a pale rage that dogged their every step. Mirrortac abandoned any formalities, sneaking up close behind the roznogh and clinging blindly to him as the wild storm vent its fury. The roznogh stumbled on, undaunted, the tinkle of his anklets muffled by the roar of the wind. Snow streamed over their bodies and was whipped up into eddies. The erfin was fast becoming numb all over, every step an increasing effort of will. The noise of the storm was all he could hear; the chill like a fire in his bones.

Mirrortac was struggling to concentrate after a few more hundred erfin-lengths. He fought against losing consciousness, but the blizzard was fast winning the battle. He could no longer feel his feet and was totally disoriented. He could hear the roznogh's voice in his head – '*Hold on, Mirrortac. We are nearly at clan-place.*'

Mirrortac blinked into the gloom. The faint outline of a roznogh was silhouetted against the dim light, standing over him where he lay. Gradually he was aware of the muffled sound of the blizzard somewhere beyond his dark surrounds, which seemed very warm and comfortable. Noticing he was awake, the roznogh leant closer, accompanied by the brief tingling of pebble necklaces and circlets.

'*Mirrortac,*' sounded a feminine voice in his head. '*This one be Swarg, maja-tak of the roznogh clan of Erga. You are safe now as this one has placed the Stone-Circles-of-Yidu about your feet and meshed you with a warming spell. Yidu has decided to spare you, strange one. Aghfa carried you within the hyfnu near three thousand steps to bring you here.*'

The erfin stretched himself a little on the bedding of material that he now realised was hyfnu. The odour of the weed filled the small cavern; a snuffling sound from behind him betrayed the presence of the hyfnuk who rested in the corner of the cavern. Mirrortac winced at the terrible ache in his head. He squinted up at Swarg's silhouette.

'*I owe my life to the one named Aghfa. This erfin has travelled through many worlds and seen many weirdness ways. I am amazed how alike to the erfins the roznogh are, and this brings many questions to my mind.*'

Tiny glints of light reflected out of Swarg's eyes as she inclined her head at his words. *'This one knows naught of other worlds beyond Yidrogh yet the paths within your mind are many and long, mooniths more than the reach of this holy maja-tak. There is much about you to discern before you can be allowed to walk among us.'*

The erfin felt a rising sense of fear. He did not want the maja-tak to enter into the privacy of his own thoughts, but he could already feel her mind pressing at the edge of his awareness. Suddenly, there was a sharp snapping sound, or so it seemed, and he was instantly asleep. When he awoke again, the maja-tak was standing across from him, hardly discernible except for the dim outline of shadow. He shivered despite the warmth. Swarg came to him when she noticed he was conscious again.

'Never have I faced such a task as this discerning.' The maja-tak's tone sounded weary. *'Your memories carry visions which I would fear to find in my dreams let alone in the real world. I found many of the ways barred to me though I had spelled you to sleep ... all passages should have been open. You are bound with spells unknown in Yidrogh. You told Aghfa that you were a holy one – a maja-tak such as I, yet I know no such maja-tak of Eol, or the erfins.'*

Swarg appeared to be shivering herself as she bent closer, and it wasn't until her face was almost next to his that he could see that she was afraid. A strained whisper urged up from her throat. 'Who are you, Mirrortac? What do you want with us?'

'Have you heard of the Werdstone?' he asked simply.

Swarg shrugged with surprise. *'Who has not heard of it? It is the Eye of Yidu ... the Most Sacred ... stone of wisdom and knowledge. Why do you ask me such a thing?'*

'I have come to venerate it. News came of it in Eol. I have been searching for it to ask for answers,' the erfin lied.

'Then you have found it, holy warrior. How is it that you came to our clan just at the time when the Maja-tak of the Werd brings the Werdstone to us?' There was an edge of excitement in her tone but fear still lurked in her eyes.

'You are not the only one to discern the truth from others, holy Swarg.'

Swarg stood up stiffly. *'I shall have to discuss your request with the elders. We must know if your intentions are as you say. The Eye of Yidu can see everything.'*

'Then bring me to the stone, so that you will know that I speak the truth.' Mirrortac had no idea about the power of the Werdstone, but whatever the outcome, he had to access it.

Swarg left the room, leaving the erfin alone with the snoring hyfnuk. Mirrortac had drifted off to sleep by the time Swarg had returned, wearing a resigned and solemn expression. When he was awakened, he already guessed at the decision of the elders. Swarg remained standing as she addressed his mind.

'*Mirrortac, holy warrior. I have discussed your request with the elders, and we are of the mind that you hail from clans that left here long before the rise of Yidu, and I could not reassure them that you were naught in league with the renegades. The demons you fought may have possessed you, I can naught be sure. The Eye of Yidu must naught look upon you.*'

Swarg summoned Aghfa, who was now awake. Their minds met but Mirrortac could not 'hear' their thoughts – only see them both look back at him from time to time during their discussion. Swarg then retreated to a corner of the cavern while Aghfa approached and took Mirrortac away into the gallery of caverns. They marched through dark passages, hewn out of the ice and frozen rock. A faint light issued from one of the doorways where Mirrortac could hear the snapping and munching sounds of a group of roznoghs eating. The odour of hyfnu weed and snails was almost overpowering.

They entered the cavern, and immediately Aghfa reached down and grabbed a fistful of hyfnu weed and handed it to the erfin. 'We eat.' Aghfa squatted on the floor and grabbed another fistful for himself. Mirrortac mixed some snails with the weed and cast it into his mouth. The hyfnu tasted very bitter but sufficed.

'*So, Yidu is your god?*' Mirrortac asked feebly.

Aghfa's eyes glowed a pale yellow as he regarded the erfin. '*Yidu is Sky-master, Father of the Werd, empty one,*' he scowled.

'*Indeed, Yidu must look with favour upon you, Aghfa, for saving my life. It be the custom of our clan Eol to grant you a task of your choosing. I stand to do your will,*' Mirrortac offered.

The hyfnuk's tone lightened slightly. '*And so shall it be in Yidrogh! I will choose your task, short one, when I am ready.*'

Mirrortac smiled at the reference to him as the 'short one'. The hyfnuk was tall, yes, but even the other roznoghs were taller than the erfin. Swarg was the shortest he had seen so far – being almost his own size. He saw the chance now to press the roznogh for more information while the mood was right.

'*You must be in good spirits that the Maja-tak of the Werd is coming here with the Werdstone. Do you know much about him? And the stone?*'

'Yea, we see her only in the ninth cycle of the seasons,' Aghfa replied, filling his mouth with another fistful of the weed. '*The Maja-Tak of the Werd carries the knowledge of the Ancients with her in the Eye of Yidu. She is the spell-master of all the clans of Yidrogh. But it be the elders who know more about her and the stone. What does a lowly hyfnuk know?*' He shrugged and showed green teeth in an attempt to smile.

Mirrortac nodded, previously unaware that the maja-tak was a female. He had assumed that one of such import was a male, as was the case in the patriarch ruled society of Eol.

'*Then I must see this Maja-tak of the Werd for myself,*' Mirrortac decided, more as a rhetorical question rather than something consciously projected to the roznogh sitting next to him.

Aghfa's brow rose. '*This I would doubt, short one. You are forbidden to see the stone … much less see its keeper. You must forget such ideas; it will mean more trouble for you.*'

'*I did naught come across the thresholds of many worlds to be turned away when I am in sight of the great Eye of Yidu,*' Mirrortac boasted, slipping the last of the snails down his throat.

Aghfa looked the erfin up and down then continued eating. '*I did not "hear" that,*' he stated before his mind went silent.

The two continued their meal alone with their own thoughts while those around them discussed the newcomer in secret, casting suspicious glances at the erfin. Mothers and their children were segregated to one part of the large cavern. Young roznoghs scampered about the cavern and through the passages, their pebble anklets jingling as they ran. Occasionally one would stop in front of the erfin to giggle at his comparatively small feet and stature. Aghfa growled at them between his teeth, sending them fleeing into the nearby passages.

The Maja-Tak of the Werd had been travelling for 40 days since leaving the Springs of the Werd. The moon of Mogog was just a dim crescent when she had set out for Erga, accompanied by her hyfnuk Evarngar and two clan elders as advisors. They carried with them the sacred Werdstone – the Eye of Yidu – wrapped in animal hide. The Season of the White Veil continued to blanket the world of Yidrogh in layer upon layer of snow, forcing the maja-tak, Ameece, and her entourage to seek shelter with a clan still some way from Erga. There she joined those sleeping, and the only thing that stirred in the storm was the strange lump of stone under the hide, pulsing with a weird faint glow. And above the darkness of the storm, distant suns winked into the eternal vastness of the Greater Sky – unseen eyes gazed out across the distance, watching the gentle roll of the Greater world of Mareos in which erfins, faugs, petros, meretees and roznoghs shared a common sky. Other eyes also gazed up from another world across space, noting the pattern of suns that made up the shape of the warrior. Clever eyes could see the sun of Luma, but the planet of Mareos was unseen, as its feeble reflection could not be detected over such a vast space. In the third world linked by the stones, bitter eyes beheld the struggle between two suns that fought to gain control over this planet. Tongues cursed their many enemies while even the earth underfoot was in disquiet with quaking and fire and burning stones. Yet, as vast as the distance that separated these three planets, the experiences of the peoples in them were woven into the dreams of their far-flung brothers and sisters. In his own sleep, Mirrortac dreamed again of the haunting visions of the planet Nerthule where a great and terrible war brought death and misery to many millions of the people there. There were magical staffs that thundered and spat fire, weird craft that defied the sky and carried eggs of death. All the waters of Nerthule were awash with the stain of blood; the sky with poisonous smoke. The hearts of the women were tortured with sorrow while the leaders of the big clans bickered among one another, arguing over the division of the land while more warriors met their deaths on the battlefront. Nerthule reeled under the darkness while the residents of all the worlds in all the reaches of space wept in their dreams. But the erfin would remember nothing when he woke up. And neither would Ameece, who dreamt of a stranger who would steal the Werdstone from under her nose and later kidnap her along with her servants. And she would let him do it.

It was days later that the clan-master convened a meeting of elders and invited the erfin to sit in witness among them. The clan-master's youthful face betrayed neutrality while the elders were much older, having gained office through their experience over many cycles-of-the-seasons. They had survived many bleak seasons of the White Veil, and in the wrinkled lines around their eyes and faltering stoop of their bearing dwelt such wisdom as only time could deliver. However, age had also made them stubborn to change and fearful of anything new or strange. Their disapproving stares had made their judgment on Mirrortac, who shuffled uncomfortably in his seat of rock.

The clan-master bowed before addressing them.

'Greetings, elders of Erga, and Mirrortac from the lost clan of the erfins. Perhaps you hail from the Uzdree who left Yidrogh in ancient times before Yidu proclaimed his protection. My elders have no concern for a descendant to drag up the dead from their places of forgetfulness. You have told us naught of this sacred purpose of yours, erfin, yet you speak of venerating the Werdstone.'

A sea of eyes turned towards the erfin, glinting in the semi-darkness like moon-drops. Mirrortac breathed out a stream of warm mist that curled away lazily into the gloom.

'We are indeed kin from a common ancestor,' Mirrortac began. *'How fear guides you as it does others. The real purpose of my presence here can only be discussed with she you call the Maja-tak of the Werd. I am sure that she has the right discernment.'*

Some of the elders stifled mock laughter while others brooded in silence. One of the mockers remarked, '*The erfin is clearly a fool who Yidu has sent to test us. When She of the Werd has seen him, she will also see this, and he will be cast out to feed the wooils, if he survives the veil!*'

'*Then why not cast him out now?*' another scowled.

A debate ensued among them until the clan-master raised his hand to stop them. '*I have heard enough!*' he said, peering towards the erfin. '*He may yet have a purpose here, I cannot say for sure. In the meantime, the erfin Mirrortac will take his tasks from Aghfa who holds his favour ... until She of the Werd arrives, then she may decide what to do about him ... be there matters before this council of elders to attend?*'

One of the elders stood to gain attention. '*Yea, the young Fervik has been smote by the demon of darkness. He must be seen safely over to the Otherworld; Swarg can naught undo the demon's spell.*'

'*Then bring Fervik here. This is a sad task that befalls us.*' The clan-master shook his head with dismay.

All heads turned as the sound of whimpering issued from a nearby passage. Two shadowy forms emerged, one of a hyfnuk leading a much shorter form, no more than a child. The young roznogh was shivering and whining piteously while his mind was choked with a terrible fear of foreboding. Mirrortac was touched and wanted to offer some comfort to the child whose eyes gazed ahead unseeing. The hyfnuk led the child by the hand, with his own head bowed, desperately holding back tears that snuck out from his dark eyes. Mirrortac was shocked to realise that the child's sentence to go to the Otherworld meant only death. The clan-master reached out for the child and laid his hands on his head. And for the first time since the erfin's arrival here, uttered out loud, his voice booming and echoing throughout the many passages. Mirrortac was suddenly alert as he recognised the ancient tongue that was the preserve of the priests of Mateote – the tongue known as Maja.

'In yarg du Yidu mun shushim insta lumen duk! – May Yidu light and protect this one's path to the Otherworld!'

The clan-master nodded to the hyfnuk who took Fervik by the hand again and led him to another passage that went to the exterior where the blizzard still raged. The hyfnuk shoved the child roughly into the passage then turned before half running to a corner where he wept without solace. The child now was standing alone inside the passage, shaking and wailing before obeying the will of the clan. He stepped forward, his thin layer of fur bristling against the frigid air that whistled up the passage.

Mirrortac could stand no more. He leapt up, pleading. 'Why must this child die?' His voice startled the assembly of elders. They pierced him with cursing eyes, but his concerns were with the child. He stood and started towards the passage.

'*Sit down erfin!*' The clan-master registered pain in Mirrortac's head. '*There is nothing can be done. The child has been smote with the demon of darkness and carries it with him ... we cannot allow him to desecrate us. His spirit will be safe with Yidu and will again enter a clean body.'*

Mirrortac continued his plea as he edged towards the passage. *'Just allow me to speak with the child ... comfort him ... perhaps I may find the demon and convince it to release the child from the darkness.'*

The hyfnuk, who had brought the child, now lifted his head and saw a glimmer of hope in the erfin's words. *'Oh clan-master, will it do any harm if the stranger wishes to comfort the child?'*

The clan-master's face was a grim mask. He considered first the stern-faced elders then the pitiful hyfnuk. The child had kept walking and was now approaching the opening of the numbing blizzard. The clan-master's gaze finally rested upon the erfin. 'Do what you will. Speak with the demon if that be your power but beware that it does not choose you to trade the darkness. I will not hesitate to send you out into the storm with Yidu's blessing.'

Mirrortac was moving before the roznogh had finished speaking. He ran up the passage, hoping to catch the child before the blizzard claimed him. He caught up with the child and took Fervik's hand in his own. The small body shuddered, and its head revolved in the general direction of the warmth radiating out of the erfin's body. He was uncertain as to why he had been stopped or who it was who stopped him. The roznogh gingerly reached out his free hand to touch the erfin's chest, feeling the shaggy green fur. His tiny mind spoke.

'Who are you? Has Yidu found me already? Am I dead and know naught of it?' Fervik enquired, squinting vainly to see.

Mirrortac's heart was breaking. *'Nay,'* his thoughts said, quietly. *'It be naught Yidu who takes your hand. I am a stranger here, but I have some knowledge of those places where spirits dwell. I know you naught, Fervik, but I regard you as I would my own child. If only the great calm one who calls himself Light of the World could bring the light back to your eyes. If there be a demon here, let it answer to the anointed one and return to the Netherworld ... to trouble us no more.'*

He looked upon the still sightless eyes of the child and sighed. *'Blessings upon you little one,'* he said as he turned with a sigh back up the passage, tears streaming down his cheeks. He stumbled out of the passage, defeated and feeling utterly foolish. The child stood motionless where Mirrortac had left him, his young mind grasping at the weirdness of this stranger's words.

Mirrortac returned to his place among the elders. The clan-master would not meet his eyes while the hyfnuk fell shattered over a rock. After a tense silence, the clan-master calmly said: *'Be there any other matters? Otherwise, I think we have seen enough this meeting.'* The question was almost rhetorical.

The elders were already rising when there was a sudden scream from out of the passage. The hyfnuk rose up and twisted around urgently. Mirrortac felt his heart jump and leaped up from his seat. The hyfnuk approached the passage and was peering inside when he turned around, his face transformed with awe. 'Great blessings of Yidu!' he proclaimed. There was a rush of excitement in the assembly when they saw a small body rush out of the passage and embrace the hyfnuk. 'The demon has released Fervik from the darkness! I can see again! I can see again!' he shouted at the top of his voice.

Mirrortac grinned. 'Praise the Light of the World!' he yelled. And the elders too were amazed. 'Yea, praise to Yidu, the light of the world!' one proclaimed. But the erfin's actions had done nothing to allay the elders' suspicions about him. They now were uncertain whether he wasn't a demon himself or an agent from Yidu come to test them. Mirrortac could only resign himself to the facts as the roznogh people saw them. However, he had won a friend in Fervik who went about telling everyone of his power over the demon of darkness. Curious young roznoghs followed the erfin, prodding him for stories of his adventures, but sceptical parents removed them. Only Fervik was not discouraged, and was allowed to accompany Mirrortac wherever he went, plying him with many questions. Soon the child was privy to many things that the erfin had told no-one else, and they became inseparable companions. Mirrortac found comfort in telling a wide-eyed young roznogh about the many worlds he had encountered, and in turn learning about life in this icy wasteland.

Time moved immeasurably slowly in the tedium of the blizzard as it raged in the long night of Yidrogh. Hyfnu weed supplies were rationed and more time was spent merely sleeping the time away. Still a long distance away, across the snow-swept fens there struggled a small band of roznoghs, protected within a shield of magical light. Mirrortac had slept for three days when the echo of shouting inside his head, and the rough shaking of large paws, aroused him. He raised a heavy eyelid to spy Aghfa peering down at him with those bulging eyes of his. *'Awake, short one! I have a task for you.'*

The erfin tried to ignore him but the shouting in his head would not stop. He curled over the floor, stretching and yawning while he forced open his eyes and shook the fuzziness from his mind. The floor was cold and uninviting, his feet protesting as he tried to stand. He smirked at the hyfnuk.

'The seasons are a burden to this body. What is this task that you would have me do,' he muttered.

'The White Veil has lifted,' Aghfa said. *'We must gather hyfnu. There is naught time to waste. The Veil may return at any moment.'*

The erfin regarded the hyfnuk with incredulity. *'How can we gather hyfnu? The stone numbness covers all!'*

The slightest hint of a smile crept over the hyfnuk's face. '*You are such a silly one, shorty! Aghfa and his fellow hyfnuks are strong; we will break the stone numbness with our feet. All you need do is help us carry it.*'

Mirrortac chuckled. '*So, now I can help you carry your burden! You who would crawl on your belly to carry this burden for Yidu!*'

Aghfa frowned in mock annoyance. '*You will not be carrying my burden, short one. I will carry three or more to the one you carry!*' The hyfnuk puffed up his chest and strutted out of the sleeping chamber that the roznoghs called a hollok.

Mirrortac shuffled in behind him and gave the hyfnuk a friendly slap on the shoulder. '*And how strong would your feet be to climb a mountain?*' he challenged.

Aghfa looked at him uncertainly. '*Tell me first ... what is this mountain?*'

'*Like a very high hill ... up as far as you can see.*'

Aghfa threw back his head and laughed. '*Hah! I would run up the mountain and back down before you had come half way.*'

Mirrortac's face lit up. '*I should like to see such a thing.*'

The two continued to challenge each other as they made their way through the passages and past holloks where roznoghs slept on – some not to awaken again until the long Season of the White Veil had come to an end, and the sun of Luma had returned to the sky. Swarg was waiting for them on the outside. There were also other hyfnuks who had all gathered in a huddle around the maja-tak. She wandered among them, stooping to touch their anklets while she whispered incantations of protection. When it came to Mirrortac's turn, she looked up at him with a mixture of fear and curiosity. The maja-tak of Erga nodded to him without any exchange of words.

Outside, a faint twilight illumined a sky that was troubled with the march of more snow clouds from the north. A thick mantle of snow covered the landscape, slowing their progress as they sunk almost up to their thighs in places. With no time to lose, the hyfnuks forged ahead with determination, their faces now set grim like stone. Mirrortac had not forgotten the importance of tasks, and shed the jovial banter with Aghfa, his mind focused on the job at hand. Despite the difficulty, they managed to travel some distance, passing up several smaller bogs until they came to the one that they finally selected. Aghfa ordered the erfin to wait on the shore while he and the other hyfnuks proceeded onto the ice-covered pond. He watched them search the ice for the telltale faults that the many seasons of experience had taught them to find. Finally, they each took up their positions, flexing muscles and joining minds in the one purpose. Tension hung momentarily before the hyfnuks heaved their huge bodies into the air to come down in a crash upon the ice in a single tremendous thrust. The surface of the pond thundered with the combined weight and strength of 20 hyfnuks but would not yield. Again, the hyfnuks steeled themselves, filling up their lungs until their chests were expanded tight. Then, with a deep-throated roar, they leapt up and thundered back down onto the ice. Again, they repeated their efforts, and again there was the roar and the horrible thud of their feet as they simultaneously hit the ice. This went on for several more attempts until there was a sharp crack as the ice splintered and separated. They were left wobbling on chunks of ice, which they quickly cleared until there was an area of clear freezing water large enough for them to dive in. Soon they were all disappearing into the water and emerging with large bundles of stinking hyfnu weed.

Aghfa emerged dripping in the mud of the bog and carrying a small load of hyfnu. He grinned wickedly at the erfin as he transferred the load onto Mirrortac's shoulders. The erfin almost collapsed with the weight of it even though it was nothing to the hyfnuk. Aghfa then dived under the water again to return with a larger load for himself. The other hyfnuks were soon all loaded up and preparing to return to Erga. Fervik's father, Shuth, was also among them. He caught the eye of the erfin for a moment and nodded silent thanks for saving his son's sight and life. Mirrortac smiled and nodded as best he could under the weight of the stinking weed, which dripped black mud all over his green fur. A light fall of snow had begun but the chill of the wind was lessened by the warming spell. Nevertheless, Mirrortac longed for the warmth of Eol and dry earth under his feet.

A swirling mist drifted across the party as they moved slowly through the snow. Mirrortac squinted ahead, losing sight of them for a few moments as the mist thickened around them. His back ached under the load. There was something ominous about the mist and the sudden feeling of wariness that had crept into all their minds. In the next short moments, the hyfnuks abruptly dropped their loads and scattered, warning 'Wooil! Wooil!' They ducked for cover, raising their heads only a little to watch anxiously into the mist-covered ground ahead. Mirrortac was flung roughly into the snow as one of the hyfnuks fell in beside him.

The erfin did not have to wait long before seeing the cause of this reaction. It appeared at first like a small hill of snow moving towards them, but as it neared, he could see its four beady dots of eyes, which glanced furtively from side to side. The wooil thrust up its shaggy white head and sniffed the air. Puffs of mist blew out of its jaws that were armed with a dangerous set of slim pointed teeth. The creature mooed and grunted, stamping and heaving with hunger and impatience. When it saw the abandoned piles of weed it sauntered over to them and sniffed at them with interested grunts. They all watched from a safe distance, a wary head raised here and there as one or another gained courage. While they were clearly afraid, there was also another element in play – the racing blood and keen-eyed mark of the hunter.

Muscles steeled as the wooil worried at the hyfnu, maddened by the scent of roznoghs. It pawed the weed with its heavy set front feet, tearing out pieces and tossing them in a litter around it. The wooil's body was huge and white and furry like a bilk (six-legged creature of the desert land of Petrosium), sloping up above its thick neck in powerful shoulders then falling back into smaller yet still powerful hindquarters. It was too preoccupied with the hyfnu at this stage to notice the cautious approach of the hyfnuks who had surrounded it and were focused on a combined attack. Mirrortac shivered with awe.

Without warning they leapt up and charged the beast. Startled and stirred into a fury by the attack, the beast reared up on its hind legs, dwarfing the hyfnuks as it stretched up to its three erfin-lengths in height above them. The wooil's deep snarling growl shook the air, mingling with the wild shouts of the hyfnuks who were charging at its belly and jumping on its back. They punched into it with their big fists and tore into its short fur with able claws. This angered it even more, provoking it into a rage as it tried to shake off its attackers. It rested its beady glare onto one of the hyfnuks, and with a lethal swing of its powerful paw, clipped the top of the hyfnuk's head as he tried to duck out of the way. Lumps of his fur sheared away, exposing raw pink skin. Shuth was behind the wooil when it kicked him squarely in the chest, winding him severely and throwing him into an untidy heap. Aghfa charged into the lower belly of the beast, putting his whole weight into the thrust. The wooil let out a sharp bellow of pain, falling in among the hyfnuks below it and lashing out at them with his paws. Large tufts of fur and flesh flew into the air. Aghfa slipped out from under the beast a moment before the huge belly came down, pinning one of the other hyfnuks. In a killing frenzy, the wooil sunk its teeth into the hyfnuk's neck, and with one quick flick of its head, tore open his throat. Blood gushed out in a fountain. A hyfnuk leapt up behind the beast and started bashing his fists into its head. Other hyfnuks quickly joined in the melee, crowding over the wooil and beating at it until their knuckles started to bleed. The wooil tried to shake them off, snapping at them but without effect. Finally, it satisfied itself with gorging on the body of the dead hyfnuk. It disemboweled the corpse in front of them all and buried its head deep into the warm innards. A distraught friend of the deceased tried to retrieve the body but the wooil back-handed him with a simple sweep of its front paw, instantly breaking his jaw.

Alarmed at the carnage, Mirrortac aroused himself and braved forward. The hyfnuks continued screaming and beating the beast with their fists while the wooil ravaged the body – its snout moist with fresh warm blood. Hunger obsessed its whole purpose and it stopped from its feeding only to snap at another hyfnuk. Still, the hyfnuks clung on like fierce insects, determined to bring it down. The injured limped about or lay on the snow, nursing bruises, wounds and broken bones. As though mirroring the mood of the scene, the wind strengthened, sweeping up clouds of snow which stung like arrows. Mirrortac halted within a short distance of the wooil, glancing at Shuth who was resting on the snow nearby. The hyfnuk winced with every breath he took, and his chest was out of shape, as though a hole had been made in his ribs. Shuth's eyes regarded the erfin with concern. *'Do naught challenge the wooil, Mirrortac. You will be dead in an instant.'*

Mirrortac considered the wooil and turned his mind to Shuth. *'I will naught resist this beast, friend. But I must put an end to this madness. I will try and speak with its essence.'*

Shuth's eyes darkened as he looked upon the erfin with uncertainty. *'You are weirdness, erfin. Take care!'*

Mirrortac breathed in deeply a few times before resting his gaze on the wooil. He emptied his mind of stray thoughts and opened to the essence before him. Then in the silent vacuum of some greater mind, he made contact.

'Spirit of wooil, still the beast's hunger!' he commanded.

The beast broke off from its eating to look up. Its head turned towards the erfin and eyes met. The wooil had two eyes placed normally, and another two placed together on its forehead – their bead-dark lustre winked as the beast paused, somehow distracted. The hyfnuks froze as they realised something strange was happening.

'Who speaks to the spirit of wooil?' replied the beast's essence. *'The wooil is hungry. Many are the ways and long are the days since this creature has eaten. The beast wishes to survive – flesh to flesh, soul to soul.'*

'To each is given its portion. The weaker flesh yields to the stronger. One flesh dies so another may live. The wooil has earned the flesh it feeds upon. If I can stop the attack on the beast, will it go with the blessings of our Master?'

The wooil shook its head. *'You ask much of the spirit of wooil. I cannot grant this request but to my brother I will give the body of this beast as the spirit can find another, and the balance will be made up at another time, another place. You must strike it behind the ear to kill the wooil. It knows only survival. Do not ask of it something that is beyond its design.'*

Mirrortac blinked as the wooil returned its attention to the corpse. It buried its head into the torso and continued to gorge itself on entrails. The hyfnuks also resumed their attack while Mirrortac approached slowly from behind, careful to stay out of reach of the lethal paws. Spying the erfin, Aghfa grinned. *'Come to offer your own fists, short one!'* he mocked. *'Save your strength. Only hyfnuks can kill such a beast as the wooil!'*

Mirrortac showed no emotion as he slipped in near the animal's head, and with an abrupt blow of his fist, struck the wooil behind the ear. The beast suddenly jerked into spasm and collapsed. The thumping and cries of the hyfnuks continued on for a few moments before they all realised that the creature was dead. Shuth, who had been watching the erfin the whole time, looked up at him with amazement. *'I saw him, the erfin Mirrortac; with one fist he killed the wooil!'*

There was stunned silence as the hyfnuks regarded the erfin in a new light. Aghfa was repentant. *'If these eyes had not seen it, I would call it a tale to tell the little ones,'* he said.

All nodded their agreement, and were in awe of the mysterious erfin, when a rise in the wind reminded them of their need to return to Erga before the storm was again upon them. Aghfa and several others put their shoulders under the body of the wooil and lifted it up. Shuth rose painfully to walk behind, his breath rasping with his every step. Those of the injured who could still walk, limped in behind while the less fortunate were left in the snow to die. Those four peered skyward to offer their souls into the protection of their god, Yidu. Mirrortac sighed as he regarded the helpless kin.

'Why leave your brothers to die. Will nobody help me carry them back to their holloks?' he asked.

The mind of Shuth replied: *'There are naught spells to mend broken legs and naught demons to command. A roznogh without legs is a burden to the clan, and none of us wishes to be useless. Even your great spells could naught fix bones. It is Yidu's will.'*

A wave of despair swept over the erfin as he considered the harshness of this cold desolate place. He thought of how he had to leave his own friend Fillytac to the mistress of death and start out on a journey from which he would never return. And now, as he watched the resignation on the faces of the four left behind, he thought of the slow painful death that awaited them as they lay at the mercy of the elements. His stomach knotted with frustration as he looked ahead at the diminishing party. *'I can naught leave you to this!'* he said, gesturing up at the storm. He strolled back to the prostrate forms and squatted beside each one to examine their injuries – snapped portions of bone protruding through flesh, broken jaws, legs bent back at unnatural angles. It was useless. He sensed their pain as they lay quietly, enduring without complaint. Eyes followed him with incomprehension as he shoveled up handfuls of snow and piled it on their wounds and broken bones. They could only shake their heads at him and say: *'Stranger, leave us at peace with Yidu. Can you naught see that your efforts are in vain.'*

And he knew they were right.

The erfin padded off a short distance before he collapsed to his knees. Fresh snow began to fall as the grey clouds swept over all of Yidrogh. 'What cruelty be upon this world!' he cried, shedding frozen tears down aging cheeks. 'What despair abandons these to this numbness!'

Mirrortac peered up through his distress to address the heavens above him. *'You, the greater Master. If we are truly of the one essence, then surely I might be so bold as to ask that these ones be made whole again. Must they go by this gateway?'*

The storm seemed to flush up in anger at him. A gust of wind chastised his fur and stirred up the snow into frenzy. Then with a flash of insight, he had the answer – if all is of the one essence, then all he needed to do was believe and it would be done.

So, with a flourish of drama, he stood up and shouted: 'In the name of the Master of all masters, the one who is Creator of all, I command that these hyfnuks be made whole again!'

He felt a great surge of heat fill up his paws, and immediately trudged back to where the four hyfnuks lay. Although no words had formed in his head, he knew what to do. Without hesitation, he placed his paws over the snow-covered wounds. His fingers tingled as the heat surged out of his paws and into the wounded hyfnuks, melting the snow into a mist, and melding bone and flesh into healthy tissue once more. The hyfnuks could not believe what was happening. Pain left them and they all stood up in their turn after the erfin had finished with them. Mirrortac's tears of despair turned into tears of joy as he fully realised that he was only limited by his own perception of what he could do. But for the hyfnuks, the erfin had risen in status to god, and they began worshipping him and fussing. 'Praise to the master!' they all cried. 'Yidu has come among us!'

Mirrortac backed away in embarrassment. '*Nay, do naught praise me. It be the greater Master who works this wonderness through me. Do naught mistake me for Yidu. You must never call me that or show such praise to me,*' he insisted.

Still bewildered and amazed, the hyfnuks took the erfin upon their shoulders. '*Then we grant you full service for all the seasons of your life ahead and shall carry you to Erga upon our strong shoulders!*' one of them said, and they all nodded, grinning widely.

Mirrortac smiled back, warmly. 'As you wish. I am no burden to hyfnuks.'

Soon, the thoughts of the four hyfnuks were conveyed to those carrying the wooil carcass, and there was much amazement and consternation among them. The four carried the erfin high, venturing every now and then to touch their healed wounds and limbs. Mirrortac soaked up the attention. This may give him the edge to gain the Werdstone. The elders must surely lend him their support now.

After a long march, they came within sight of the holloks of Erga, defined by a series of small hills. A small group of children and mothers were waiting, and with them was the slimmer form of the clan-master, who was grim-faced and clearly troubled. Mirrortac couldn't believe that after all that had happened that the clan-master would still be opposed to him. But for now he had no care for stubborn roznoghs. His grin of elation only served to deepen the frown on the clan-master's brow, and he shot the erfin a dark glance. '*You! Erfin! Meet me in my hollok now!*'

Mirrortac indicated to the hyfnuks to put him down before he followed the clan-master into the nearest opening into the hillside. There was only the clan-master and himself in the hollok. The clan-master stroked his bearded chin worriedly, sighing and regarding the erfin with muddy eyes. The elders had gone to their holloks to sleep out the remainder of the long night of the White Veil. Mirrortac was still euphoric and indifferent to the clan-master.

'*It be fortunate that the elders are sleeping and have naught heard of these deeds of yours, erfin,*' he began. '*They would accuse you of working with the power of demons though you be illumined with the blue sheath of Yidu. I know naught of what gods gave you these great spells, but it be best that you use them naught while you stand in Yidrogh. Let them die who must die. It be all our hopes that Yidu naught be angered at this. It be his decree that these hyfnuks go to the Otherworld. What shall be his mood when he sees that their souls did arrive naught?*'

Mirrortac shrugged. '*If it was Yidu's decree for them to die, then this erfin would surely be useless against the might of a god. Nay, I am sure I acted on the master's wishes.*'

The clan-master leaned forward, menacing. '*Who are you to know what the Sky-master wishes? Would you dare boast to me that you have special favour with Yidu? How you test me and vex me deeply. I must command you to cease the practice of these spells while under the protection of Erga, or I naught can promise that the decision of the elders will support a further stay here.*'

A sly inkling of a smile crept over the erfin's face as he replied. '*You shall have your wishes. There naught will be any spell come from me.*'

The clan-master's eyes narrowed. '*I see trickery in this! Whatever name you give your spells, be warned that if I hear of any more of these wonders of yours, you will be cast out into the numbness and left to the whims of Yidu.*'

Mirrortac sighed as his former euphoria dissolved. '*Clan-master of Erga. I can naught allow ones to die when there be hope that they may live. I tell you that I will practise naught of spells because these wonders be naught conjured or trickery. It be within each one of us to join with the Oneness that goes beyond all things. All you need do is believe and it be so.*'

'*Oneness? Your speech is full of the riddles of other worlds. This is too much for us. Challenge naught with these vexations, Mirrortac!*' the clan-master urged, almost pleading.

The erfin understood the fear. He had been as dubious himself when faced with the truths of other worlds, and especially the greater Truth. '*You are a strong leader, clan-master of Erga. As long as my feet are in Erga, I will bring naught further trials to you with these "spells" as you call them. But it be with ill-ease that I comply.*'

Within the semi-darkness of the hollok, the begrudged promise of the erfin was accepted. The clan-master's undirected thoughts hung pregnant in the musty air. Both knew that the erfin must leave Erga. Sooner or later, the clan elders would hear of the erfin's deeds and a worse fate would be dealt him. Thus, the four hyfnuks would be sworn to secrecy while the death of the wooil would be credited to the might of the hyfnuks. The clan-master rose and led Mirrortac back to his own hollok. He looked the erfin up and down, and took the erfin's paw, studying it. Finally, he said, '*You killed a wooil with that!*' He shrugged the paw away and left, shaking his head, a hint of a smile tugging at his mouth. Nothing more was said of Mirrortac's abilities.

Mirrortac rose up out of his deep sleep like clods of pond scum that lazily lifted off the bottom to the surface. The sound of roznogh activity filled the passages of Erga as preparations began for the feast of the wooil. His mind filled with excited thoughts of celebration, the return of the sun Luma to the skies over Yidrogh, and the imminent arrival of the Maja-tak of the Werd. It took a few moments to re-orient himself as he arose groggily and stumbled about. *'You awake then, master Mirrortac!'* came a voice from the entrance of the hollok. A hyfnuk's head appeared from around a corner, and Mirrortac recognised the scar on the hyfnuk's face. He was one of those that had been healed, and in return had sworn life-long service to the erfin.

'We shall save the best meat for our erfin,' the hyfnuk continued. *'It will be a fine feast to welcome the return of Luma, the bright one!'*

The hyfnuk abruptly disappeared with only the 'cluth cluth' of his heavy feet echoing down the long passage. Mirrortac yawned and stretched but winced as he attempted to stand up straight. The cold was no friend to an ageing body, and he was forced to favour his left leg when he walked. He lumbered wearily into the passage, joining others as they made their way to the feasting area. The floor was wet, and the walls seeped with thousands of icy droplets. Child roznoghs splashed and danced through the many puddles, easily escaping the clutches of their frustrated parents. Daylight filtered through in some places, creating glaring reflections that forced everyone to squint as the glare struck their unaccustomed eyes.

There were many already assembled in the feasting area when the erfin arrived. Elders would not look at him while the clan-master gave him a stiff nod, retaining a grim face and formal bearing. The four healed hyfnuks appeared from out of the crowd to fuss over the erfin, plying him with hyfnu weed and clearing a way for him to move through the crowd and sit down at a place they had reserved for him. The clan-elders looked down their noses at this, swapping thoughts on this unseemly display of servitude to this suspicious stranger. Mirrortac felt the sting of their minds yet could not tell what they were thinking to each other. Their thoughts were shut off from him.

A space was cleared in the centre of the cave where the younglings busied themselves carrying in large chunks of cured wooil meat and arranging them into a mound. Everyone was licking their lips at the sight of the meat and started to debate over the best pieces. Mirrortac watched the mound grow as more and more armfuls of meat were brought in from through a hole in the wall where he could hear the muffled thud of the cutting task. Fervik appeared with meat spilling from his arms as he proudly mounted the mound and placed the chunks at the top. The child paused for a few moments to admire the juicy steaks before walking off with a self-satisfied grin.

Mirrortac's heart lifted. '*It gladdens me to see you, Fervik. I trust you had many happy dreams,*' he thought out to him.

Fervik halted and swung around to peer into the crowd, searching for the erfin's face. Mirrortac lifted a paw high then stood up so Fervik would catch sight of him. Fervik brightened while his grin broadened as he saw his benefactor.

'*It gladdens me to SEE you, too, my dear brother! I shall finish this then come eat with you.*'

Fervik kicked up his heels and ran into the hole in the wall. He soon emerged with such a large load of wooil meat that his head was obscured. '*This will be my last, then my task is complete!*' he said.

One of the hyfnuks leaned towards Mirrortac to offer him some hyfnu. '*This will seal your belly while we wait for the wooil meat.*'

He accepted it and chewed at a small stem of weed. They exchanged pleasantries until Fervik joined them, bundling himself immediately at the feet of the erfin, still grinning widely. Mirrortac stroked Fervik's head and was reminded of his children now in the Faug Forest where he was forced to leave them. He realised with an ache that he was missing them growing up. Would he ever see them again? Fervik noticed the erfin's solemn expression and touched him tenderly. '*Be you of heart to enjoy the wooil meat with me?*'

Mirrortac glanced down at the young face and absently toyed with the fur on his cheek. '*The seasons begin to weigh on this erfin, young one. My thoughts stray to my home world and of kin seen naught for the many watches of Luma.*'

Fervik snuggled his head into the erfin's chest in unspoken sympathy. Around them, the excited activity of roznoghs greeting one another had died down as all attention centred on another darker hole in the wall – an entrance at the far side of the cave where the maja-tak of Erga would soon emerge.

'*Welcome roznoghs of Erga!*' Swarg's thoughts preceded her entrance.

'*Welcome from the darkness of the Season of the White Veil! Let us now celebrate the return of the daughter of Yidu, Luma, who shines her light over all of Yidrogh. She has again conquered the Veil of Darkness!*'

Swarg appeared draped in a cape of wooil while her many pebble necklaces, circlets and anklets tinkled noisily as she walked. In her hand she grasped the leg bone of a wooil as a staff. Her grey erfin-like fur was neatly groomed. She approached the mound of meat, straightened her short but full height, surveyed the crowd and spoke in the sacred tongue of maja. Her voice was harsh and broken, strange in a voiceless place.

'Yidu willim lumen sa tuppung Luma!' She touched the mound with the knob of the bone then bent down and picked up a piece of meat. Lifting it up to the crowd, she smiled and cast it into her mouth.

The signal to eat had been made; roznoghs from all parts of the hollok rose and converged on the mound, and soon were throwing chunks of wooil down their throats with abandon. Mirrortac was about to rise when one of the hyfnuks forestalled him. '*You must stay seated Master Mirrortac. We will bring you the best parts of meat ... all you can eat.*' He left promptly, muscling his way through the throng until he and the others too had reached the mound, and they scrambled to be the first to bring him the choicest cuts. Fervik meanwhile had returned with enough for himself, but noticing that the erfin had nothing yet, chose to give him the largest piece. Mirrortac nodded as he bit off a piece and tasted it. Fervik watched as the erfin showed his approval with satisfied grunts. The hyfnuks returned, all carrying a share of meat which they dropped at the erfin's feet. Mirrortac needed no further encouragement. The flesh had a strong and agreeable flavour which was hard to resist. Fervik teased his pieces of meat with exploring claws, tearing it this way and that, and examining it before he chose to eat it. His mother, who was keeping a close eye on him from among the crowd, chided him for playing with his food. Fervik grunted his defiance, screwing up his face before he relented to swallow the meat whole. Mirrortac chuckled softly and patted the young roznogh with affection.

'*You are as I was in my youngling time,*' he said. '*I have memory of a time when I did tease a wood-finch for half of the passing of Luma before I killed it. But I ate naught of it and left it where my mother later found it. She was much angered at me; naught for killing it but that I had wasted a good meal. She then went out into the woods and caught as many of the birds as she could and fed them to me at every rising until all of a cycle of the moon of Mogog had passed. I never killed another wood-finch nor ate of one from that time to this.*'

Fervik inclined his head a little bemused. '*What be these woods? Tell me of your world of Eol.*'

Mirrortac warmed to his role as the wonderful adventurer. He told him as much as he could about the world of his birth. He told of the fields of nif-grass where the poultry bird, fote, bobbed up their heads while searching among the roots for worms. He told of the trees of the woodlands and the snowcapped heights of the mountains that towered high above all the villages. With the ability of mind contact, he was able to transmit images of all these just as though the child was there in Eol himself. Fervik beamed with delight and awe at all these fantastic visions which he relayed to all his young friends. Soon there was a small crowd of younglings seated around the erfin, who was careful not to transmit anything to do with spirits, demons and alien magic.

After the feasting was over, Swarg, the clan-master and elders led them all out into the air. All thoughts of the stranger among them were forgotten as they were greeted with the shining visage of Luma hanging above the far horizon. A brisk cold breeze greeted the party as they shrugged off the old season. Their feet sunk into the wet snow as thin streaks of cloud fanned out in the sky above them, forming a fine veil to remind them of the many days of darkness and snow just passed. Mirrortac took a deep breath, sucking in the cool crisp air until his lungs expanded, then he exhaled with a forceful gush that Fervik mimicked, grinning back with a cheeky gleam in his eyes. This made Mirrortac laugh and soon they were both laughing. The hyfnuks also laughed, but the sound of them only served to add to their amusement. The hyfnuk with the scar made such a peculiar sound when he laughed that this brought the two into hysterics until tears were streaming down their cheeks. Swarg, seeing the comical sight of all this hysterical laughter, could not withhold her own mirth, adding her own strange cackling to the throng. This prompted a chain reaction of laughter as the clan-master and even the stern-faced elders all broke into their own unconventional chuckling and cackling. *'Why are we all laughing,'* one elder said. *'What more joyful way to greet the great Luma!'* Swarg replied.

The meat of the wooil was served out over several days as the celebrations continued. Hunting soon resumed as the hyfnuks set out after the slower moving and smaller nimply-wiks that foraged on the fresh shoots of vegetation. Mirrortac was still tasked to Aghfa to carry hyfnu weed but he was allowed a lighter burden. His loyal hyfnuks brought him nimply-wiks which tasted better than muddy weed and bland snails. Fervik also joined in the hunt whenever permitted, curious about the magical sense of the erfin and his silent moods when he stood alone, eyes glazed and mind somewhere beyond reach.

Preparation for the arrival of the Maja-tak of the Werd began in earnest. Fatty wooil grease was rubbed over the walls, floors and ceilings of the passages and holloks after the grease was first imbibed with a protection spell. Mirrortac and the hyfnuks were responsible for providing the best food that could be found in Erga – the best cuts of wooil were kept aside; nimply-wiks that were fat and healthy; fledgling zarnok birds stolen from the nest – all food fit for the equal of a princess in other realms. The clan leaders had returned to their sombre and grim demeanour but the loyal hyfnuks were as anxious as ever to please the erfin, yet there was a disquiet and nervousness about them as though something was bothering them.

KEEPERS OF THE WERD

Colour reflected off the long icicles that hung from the roof of the entrance to Swarg's cavern as she stood at the entrance witnessing the new dawn. She had been meditating for much of the night as the vyndroolsh (aurora) flared and rippled through the twilight sky, lighting up the earth in moments of blazing yellow, red and soft blue. It was the day for which she had prepared for some time. The One of the Werd was coming to her clan. Most of the clan was still asleep after a wearied day of final preparations and Swarg had used the quiet time of the night to concentrate her mind and clear it of all unneeded thoughts. And now, as the sun of Luma broke over the horizon, she prepared to link minds with the Maja-tak of the Werd.

'*Spell-master of Yidrogh, she of Erga greets you,*' she said, beginning the formal greeting that ancient ritual required of her. '*I am out of my father, Tanuk, who was maja-tak before me, and he was from the Ergane line of spell casters who herald from Urguthra before the Great Numbness. I mesh this spell of Finding within you so that your steps will lead you safe to Erga. Do you accept the spell?*'

'*The One of the Werd accepts greetings and the spell,*' came the reply.

'*Then in these words – mufti du raha py – The spell is meshed and each step forth is closer to Erga. May Yidu protect you!*'

'*I wish to see this stranger among you, who calls himself an erfin. He is powerful like a maja-tak and must be watched. He is not all that he seems. My mind is set in confusion when I see his thoughts. I must discern him and see if he is a danger to us. I see all yet this one is like a swirling mist ... take him to your hollok and seal all the ways before you leave. I will feast with the clan but the erfin is not to feast. Then I will see him, and no-one is to disturb the discerning.*'

Swarg bowed absently. '*I will do this right away One of the Werd.*'

'*Then look for me as Luma passes down to Yidu-Brwg. May the blessings of Yidu follow you!*'

Swarg blinked a few times as she became aware of her surroundings again. A nimply-wik scurried out from a burrow and hurried past as Swarg turned back and re-entered her hollok. Swarg donned her ceremonial wooil robe, brushing it absently as she entered the passage. Mirrortac awoke with a start as she swaggered into his hollok. She gestured to him to follow her and he staggered to his feet as Swarg swept out of the hollok and made her way back down the passage. He limped in behind her, still shaking off sleep. '*What do you want with me,*' he queried as he regained his senses.

'*I want nothing, but it is She of the Werd who wishes to discern you,*' she said plainly.

When they reached her hollok, she motioned for him to sit down. '*You are to wait here for She of the Werd but eat naught until after she has seen you.*'

As Mirrortac seated himself down, Swarg picked up a wooil bone; and facing him, raised it to the ceiling and shut her eyes. She began muttering an invocation in maja as she moved about the hollok, waving the bone around the threshold of each entrance and corner. The erfin felt a drowsiness overwhelm him, and before he knew it, he was again asleep.

A soft voice urged Mirrortac out of his slumber. He squinted up at the silhouette in the semi-darkness; gradually realising there was a stranger in the cavern with him.

'*Now I see you, the one of the erfin clan, there is resemblance to us. I am Ameece, Maja-tak of the Werd.*'

Mirrortac was surprised at the youthful tone Ameece conveyed to his mind. He strained his eyes to see her face but there was a distracting aura that simmered around her form.

'*Welcomeness She of the Werd. This erfin is named Mirrortac.*'

'*The name is unfamiliar, yet it seems I have known it always,*' she answered vaguely.

There was a pause as her aura pulsed with a strange light. Then she said, '*I am about to take you on a journey into your past. Do not be discomforted by the many images you shall be seeing. They offer no harm now.*'

Ameece reached down and lifted up a small bundle at her feet. She began unfolding it, and as she did so, a soft light escaped, revealing the rough shape of a large stone that generated its own luminescence. It illuminated the maja-tak's youthful face. Her fur was as white as snow and her eyes like bright blue jewels.

'*Mirrortac, I want you now to look into this stone and place your mind at its centre.*'

But the erfin seemed not to hear as he continued to study her face.

'*Mirrortac, look into the stone,*' she said, still patient.

'*Look into the stone?*' he queried, absently.

'*Yea erfin … look into the stone; the Werdstone.*'

'*Werdstone!*' Mirrortac's eyes leapt to the glowing stone. This was the stone of the knowledge of the Ancients, he thought guardedly to himself.

He admired the stone and silently wondered at the strange luminosity which began to change in hue as he stared into it. Fascinated now by the stone, Mirrortac was almost unaware that it was drawing his mind into it, through the rainbow of yellow, green, blue … and finally, into deep violet. Everything else around him was lost to his sight until the only reality was a streaming tunnel of violet that spun and twisted past him as he sank deeper under the spell of the stone. He could feel the strong presence of the maja-tak beside him although he saw nothing. They seemed to travel onwards, deeper and deeper into the tunnel while the voice of Ameece echoed around him, reassuring him.

'*Be naught alarmed, Mirrortac. What you are about to see, and feel, and hear and taste and smell will seem real, but it be just a vision of the past. Pay no heed.*'

Her voice was swept away as the tunnel appeared to explode all around him. There was a brilliant display of flashing colours which sprang out of the centre of the tunnel, gradually filling it with the most startling of visions. Indeed, despite Ameece's warning, Mirrortac could only gasp with the incredible realness of it all. It seemed that he was standing in the forest of the Divine Green and ahead of him were the floral-clad meretees, dancing along the forest path, hugging trees and singing praises to the forest and its animals. Mirrortac could see the familiar wise form of Shubek ahead of him and felt himself acting out something that had happened so long ago now. He tried to pick up the pace but discovered that he had no control – he was simply the observer now. He witnessed himself question the female meretee about why she had spoken to the tree, and remembered now, with amusement, how she replied and his own reaction at the time. Time fluttered in flashes as highlights of his journey on the islands of the Meretees were re-enacted – his many talks with Shubek, their arrival at the Pyramid of Ra-Los, the meetings with the Ra-finelles, the journey to the Palace of the Pool Stones and all the strange experiences except for those in the etheric realms. The visioning took him once again to the beach where he was first taken into Hopocus, but again the memories of this astral world were not revealed in the discerning. He was then taken back to Petrosium where he again faced the horror of the monster Beeble-Zub. He could smell the stench of the monster and hear again its eerie chorus of voices, and its scowling words 'Darkness is safe, darkness is free'. He quickly re-experienced the last battle with the monster before he was back in the Wastes of Nug, then the Faug Forest and the battle against the snerks; and finally, the Royal community of Greenfaug. And his departed wife who died after giving birth to triplets. He felt again the pain of his loss and could feel tears gather and run down his cheeks.

As the vision faded, he could sense the Maja-tak's own empathy. *'We must go on. There are many lives to see,'* she whispered.

Mirrortac's first life came as no surprise as its spirit had been his companion during his journey to Hopocus. On either side of him, Mirrortac could see a great army of erfin warriors, their many swords gleaming sharp silver in the light of Luma. The warriors were in the battle dress of wolf-hide belts and breastplates of tempered metal inscribed with the maja symbols and the head of a nite-wolf. He could feel the weight of his own armour, sharing the sensations of the warrior he had become. And letting out a cry of defiance, he heard himself shouting, 'Warriors of Erfin! Before Luma reaches the end of the earth, we will drive the Madin out of their caves of dung and beat their flesh into the stone of their mountains. Death to all the Madin!'

The warriors answered in chorus: 'Death to the Madin!' their angry voices carrying across the plain and up into the foothills of the mountain range ahead of them.

One of the warriors nearby turned towards Mirrortac and said, 'I say to you, Merftac, why do we stand here wasting the light of Luma when our blades ache at our sides. Let us be rid of these hairy-sons-of-the-Netherworld. Let us splatter the rocks with their blood!'

Merftac's voice answered out of Mirrortac's mouth. 'Yea, you need be patient no longer, Narssup,' he said, and unsheathing his sword, stabbed it out towards the mountains. 'Erfin warriors! Let us show these Madin the might of the empire! To the hills!'

With these words, the warriors let out loud hoots, baring their teeth in rage. In a single mass they charged towards the foothills. A call rose up from behind a series of boulders ahead. Madin warriors leapt into the open, answering the erfin charge. The erfins fought fiercely, driving the Madin back. Metal blades clashed, and the ground was soon littered with the bodies of warriors from both sides, their blood mingling and dripping over the stones. The Madin were like erfins in general appearance but their hair was long and coarse, and they were a few erfin-lengths taller. Their swords were of smoky quartz and they wore animal hides bearing the symbol of the great bird, the gakar, wings outspread, cut into the leather.

Merftac and his warriors drove the Madin farther and farther into the foothills where they were ambushed. Many warriors were lost but the fury of the erfins and the superior might of their metal swords and breastplates eventually overcame the brave Madin warriors who turned and fled towards the safety of the high mountains. But Merftac and his warriors set after them, keeping close behind their heels as they traversed a thick and foreboding woodland and up the slopes of the largest mountain they had ever seen. Mirrortac recognised it immediately – the sharp ridges and the mists that haunted its summit were of the great Mateote.

Upwards went Merftac and his warriors, unafraid and filled with the battle rage. The Madin scattered but none could escape the relentless net of the erfins as they encircled every avenue of escape. The bravest of the Madin warriors, Golak, turned on his pursuers and was able to kill and wound eight erfin warriors before he ducked between his pursuers and escaped into the same cave that Mirrortac had entered at the very beginning of his journey. Merftac ran after him, leaping down from a rock ledge above the cave and wading ankle-deep in the cold waters of the stream. When he reached the cavern, he caught sight of Golak's feet scrambling into one of the narrow tunnels that led out of the cavern. Merftac crawled in behind him, shuffling on his belly in the darkness. Around a bend, he saw the Madin in a shaft of light and realised he was trapped at a dead end that opened above a cliff. Grinning at the helpless Golak who was unable to turn around in the narrow tunnel, Merftac shouted curses at him and received curses in return.

Merftac tried to dislodge his sword but found he couldn't in the tightness of the tunnel. Golak crooked his head around and cried out, 'What vexes you wolf-dung? Have you forgotten that the Madin are kin of the mountains? Kill me and I shall take you into the Netherworld with me!'

Merftac flew into a rage, and shouting at the top of his voice said, 'Cursed seducer of demons! Merftac be naught afraid of mere spittle of gakar such as you! I will fight you with my bare hands and send you to the Netherworld alone!'

The two fought in the confines of the narrow cavern until that moment when Golak was hanging out over the steep cliff where the passage met the outside again. Mirrortac remembered the look of incomprehension on Golak's face just before he let go and fell out of sight into the cloud below. Merftac then returned to his fellow warriors after the last Madin were tossed over the cliff or killed with a sharp blade.

The startling vision dissolved like a disturbed reflection on water before he again joined Merftac in the Faug Forest. There was a group of warriors with him, but they were wearing only light armour and carried lesser swords. Figures of demi-gods who wore strange close-fitting robes that shone bright silver like a mountain stream, were leading them to a clearing where there was an enormous golden stone with edges worn smooth and shining silver. These hairless ones were like the Nerthulians yet were wondrous in the way of gods. They told them that only 50 of their number could enter the golden stone and the rest would have to return to Eol. Merftac chose 50 of his warriors to go with the demi-gods but chose to stay behind himself along with his most trusted he-erfins. The chosen ones bowed their obedience and filed into a hole that suddenly had appeared from the underside of the stone which was supported in its place by columns made like legs of some monster. When the last of the chosen had entered the stone, the demi-gods withdrew, and the hole closed up again as though it had never existed.

Mirrortac observed through the eyes of Merftac as the stone generated an eerie alien sound that shook the air around them. It was then overcome with a dazzling light like fire and its columned legs retracted into the structure, leaving the stone floating in the air. Then, with an incredible burst of speed, the stone shot up into the sky and disappeared into the heavens.

They were left wide-eyed and disbelieving. Merftac was overwhelmed at the sight and fell prostrate on the ground, proclaiming: 'My warriors have gone to the home of the gods!'

Merftac and his warriors acknowledged the mighty forest where the trees touched the sky while the earth reeked of decay and mould. Before returning to Eol, they decided to do some exploring, but had not advanced far before finding their passage blocked by a stream. Mirrortac knew what horrors Merftac and his warriors could find in the Faug Forest and felt a sense of dread as the warriors caught sight of the giant leech-like gorkles. They abandoned their exploration only to encounter a mass of minor snerks, still exceptionally large, slithering out of the tree branches around them, and hanging their large serpent heads above them, menacing.

Fearless as in battle, Merftac and his warriors withdrew their swords and prepared to fight their way out. Hissing and scowling with gaping jaws, the snerks descended quickly to the ground.

'Try to blind them!' Merftac commanded as the first of the snerks rumbled upon its great belly, scraping over the dark leaf matter in its path.

Merftac danced around in front of it while he directed one of his warriors to sneak in behind its head. The warrior was almost at the serpent's side when the snerk detected his movement, and with a deft flick of its head, grabbed him in its jaws. The warrior let out a horrible cry just before the huge jaws clamped down on him and broke his ribs with a loud snap. And with a toss of its head, threw the erfin into its gullet and swallowed him whole.

This sent the other snerks into a feeding frenzy as they fell in among the erfins, snapping them up in their jaws while the warriors feebly replied with their swords that barely were able to pierce the thick leathery skin. Merftac dodged an attack and leapt onto the back of one of the snerks. He crawled up to the head, resisting violent swings of its body in its attempts to dislodge him. He managed to thrust his sword up to its hilt into the eye of the monster but had to bring up his leg quickly as the head tried to bash his body against a nearby tree trunk. He grabbed the hilt of the sword and was trying to withdraw it when another snerk sighted him and came in for the kill. He watched helpless as the gaping jaws closed in on him, then shook with relief as its body abruptly rolled out of sight. There were great gashes on the serpent's body, and Merftac knew that neither he nor his warriors had caused them. Above him came the sound of a host of grunts as an army of faugs glided out of the uppermost branches to fall in among the snerks, hacking and slaying as many as they could with their double-bladed axes of quartz.

The faugs rescued Merftac and the wounded from the snerk menace, to take them up into the canopy where the faugs had built their tree-top communities. Merftac was never to return to Eol, and along with his remaining warriors, spent a pleasant life among the faugs under Princess Parthena in the Royal Halls of Greenfaug.

Merftac had hardly drawn his last breath when Mirrortac and Ameece were taken back through the void and into another life. It was to the erfin's astonishment to discover that his seventh life was spent as the Madin warrior Golak who lived with his people in the caves within the mountains that traversed the land in a long range of peaks and hills. Golak was as proud and courageous as Merftac, but his courage was a response to his need to protect his family against the fierce erfins who had taken all the plains and valleys as theirs to command. The Madin conducted raids of outlying erfin villages, defending their mountain home against being taken in the relentless spread of the erfin empire. Each time the moon of Mogog came to fullness, the erfin villages encroached nearer to the mountains and the swords of the erfin warriors were bewitched with spells that gave them the strength of gods. Golak had simple tastes, nurturing his family with the sparse pickings of the mountain. The raids provided them with the meat of fote and other animals that the erfins killed, along with fruits from the trees that grew on the vast plains to the south. Mirrortac relived Golak's last desperate dash for cover under the summit of Mateote, and in those last moments, as Golak clung to Merftac above the yawning abyss, Mirrortac finally understood why the Madin's face paled – he recognised Merftac and he were of the same soul and their only hope was to allow Merftac to live.

The fire in Golak's eyes was barely extinguished when Mirrortac found himself seeing through a child's eyes. The young male Madin stumbled on his unsure feet while outside the hut of his parents. Behind, the mountain peaks paraded across the landscape, tumbling into the smaller foothills and the boulder strewn downlands where his family lived. Cuf explored his surroundings with an eager curiosity, wandering a little farther each time he ventured out. His mother watched him with proud eyes as she skinned fruit with a sharp stone. Cuf picked up a white pebble and struck a boulder with it. The pebble left a white mark where it had struck the rock and Cuf stopped to examine the mark. Transfixed by his own creation, he did not at first take heed of the nearing sounds of battle.

The air all around him exploded with shouts and Cuf wheeled around in time to see his mother fall screaming as an erfin warrior run her through with his sword. Several warriors were destroying the hut while another walked towards him. Cuf shrieked and tried to run away but the erfin grabbed him in one hand and let him hang by the fur of his back while shouting to the others, 'What shall I do with this little

Madin worm?' and one of the others answered, 'The Madin have naught protection. He must have nine demons in him already. Kill him!'

The warrior holding Cuf sniggered. 'I shall see how far I can throw him!' he said, and grabbing hold of his little feet, swung Cuf around until all he could see was a blur of green and brown. The young Madin struggled against the might of the warrior but to no avail. The warrior let go and Cuf glimpsed the boulder where he had left his mark, racing towards him. Mirrortac shuddered as he shared the intense pain as Cuf's small body collided with the rock. He felt the bones break in his chest and the taste of blood in his mouth. His head seemed to explode with a bang that sent the senses reeling.

The morbid game continued as each warrior vied to throw Cuf the farthest. Death came to him in the third throw, as his body crumpled into the dust, his blood spilling in gurgling streams out of his mouth. Mirrortac was revolted that his own erfin ancestors would do such a thing.

'I do naught wish to see any more,' he pleaded.

'Each life brings lessons and not all lessons be pleasant, my he-one. The greatest lesson for the life of Cuf would be forgiveness. Forgive them and you can forgive all,' Ameece softly reassured him.

Mirrortac then experienced memories of three lives as females, each taking them further back into the ancestry of erfins. Strife was ever-present between the clans as they vied against one another, ruled then by powerful maja-taks who reigned using strong spells. The lands were themselves rent with unrest and upheaval; mountains of fire brought terror and the Monsters-of-the-Deep-Earth rampaged and devastated the world. Finally, the moment of confirmation came as Mirrortac looked through the eyes of his second life as an Uzdree maja-tak whose name was Harka. The Uzdree had settled in well wooded lands south of Yidrogh where the Great Numbness had divided the world. Harka experimented with new spells as did other maja-taks of the clan-race and there was competition between them. The rivalry, friendly at first, grew more intense as the maja-taks sought more freedom to exercise their newfound spells. The clan elders objected to the use of the new spells and arguments were heated. In a daring show of defiance, the maja-taks overthrew the clan elders and sent them and the clan-master into exile. Arguments broke out between the maja-taks on who should be leader and the Uzdree were split, forming the Urdin and the Madree. Relations between the two clan-races became frayed as the power game continued. The Madree finally gained control and formed into a powerful ruling clan-race which still ruled in Mirrortac's third life as a female Madree called Loreel.

When his first life focused into being, Mirrortac found himself in the body of a roznogh known as Browagh – a stubborn male who would not believe that the Viyu

– the Great Numbness – would truly be a threat to his native Yidrogh. Browagh had ignored his mother's warnings of the coming of the Viyu and had stayed at the clan-place until he had seen the great river of ice with his own eyes. Only then did he follow his family who had left many moons before for the Springs of Luma. But he had waited too long. The river of ice had cut off the path to the warm springs and he was forced to follow it along to make his way around it. He travelled farther away from the familiar country of Yidrogh to a mysterious land enveloped in a thick mist. Clambering through the mist, Browagh found the end of the ice river – its feet melting away into a frigid stream that flowed through a valley of ordered trees, quite beautiful and alien in their twisting trunks and slim elongated pine needles. Browagh was awed by all this as he had never known trees before. He tried to eat the bark but found it unbecoming to his palate and spat it out. The pine needles likewise were tested and rejected.

Browagh crossed the stream and stumbled onto a path leading deeper into the woodland. Someone had taken great pains to fashion a path, as it had been paved in flat sections of rose-coloured stone. Browagh followed the path, unable to withhold his own curiosity. He followed its straight course into the wood and between the rising ridges of stone that flashed with fire and blue wherever the sunlight struck it. The trees assumed magnificent shapes and a soft fine mist swirled about their upper branches. Faug-like beings watched from on high, their manner contemplative. At last Browagh found himself in a box canyon with steep walls of stone on either side and ahead, standing above a flat ring of mist, was a plateau. The path stopped abruptly at the wall of sheer rock, where the roznogh was forced to stop.

Weary from his long walk into the wood, Browagh curled up against a stone and went to sleep. However, he was no sooner asleep when he was awakened by the rough prodding of one of the faug-like beings who was grunting and gesturing to him to come with it. Browagh was ill-tempered from being disturbed from his sleep, and scowled at the faug. It tried to pull him away with it but this only made him angrier. He threatened the being with closed fists until the faug sighed, shrugged its shoulders and left him. Browagh settled back to sleep but was again disturbed, this time by a grinding noise nearby. He opened one wary eye, searching for the source of the noise and was alarmed when he saw the wall where the path ended rumbling loudly from within. He jumped up as the wall slid outwards, revealing a large hollow space behind. And out of the cavern came a demi-god robed in a garment of glistening crystals that changed colour with each movement of the robe. When the demi-god saw him, Browagh fell prostrate at his feet in fear.

'How did you come to be here?' Yidu asked him.

Browagh told his tale and waited for the sentence of the god to be proclaimed. Yidu peered down grimly.

'It is indeed Yidu who speaks to you, roznogh. Do naught lie upon the ground like a worm, Browagh. Rather stand and look into the eyes of your master?'

Browagh rose on trembling feet, his eyes still averted. 'You are the great Sky-master. How can this roznogh dare be in your presence, let alone look upon your wonderment.'

Yidu said, 'Such a young soul can be so stubborn. Look at me, Browagh!'

Browagh forced up his eyes and looked upon Yidu in his splendour. The crystal garment changed colour to green then reflected yellow and blue then back to red.

'Now, look into my eyes, Browagh,' Yidu commanded.

The roznogh raised his eyes slowly to the being's face. Three sapphire-blue eyes stared back and Browagh felt them penetrating him. Mirrortac witnessed the scenario with interest tainted by apprehension. Yidu smiled and his eyes flashed wide with an incredible sense of power and mystery. He reached into his robe and took out a glowing stone of crystal – the Werdstone. Then peering seemingly into the heart of Mirrortac himself, Yidu said, 'Take this stone, Browagh, and return to your people. If you can naught find the path to the Springs of Luma, then look into the stone and the knowledge of the path shall come to you. Keep the stone and find a she-roznogh to whom you can be joined. But do naught be joined without consulting the stone as it is to be a sacred joining and blessed by me who will send you the ritual of the joining through the power of the stone. After your joining you shall have a daughter whose name shall be Lumerday which means "the one of light and wisdom" and when she reaches her 10th Season of the White Veil, you shall give her the stone after a ritual given by me through the stone. The stone is empowered with the wisdom of Yidu, who holds all the knowledge of the worlds since before the beginning. I am Father of this knowledge which is called the "Werd" and the stone shall be named for it – the Werdstone.

'Your daughter and your daughter's daughter and her daughter after her and all the daughters of the Werd shall be guardians of the Werdstone which shall bring the roznoghs the wisdoms to speak with their minds across the distances of Yidrogh, and many protections and blessings which I shall grant beyond the spells already known by your maja-taks.

'And as for you, Browagh, you shall take many forms and when you are in your last body, I will call you back to me through this stone which will reveal your past. You must then return to me with the Werdstone when we must prepare for the joining of all worlds and all peoples. As Browagh, you shall forget these last words as soon as your feet leave the path of rose stones, and even my face shall be forgotten to you. This is as it should be.'

Yidu wrapped the stone in its hide of wooil and presented it to Browagh who took it with great reverence and awe. 'I shall do all you say, great Sky-master, Father of the Werd!' the roznogh cried, bowing several times while backing away along the path.

Yidu grinned and his eyes flashed from beneath large bushy eye-brows. 'Do naught think that you came here by happen-stance,' he said. I have chosen you with great care and called you here.'

Browagh bowed again and rushed away along the path, head down and buzzing with the enormity of his sacred mission. No more of his life was revealed as the vision drew back into the void and the two observers were thrust back into reality.

Mirrortac blinked in the darkness of the hollok and stared down into the Werdstone which was now opaque and dark. The strange aura still danced around the form of the Maja-tak of the Werd who remained staring at the stone and deep in thought. Mirrortac looked across at her silhouette, feeling both elated and apprehensive.

Ameece was silent for a long few moments before lifting up her face to his. *'You were the first to possess the Werdstone, Mirrortac ... as Browagh. The stone cannot lie ... you must bring it back to Yidu,'* she said, but was hesitant to go on. *'But I cannot give it to you ...'*

'Why is that,' he posed. *'You saw for yourself what Yidu had commanded. Would you betray his command so long ago?'*

'T'would seem simple ... to you, erfin. But naught be as simple. Mogog has passed over beyond count between that day and this, and much has changed. That was Yidu's wish then ... but now, I am distressed. I must consult the stone for Yidu's wishes ... to see if they remain.'

Mirrortac frowned. *'The stone possesses you. It IS Yidu's wishes and I will act upon them!'*

Ameece sighed. *'You must be patient, he-erfin. I will consult the stone now, and if Yidu wishes, then you may take the stone. But not before the elders be consulted also.'*

Mirrortac held back his frustration as he turned away. *'Perhaps there be naught harm in that. Go and consult the stone ...'*

Ameece moved a short distance away, taking the stone with her. Mirrortac turned back towards her shadow as he glimpsed her face in the renewed glow of the Werdstone, and saw her jeweled blue eyes reflected in the light. His heart skipped a beat as he inexplicably felt he knew her intimately as his own. However, the moment passed and soon he was considering his next action should things not go his way.

ESCAPE FROM YIDROGH

It was some time before Ameece returned to Mirrortac to reveal what had transpired in her consultation of the Werdstone. She wore a worried expression, clearly in conflict about what she should do.

'*Yidu has changed his plans about you. He does naught wish for you to return the Werdstone to him. The stone says you are naught in his trust any longer. You must be cast out from here.*'

Mirrortac was smug in his assumption about Yidu. This demi-god had perhaps begun with the best of intentions but was now wholly corrupt. In any case, he was no more god than the roznoghs themselves. Though his magic was strong. It was time to act, and act quickly.

'*Yidu is naught as you expect. He is naught god … I want the stone now.*'

Ameece moved slowly and uncertainly. '*You can naught have it. I must tell the elders.*'

The maja-tak stood up to go but Mirrortac was up in an instant and snatched the hide and the Werdstone from her grasp. '*I know you want to believe in what I say, but it tests you. Come with me; we will seek out Yidu together!*'

Ameece stood motionless, her body trembling. She sighed again. '*I do naught … I must stop you. I …*'

'*I am going then … and the stone with me.*' Mirrortac rushed for the entrance but Ameece had regained her senses and let out the alarm.

Mirrortac limped as fast as he could along the passages, grasping the wrapped stone close to his chest while trying to find the way out. Heavy feet thumped up from behind, and the erfin soon realised he could not outrun them. He was soon caught and taken before the elders who wore self-satisfied expressions that their own suspicions about him were borne out. He had stolen the most precious and sacred object in Yidrogh and would pay dearly for his crime.

Mirrortac was left for dead. He could not feel his body for the numbing, freezing water of the bog with its stench of rotting vegetation. The elders had wasted no time in passing judgment on him and casting him out into the wastes of Yidrogh. He was beginning to lose consciousness as the day came to an end and the darkness of night crept upon the land like death, preparing to reap with its wide and sharp blade, cutting away the last thread connecting him to life. He had struggled feebly against the cord tied tightly around his arms and the weight of the water and weed. 'What now, oh dazzling wise one,' he mused to his guiding spirit, Phantac, spitting out bile as the nausea rose again.

'Your rescuers are at hand. The Werdstone will soon be yours,' came the calm reply.

Mirrortac was only half aware when another voice entered his mind.

'We can see you, master! We will naught let death take you. We be here to keep you safe and serve you.'

The words were that of Daghva, one of the hyfnuks he had rescued. Through blurred sight, he could soon discern the shapes of four hyfnuks as they approached the bog. He detected movement in the slush and mush around him as the hyfnuks entered the bog, and they soon were lifting him out of the freezing water and rubbing feeling back into his body. Mirrortac could not tell whether he was freezing or burning as his whole body felt like it was consumed by a freezing fire.

Mirrortac opened his eyes. The arrival of the hyfnuks had seemed like a dream, but now he found himself inside a small hollok feeling much warmer and comfortable, and surrounded by his rescuers – the hyfnuks Daghva, Rusk, Iyaji and Karn. And to his surprise Fervik was also there. The young roznogh grinned when he saw the erfin was conscious again and offered him some wooil meat.

'I was afeared you would be taken to the Otherworld before we could reach you,' Fervik said, looking sombre for a moment before his face brightened again. *'But you are alive! And we will all be together, like a family.'*

Daghva approached from a corner of the hollok and appraised the erfin. *'You be indeed fortunate to be alive. We could naught leave you to die, although you had taken the Werdstone.'*

'*Your clan will cast you out as well,*' Mirrortac said. '*Why would you risk your own lives to save me?*'

Daghva exchanged glances with his fellow hyfnuks before speaking out loud. 'We have a great secret. We be naught of the cleverness of elders, but we have no trust in them. They speak of renegades ... we are of them. We be in agreeance that the elders be unjust in their actions. And you be the one to take the Werdstone back to Yidu. It be his ... let him take it back, with all its demon spells.'

'Why would you think this of Yidu? Is he naught your Sky-master Father of the Werd?' Mirrortac quizzed.

'That be the teachings of the elders since my child-nogh days,' Daghva said, 'but we spoke with some of the Skye-clan who told of seeing Yidu. He was indeed shining with his garments like a god, but they saw he could bleed and feel pain like us, so he can naught be god.'

'Hmm,' Mirrortac mused, now sitting up in contemplation. 'That be of much interest. He must now be of immense age ... no doubt with the aid of his spellcraft.'

'They say where he lives that the seasons move slowly. It be a place of madness.' Daghva was sullen and was almost whispering.

'I use my voice here,' he said, bending close to Mirrortac's ear. 'That my thoughts naught be heard at Erga, just a half passing of Luma from here. I can naught hide them from the maja-taks.'

'Be the one of the Werdstone there ... Ameece?' Mirrortac was standing and started ambling around in circles.

'She leaves on this day. We must be quick to catch her ... to gain the Werdstone.'

'Yea. We must take her with us to Yidu. She is linked to the stone. Who be with her?'

'She has two elders only, and the hyfnuk Evarngar. They will yield to us with ease.'

Just then Fervik hopped up to them, still smiling. 'When do we go? My feet itch to find new places to see!'

Mirrortac's greying eyes glinted with mirth at the young roznogh's eagerness. 'You take much risk coming with me. Why do your kin allow this? You be a child.'

'My kin know naught. I would be in the Otherworld if be naught for you. I will follow you anywhere!' Fervik determined.

Mirrortac turned to Daghva. 'Could you naught stop him?'

Daghva shrugged. 'He is stubborn. We took him back, but he followed us again.'

The erfin scratched his head and lifted a mocking eye-brow at the young roznogh. 'You remind me of myself, youngling. This be no pleasant journey. You must stay out of the way of harm.'

'I will come to naught hurt,' he said.

Mirrortac admired Fervik's faith borne of the foolhardiness of youth. But he worried about the young roznogh and the dangers they no doubt would face on their journey to find Yidu ... or rather the first stone, Oashu, in the realm of Yidu.

After some rest, the six of them set off across the cold wastes to intercept Ameece and the Werdstone, now more than a day's passing from the greevun where Mirrortac was found. Daghva was the eldest of the hyfnuks and was more introspect in nature. Rusk, Iyaji and Karn enjoyed each other's company and took to daring each other in risky pursuits, such as the rushed attack of the wooil which nearly meant the end of them.

By nightfall they had reached a stream and decided to camp a short distance from its still icy shore. 'The Bringer of Viyu!' Fervik pointed at the stream, happy to have attained this landmark.

'It flows from northering ... many passings of Luma from here.'

In the dying light of the sun of Luma, nimply-wiks scurried between tussock bushes while small groups of zarnok birds wheeled overhead, searching for chance morsels of the food that they carried with them. The hyfnuks had bound hyfnu, nimply-wik meat and the last of the wooil steaks in hide-bound food packs that were closely watched as they did not want any to be wasted or lost. The hyfnuks dug holes in the ice for themselves to sleep in, covering their bodies with the discarded ice after snuggling into the holes. Fervik and Mirrortac slept together, covered by a large wooil hide.

When they awoke in the dawn, Luma was a pale disk of light boring through a thick mist that hung over the party throughout the day as they followed the trail left by the maja-tak of the Werd. They soon happened upon their last camp, which was fresh, as the bones left behind were still moist with saliva. It seemed they had lingered there half the day, as though Ameece was hesitant to return home. It was a good sign, and lightened the hearts of the younger hyfnuks who were eager for a fight, should there be resistance.

'We can catch them before mogog rises,' Karn proclaimed, and he rubbed his furry hands together with excitement.

'Perhaps a trap awaits us,' Daghva cautioned. 'They may have more hyfnuks with them.'

'Nay. There be but the four … I see the tracks of their feet,' Rusk assured, crouching down to examine the footprints on the ground.

'There be other clans near,' Daghva countered.

Rusk rolled his eyes. 'We will surprise them. We will watch them in hiding … and see if other hyfnuks be there.'

Fervik kept close to the erfin, all the while chattering about one thing or another of little consequence. Mirrortac happily endured Fervik's chatter for it was the roznogh's youthful exuberance that buoyed him, distracting him from the serious purpose of his journey. Daghva was becoming gloomy, struck by solitary moods, brooding in his own secret thoughts, and no doubt worrying about what they may encounter. The three younger hyfnuks, on the other hand, only became more enthusiastic, which further aggravated the elder Daghva, but he remained quiet.

Darkness came too early, but the party continued onward with the hyfnuks sniffing out the trail. They soon picked up the scent of wooil meat and hyfnu on the light breeze drifting to them from the north. It was clear that Ameece had already set up camp, unaware that she was been tracked. They found them encamped alongside a massive greevun where hyfnu grew in abundance. But the prospect of a fresh feed was still far from their minds as they used stealth to spy on the small party now in plain view from a relatively short distance away from behind some thickets.

'They sit like nimply-wiks without a hole to go to. We can take them easily,' Karn grinned, and his eagerness was infectious, bar Daghva and Mirrortac who both maintained a cautious outlook.

Evarngar suddenly stood up and looked towards them, alerted by Fervik's rustling in the thickets.

'What is it Evarngar?' Ameece communicated.

'Mistress, it be naught I am sure. I heard something, but it were but nimply-wiks in their haste. At least that be my reckoning …'

Evarngar sat down again and they all gave out a sigh of relief.

'*I feel you erfin-one,*' Mirrortac heard, which startled him.

'*If you seek us out, then be done with it now. I will naught resist … you are well able with four hyfnuks with you,*' Ameece said.

Mirrortac looked around at the others but her thoughts seemed to have been directed only at him. Daghva looked sideways at the erfin, picking up on the erfin's distress.

'What vexes you, Mirrortac?'

Mirrortac let out a breath. 'We must act now. She knows we are here. She is waiting for us to take them!'

Dagfva looked equally surprised at the erfin's revelation. 'She waits for us? Maybe a trap … but where do the other hyfnuks hide?'

'No-one hides. Come and be done with it!'

This time they all heard her. Mirrortac stood up from behind the thickets. 'We go now. She will surrender to us.'

After a moment of confusion, they all stood with the hyfnuks taking the lead to approach the small group on the ground ahead. Evarngar jumped up to defend his mistress with Ameece trying to forestall him.

'Renegades! Mistress, take the stone and run. I will try to stop them best I can,' he commanded, stepping between Ameece and the approaching hyfnuks.

Ameece remained sitting.

'Where will I run to? They will gain the stone regardless,' she said, resigned to her fate and that of the Werdstone.

Evarngar's nostrils flared as he stomped up to the approaching hyfnuks and tried to wrestle them. But he was no match for them, although he was strong and furious in his fight. Karn and Rusk grabbed his arms while Iyaji took his feet and they lifted him up. He wriggled like a huge worm in their grasp and was able to kick Iyaji off several times before their battering got the better of him. After some time, Evarngar lay on the icy ground whimpering and bruised.

'Why do you do this, renegades? Your blood is tainted by the erfin-clan one. What do you want with the Werdstone, erfin?' Evarngar pleaded, still simmering with his ire at this assault of the most sacred keepers of the Werdstone.

Mirrortac beheld the hyfnuk with a sense of pity. 'It be your duty to fight for your mistress and the stone. I understand. You know naught of the treachery of Yidu nor of his plans for the three worlds of the Greater Sky. But if you be prepared to listen, then I will try my best to tell you ... though you may not still believe.'

'Yidu is Sky-master ... Father of the Werd,' Evarngar pronounced.

Mirrortac just shook his head. 'Yeah, I have heard it all before.'

Meanwhile, the hyfnuks had also subdued the elders who were not as physical in their resistance but protested vehemently at being taken prisoner and their sacred trust violated. Ameece now stood and approached Mirrortac with the Werdstone still wrapped in its hide. She had the air of complete surrender although she was clearly conflicted and disturbed by the course of events.

'Here,' she proffered him the stone. 'It be yours now. You vex me ... I am strangely attracted to you yet afraid. I feel I must yield but I know naught why ...'

Mirrortac was glad that the maja-tak did not have to be manhandled. He too felt an inexplicable connection with her. It was as though he had known her all his life.

'You will be treated as sacred, and I will be the only one to share the possession of the Werdstone. The Eye of Yidu wishes to possess worlds yet unseen to us. My kin and others will be in servitude ... ahh, but the tale is long in the telling, and beyond your mind.'

Mirrortac accepted the stone. He carefully unwrapped it from its covering hide and beheld it as it glowed dimly. 'With this he can spy upon the roznoghs and rule your lives ... and has done so since early seasons. We will return it to his domain,' he said, disguising his true purpose for now.

He wrapped up the stone again and slung the hide over his shoulder with the sling designed into the hide.

'But for now, we rest, and eat.' Mirrortac motioned to the others to set down at the camp.

Evarngar placed himself beside Ameece to give her as much aid and protection as he could under the circumstances while the elders, Shaduk and Rimerelle reluctantly resumed camp, casting condescending glances at the erfin and his hyfnuks. They were shorter than the hyfnuks but still taller than the erfin and Ameece. Their dark fur was streaked with grey, giving them a slightly mottled appearance.

They ate of their supplies, the three younger hyfnuks maintaining a lively banter among themselves of their conquest and the prospects of the adventure ahead of them. Ameece, while kept separated from the erfin by an ever loyal Evarngar, was impatient for answers to the riddles posed by the erfin, and her thoughts were directed at him alone.

'I see no ill in you, erfin. Your lives be full of courage and valiant efforts, and I too am taken aback at Yidu's change of plans. You seem to know things that be naught revealed in the discerning ... I fear it will vex and try me, but I must know what you know ... tell.'

Mirrortac told of his meeting with his guiding spirit Phantac and what he was told about Yidu and the Three Stones of Destiny – Oashu, Darm and Einuk – that bound the three greater worlds and those living in them. While his mission was yet clouded, it was obvious that Yidu was using these stones to gain increasing power over not only their own world, but two others separated by the vastness of the Greater Sky. How he would span that vastness remained a mystery, but Mirrortac knew that somehow the means would be at hand once he had completed the first part in gaining possession of Oashu now that he had the Werdstone.

Ameece was amazed at this tale yet her mind and heart battled with the concept that Yidu was not a caring and protective god, but some power-hungry maniac set on possessing them. Had he not taken good care of them all this long time? What then was there for them in the Otherworld?

At first light, the hyfnuks entered the greevun and harvested enough hyfnu, snails and later nimply-wiks to provide rations for days of travelling ahead. They set off when Luma still shone low in the sky in the long drive following the stream to reach the realm of Yidu. When they had travelled 24 days, they noticed the landscape had started to change. Greevuns merged into one another in a vast wetland plain which almost obscured the path of the original stream while the dull blue outline of distant mountains beckoned from the far horizons. Fervik had started falling back, complaining of the great distance and frowning when told of mooniths. Evarngar took the young roznogh under his wing and steadied his impatience with tales of his own youth and his battles with wooils and zarnok parents protecting their young.

They trudged through shallow greevuns, slowing their pace to a crawl as the black clinging mud sucked at their feet. Stinging insects buzzed around them, burrowing into fur and biting the pink skin beneath. Wearied at last by the effort, Mirrortac ordered they make camp on an island in the centre of the vast swamp. Ameece had plied Mirrortac with questions that could not all be answered while the edge of Evarngar's ire had only been tempered by his growing friendship with the young Fervik. The elders had remained resolute in their opposition but accepted that they had been treated well, and with some respect.

Ameece stole away from Evarngar to appraise the erfin more closely. She had noticed a change in the coloration of his fur that begged closer inspection. Picking at his fur, she remarked, '*Your fur takes upon the blue as the sheath that surrounds you. You are like a magical puzzle.*'

Mirrortac groaned inwardly. '*This happens every time I face another challenge. It be a sign of change ... and my fur has changed hue many times now. Each time a different colour. At least the old fur does not fall like the first times.*'

'*You are a curious one, erfin. The blue now be the same as your sheath of blue.*' Ameece allowed her eyes to wander over the erfin's frame, finding it oddly pleasing.

Mirrortac frowned slightly. '*What be this blue sheath of which you speak?*'

'*Did you naught see a glow about me when I first discerned you? This be the sheath of Yidu ... It surrounds every roznogh but only the maja-taks normally see it.*'

Mirrortac considered for a moment, then remembered. '*Yea, but the colour was naught blue ... it be though a rainbow danced about you.*'

'*The sheath can take on many colours ... e'en yours will change with your mood. But it be mostly blue. That be a good hue. That be what vexed me ... you should be in Yidu's favour yet ...*' She paused. '*Why do you vex me so?*'

Their eyes met and there was recognition. Mirrortac's mind was suddenly filled with the vision of his departed she-erfin Yenic and a tear escaped before he could turn away.

'*It could naught be ... could you be ...?*' he mused out loud, and his heart yearned for the one he lost.

Ameece stared at him quizzically. '*What do you see, Mirrortac? You be troubled.*'

Mirrortac could not look at her and turned his face away. '*You remind me of Yenic, my she-erfin. She passed to the Otherworld many seasons past now. Do you have any memory of your own lives ...?*'

Ameece felt an urging in her heart. '*I am a maja-tak. I discern others with the Werdstone, but never have I been discerned. This teases my heart ... I do naught know of other lives. Perhaps ...*' She tried to deny it, but her feelings welled up like a spring from her heart.

Evarngar interrupted the moment as he took Ameece gently by the arm. '*The erfin troubles you, mistress. I fear he will bewitch you. Come now and rest away from him.*'

Ameece absently complied, but her mind was buzzing with confused thoughts and feelings. A link had been opened that no longer could be shut. She felt herself drawn ever more to the erfin and confessed a giddy excitement that she had never experienced before. Similarly, Mirrortac found himself stealing glances across at her. Her bright jeweled eyes reflected in their depths a familiar soul. He knew her as his own.

The night was a long one as biting insects made sleep very difficult, except for Daghva who awoke refreshed while the others moaned and peered out across the unforgiving swamp with red-rimmed eyes.

In the days that followed, they made their way out of the swamp and onto a grassy plain where shrubs and small trees grew in small pockets of green. The once distant mountains now loomed larger, fingering out towards them with ridges of stone that sparkled in the sunlight. A long flat blanket of mist obscured the feet of the mountains. Mirrortac's heart quickened as he recognised the landscape that Browagh had stumbled into at the beginning days. Before them lay a wide plain that led up to the verge of the mountain ridges. Numerous yellow flowers peeked up above waist-high grasses which were alive with the movements of scurrying small animals. They were all awed at the sight of the grasses, flowers, trees and the towering mountains. The Werdstone had become dark and lustreless yet remained warm in its protective hide covering.

After 12 days on the plain, they reached the edge of the great mist, and entered, as this was where the stream ended – in an untidy pile of boulders and stones many erfin-lengths high. Enfolded within the mist was a fir forest, which was the same as Ameece and Mirrortac had witnessed through the eyes of Browagh. The trees were twisted in exotic shapes and pine needles littered the ground where they walked. Water dripped from branches as the ever-present mist curled in drifts through the higher limbs. A pathway of rose quartz wove its straight way through the wood, again as in the vision, with the high stone ridges coming up to meet them on either side.

Daghva considered the forest with a suspicious sweep of his dark eyes. '*There is menace afoot in this place,*' he said.

Karn kicked one of the trees hard, causing it to shudder and shower everyone near him in water and pine needles. His furry eye-brows rose as he looked up at the tree.

'*This wooded thing does naught yield with ease. I should have to kick it a few more times to bring it to ground.*'

Rusk and Iyaji mocked their comrade with chortles, and Rusk said, '*We shall have to wait here until Luma has left for the Underworld and has returned before you kick that tree down!*'

Karn warmed to the dare. '*I will have six of these wooded things kicked down before the two of you together have downed e'en one!*' he countered.

'*Huh!*' Iyaji laughed. '*We will have 12 kicked down each while you are jumping around with a sore foot after kicking down your first!*'

Karn grinned then waved his palm graciously at the tree. '*Take your pleasure!*' he said, inviting them to start the contest.

Rusk took aim at the tree and ran up to it, throwing up his great foot as he leapt. The hyfnuk bounced off the tree and fell harmlessly to the ground. The tree shook for a few moments, sending another shower of water and pine needles down upon them. Karn laughed loudly. '*I thought it was the tree that you were kicking down, not you!*'

'*That will be the end of any tree kicking,*' Mirrortac interceded. '*There be those who need these trees for their own clan-place. A tree is naught use to anyone on the ground; it can naught be eaten as we would hyfnu,*' he said.

The hyfnuks instantly grew solemn and meekly followed along the stone pathway. But every now and then, one of them would test kick a tree, unable to resist the temptation of this new challenge to their strength. Fervik was now wide-eyed surveying all the trees around them and taking in every detail. Evarngar also watched the trees, but not in wonder, though he was impressed. He was searching for any danger to his mistress; and finally, after much scrutiny, was satisfied that she was safe for a time. Mirrortac found himself distracted by his growing interest in the Werdstone which he had seen change from dark and lustreless to a clear stone, like water, with a tiny yellow star of light glowing at its centre.

When they reached the canyon at the end of the forest, Mirrortac ordered that they make camp under an overhang, still some distance from the wall at the end of the canyon. He did not want to meet Yidu without being refreshed or prepared. He secretly concurred with Daghva's fear although the others dismissed it as the hyfnuk's usual tone of moodiness.

Evarngar kept the first watch for the night as all about him slept. Mirrortac relieved him after some time, bringing with him the wrapped Werdstone which he now would not let out of his sight. He snuck another glance at the stone and discovered the glowing star had changed shape and colour. He examined it more closely, watching as the mysterious shape broke into shards of different hues and danced inside the stone like the flames of a fire. In simple fascination, he watched the display oblivious to all that may have been occurring around him.

Mirrortac jerked, startled when a hand tapped him on the shoulder. He swung around and peered into Daghva's grave face.

'*Oh, it be only you, Daghva,*' he said. '*Be it your watch already?*'

Daghva glanced down at the stone then back at the erfin, and grimly commented. '*There be menace here.*'

The erfin flinched, hastily throwing the hide over the stone. '*You must naught surprise me as you did. Neither be the stone for one such as a hyfnuk to look upon. Only I and the maja-tak of the Werd can look upon it.*'

He rose, leaving Daghva to his musings. Mirrortac returned to bed himself alongside Fervik who responded to the movement by wrapping an arm around the erfin while still asleep. He fell asleep immediately and was still deep in slumber long after all had awakened and eaten their first food for the day. Daghva walked past the sleeping erfin and frowned. He wandered near the wrapped up Werdstone and stooped towards it. Abruptly, Mirrortac shouted out loud, 'Do naught regard the stone!' and sat up, wringing his eyes with his paws.

The hyfnuk returned a rare smile. '*I knew that would wake you,*' he said thickly.

'*The stone has selected a new guardian,*' Ameece observed, astounded.

Mirrortac shook himself and stretched. He surveyed the area and the group with a sweep of his eyes. '*We must make haste for the end of this rock place.*' he motioned to Iyaji. '*Attend me with some food. I will eat on foot.*'

The hyfnuk bowed in obedience. '*Yea, oh master. You shall have some of your own best wooil that I have kept until now.*'

Mirrortac led off, marking the way with large strides. Ameece and Fervik made swift to maintain their position near him with Iyaji passing over fat pieces of wooil meat to the hungry erfin. The rest of the party followed fairly closely, catching quick glances up at the trees which proved to be a never-ending source of wonder. The walls of the canyon were dripping from the mist. Moss was thick in some places and ferns and other wet plants also grew out of hollows in the rock and at the base. Evarngar's ears twitched. He pulled Ameece and Fervik to him. Mirrortac swiveled around and raised an eye-brow at the hyfnuk. '*What be the matter?*' he said.

Evarngar craned his neck and scrutinised the trees while everyone's eyes followed where he was looking. Mirrortac's green eyes rested on a spot up in one of the trees and his expression visibly relaxed.

'*Be naught afeared. These shall be friends if I can judge by their descendants,*' he said.

Soon they could hear the grunting tongue of faugs as the winged gibbon-faced beings glided from branch to branch and finally down to the ground near them. Despite Mirrortac's reassurance, the roznoghs all eyed the faugs suspiciously. Fervik timidly poked his head out from between Mirrortac and Evarngar. There were six of the tall beings now facing them, their bead-like eyes subjecting the party to equal scrutiny while their green mouldy fur stunk like the greevuns of Yidrogh. Two of the faugs were carrying loaded bows with full quivers strapped to their backs. Their faces were grim and alert for any trouble.

One of the faugs stepped forward and grunted something towards the party of roznoghs. Mirrortac nodded, understanding the faug tongue, though taking a little extra time to decipher the older dialect. The faug repeated himself. 'I say to you again, what be your place here at the borders of Skye?'

'I shall be the only one to understand your tongue, faug-one,' Mirrortac explained. 'We come from the waste lands of Yidrogh at the bidding of the Sky-master, Yidu, god to these people, the roznoghs. We shall be entering Skye.'

The faugs were alarmed at this and the one who was addressing them said, 'You must reconsider! It be great silliness to enter into the weirdness of Skye. Turn your feet now before you be lost in foreverness!'

Mirrortac felt the press of roznogh minds querying him. '*They do naught wish us to go into Skye. They be afraid for us*,' he translated before speaking again to the faugs. 'We come at an invitation of the great Yidu. He will clear a path for us as this journey be of greatest import. We can naught be distracted in our path.'

The faug's urgency was not appeased. 'This Yidu invites only fools. He will play his game with you then destroy you, or worse, leave you to search in vain for him for the rest of time.'

Mirrortac was displeased at this news but had fully expected that his path would be thwarted. But there was no other option.

'What you tell me may be truth but the task I am to do can naught be abandoned. There be e'en greater powers at my aid that shall see the completing of this task.'

Mirrortac prepared to move away but the armed faugs lifted their bows and pointed the weapons at the party. The faug leader said, 'We can naught allow you entry to Skye. If you do not turn back, the first arrow shall be your death, blue-fur.'

The hyfnuks tensed up and snarled back at the faugs. They had no concept of the archers' weapons but interpreted the menacing body language as a threat to their lives. Evarngar immediately stepped in front of Ameece to shield her while Fervik stood quivering in fear behind them. To their astonishment, Mirrortac threw his head back and laughed loudly at the faugs. 'Hah! If you knew of this erfin standing before you, you would naught be foolish. Do you believe these archers can stop Mirrortac! I have battled monster and demon many times your size and number. We shall naught be stopped!'

The faug leader flinched but remained resolute. 'You speak impossible things blue-fur. It be naught my wish to kill you but it be far the better for you and your friends to die here then step foot into the madness of Skye.' Then he pleaded again, 'I beg of you to forget this foolishness and return to your Yidrogh. Even such bravery as yours will yield in Skye.'

Mirrortac dismissed the plea while the hyfnuks and elders watched on in tense silence, helpless to know the meanings of the words passing between the erfin and the faug.

'You may see it as your duty to prevent our entry to Skye, but I warn you naught to try stopping us, as you shall regret the day you spurned the mighty Mirrortac!'

The erfin commanded his party to follow but the faugs immediately lifted their weapons to shoot. Mirrortac swung around and glared wildly at them. He lifted his hand towards them and shouted in the ancient maja tongue. 'Manarg hib rushimba!' Their arrows burst into spontaneous flame and melted in their hands, forcing them to abandon their weapons. The faugs all fled terrified. Their leader cursed the erfin over his shoulder as he negotiated a nearby tree. 'We will let Yidu have his way with you and your pack of demons, cursed-one. Go to your madness with our curses behind you!'

The roznoghs stood open-mouthed at the erfin's spell-casting display. Shaduk gazed at him grimly. '*Here be the proof that this erfin be a demon. E'en our greatest spells be naught to this dark sorcery.*'

'*The stone knows many such tricks,*' Daghva volunteered, his tone dry and suspicious.

Mirrortac was surprised himself. It seemed that he just knew what to say from instinct. He felt a certain satisfaction at being able to summon up such a spell at will, and he fingered the Werdstone absently, sensing the power of it tingling through him. Ameece gave him a cautionary glance. '*Your mind takes too much pleasure in your boldness, Mirrortac. You worry me though my heart excites at your touch.*'

Mirrortac smiled disarmingly, and his face softened. '*Do naught concern yourself, rainbow-child. After all I have fought against; I am surely allowed a little boldness.*'

Ameece smiled back uncertainly. Evarngar frowned. '*What did these creatures want with us?*' he asked. '*If they were so concerned for us, why did they threaten us with their pointed sticks and bows?*'

Mirrortac explained what the faugs had told him, which perplexed Evarngar and the elders since the faugs were talking of Yidu's dangerous games with his subjects. The elders considered such a suggestion as unthinkable, as did Evarngar. Ameece was beginning to question her own faith in Yidu but was still confused. Fervik was too frightened to put much thought into anything, preferring to stay near the erfin and Evarngar, glancing back fearfully at the forest as they made their way to the rock wall at the end of the canyon.

At last they reached the huge boulder blocking the entrance to Skye where Mirrortac turned to them, with his eyes resting on Ameece.

'*There be danger in the journey through Skye ... I am prepared to go alone with the Werdstone should none of you wish to go. You are all free to leave and go back to your homes.*'

Ameece raised her eyes to his. '*I am the maja-tak of the Werd. Wherever the Werdstone be taken, I must follow.*'

'*And I must stay by my mistress' side,*' Evarngar stated.

'*Then, we also must be with our mistress,*' the elders chorused.

Daghva stepped forward from the four hyfnuks. '*You be our master now. You need someone to curb your boldness,*' he said, with a hint of a smile.

'*And what say you?*' Mirrortac turned to Fervik.

'*Would you send a young roznogh off on his own to wander the greevuns? I wish to see this Skye for myself.*' Fervik grinned up at the erfin.

Mirrortac beamed. '*Then it be settled. We all go to Skye!*'

'*But how shall we do that? Our way be blocked,*' Rimerelle observed, indicated the great boulder.

The erfin answered with a knowing wink and turned to face the boulder. With one hand on the Werdstone he muttered something in maja, which gained an immediate response from behind the boulder. The ground shuddered and they all could hear a rumbling sound as the boulder slowly rolled to one side, revealing a gigantic cavern flanked on either side by two high columns of stone with a narrow stairway between. The stairway led sharply upward and was composed of unremarkable grey slabs of stone, unkempt with a layer of thin soot over them. The roznoghs gaped at the cavern and the stairway. '*I'm first!*' Fervik said, running on ahead into the cavern before anyone could stop him.

Mirrortac stepped ahead of the others, trying to catch up to Fervik with his limping gait. Fervik dropped back, suddenly afraid of what might await him up the stairway. He sheepishly turned and came into step behind the erfin. It was a long way up the seemingly endless flight of steps, with the erfin labouring and panting as he climbed. Fervik lent him his arm as the erfin paused a hundred steps up. Ameece too, stepped up and helped him negotiate the steps that spiraled out of view above.

Mirrortac felt the gentle touch of her hand and her body as she pressed up against him, and again was reminded of Yenic. If he shut his eyes, he could imagine it was her alive again.

The others followed not far behind. There was a distant rumble below as the boulder fell back in its place, plunging them into darkness. They all halted for a few moments while their eyes adjusted to the thick blackness. Their breaths wheezed in the dank environment. Soon, they were marching upwards again, grasping at the walls to orient themselves.

At the count of 3000 steps, the stairway abruptly leveled out and the ceiling shallowed out so much that they were all forced to crawl the last few erfin-lengths to the exit. A burrow-like opening let in a stream of light as they bellied out into the air where they were able to stand again. Once their eyes adjusted, they found themselves on top of a flat plateau where carefully arranged rows of small trees dotted the landscape on either side of a pathway stretching out in front of the opening in the rock. The branches of the trees were laid low with oval-shaped fruit while swarms of bees buzzed around pink flowers wafting a perfumed scent in all directions. The weaving pathway gleamed bright yellow under a sun perched high above their heads.

The roznoghs were stunned by the brightness as they were unused to seeing Luma so high. Daghva shielded his eyes as he peered up towards Luma, then peering around him with his typical air of gloom, said, '*This world be too unfamiliar to this hyfnuk. There be menace here unseen.*'

Fervik took one look at the trees with their bounty of fruit and aromatic flowers and let out a hoot of delight. '*It is so beautiful! These trees with their fat flowers that smell of sweetness to the nose!*'

This made Mirrortac laugh. '*They be naught fat flowers, my dear Fervik. They be fruit which we may test as food, as much fruit can be eaten.*'

Fervik giggled as he charged up to a nearby tree and picked the fruit.

'*Chew away the covering of the fruit, and taste with care. I do naught wish to see you poisoned,*' Mirrortac gestured hastily.

Fervik handed out a few of the fruits to the hyfnuks who were also eager to taste something they have never seen before. The young roznogh bit off some skin from the fruit and sunk his teeth into the flesh beneath. His face abruptly contorted as he tasted the juicy contents, his reaction mirrored by the hyfnuks who coughed and spat out bits of the fruit.

'*The flesh stings the tongue!*' Fervik smirked.

Mirrortac plucked a fruit for himself and tasted it. '*You be all silly!*' he reprimanded. '*The taste is quite becoming ... sweet. You eat only bitter hyfnu and meat; you must endure the sweetness as you will find it quite acceptable in time.*'

'*Allow us bitterness,*' Karn said. '*This sweet thing be unbecoming to the tongue!*'

'*Then we shall seek out bitter fruits for bitter tongues,*' Mirrortac chuckled as he sucked at another knob for the fruit.

Ameece took a piece of fruit from Fervik and tried it for herself. Her eyes flashed wide and she nodded appreciatively as the juice dribbled down her chin.

'*Mirrortac and I shall have this fruit all to ourselves. It is so refreshing!*' she said.

It was the first time Ameece had been inclusive of the erfin, a fact that did not escape Mirrortac's notice. The elders were sampling the fruit now but similarly rejected it after a few sucks of juice. '*You are welcome to it!*' Rimerelle said, prompting nods of agreement from the others.

Their attention was diverted for a few moments by the plaintive croaks of a flock of white birds overhead. The birds soared in lazy circles, their long necks stretched out before them while spindly long legs trailed behind. Mirrortac tried to tune in to their essence but could get no response; only a sense of dispassion as the birds continued their course to the west. The edge of the plateau was nearby, overlooking the vast icy wastes of Yidrogh far beyond. The view, however, appeared filtered and unnatural, suggesting that Skye had been assembled with the aid of great spells.

Fervik dashed off when he saw the wondrous panorama. He ran himself frantic to reach the edge of the cliff but discovered it remained out of reach – an illusion to bewilder and test the roznogh. He gave up finally, turning heel to trudge back to the party in disappointment.

Fervik shook his head. '*It looked so near. I do naught understand. What weirdness!*'

He held onto Mirrortac as he regained his breath. The elders exchanged anxious glances as a strained mood fell upon the party. Mirrortac turned and motioned them onward along the yellow path.

'*We must make haste before Luma enters the Netherworld,*' he said, but he needn't have worried as the sun was slow to change its station in the sky above.

The landscape proved equally challenging. All the trees were identical in every aspect, to the extent that the fruit on them ripened at the exact same place as every other tree in this never-ending orchard. Every curve in the path was the same as the one before while the trees spread out in the same arrangement of rows around them. The only way to tell that any progress was being made was to look behind them at the opening in the rock where they had started, and watch it gradually diminish until there was no further reference left to indicate how far they had advanced. The normally light-hearted younger hyfnuks were becoming increasingly unnerved by the maddening monotony in the landscape, and their moods grew darker by the moment.

'*This woody place makes me afeared,*' Iyaji admitted, shedding his mask of bravado.

Ameece regarded the wearied faces of those around her. She urged Mirrortac to stop. '*We have gone long enough for a day. Can you naught see that the hyfnuks be losing their spirit. A good rest shall give them renewed strength,*' she pleaded.

'*Yea, it be truth … I detect the workings of many spells in the making of this place. It be maddening indeed. We will rest for now.*'

They all slumped beneath the shade of the trees and were asleep in moments. Although it was far warmer than in Yidrogh, there was no fierceness to the heat, with a cool breeze proving to be most invigorating.

Ameece awoke earlier than the others. She wondered at her strange feelings for the erfin and how she wanted to trust him but was confused. She crept over to his side and regarded him as he slept. He had spoken of his beloved Yenic, and how she reminded him of her. Ameece searched her spirit for any memory of a past life. Vague images came of an erfin life … fir trees, nif-grass, child-fins … girls … a face of a he-erfin … was it Mirrortac? The images dissolved too quickly. Yet the yearning did not fade. '*I think I love him …*' she thought absently.

Mirrortac snuffled awake and yawned. He opened his eyes and saw Ameece staring at him. '*It be comforting to see you here, rainbow-child,*' he whispered.

Ameece allowed a smile. '*And you ... though you vex me.*'

The others were awakening too; glad to have shut their eyes on the bizarre landscape for some time.

Fervik patted his furry belly. '*I be hungry ... be there any wooil left?*'

Evarngar handed over a small piece of dried meat. '*Here ... this be the last.*'

They all ate their fill from the supplies while Ameece and Mirrortac also ate some of the fruit from the nearby trees. Luma held station much at the same spot it was when they had gone to sleep, but clearly much time had passed, perhaps half a day in the reckoning.

Soon, they all stood and Mirrortac gave the order to march on. It was perhaps a full erfin-day again before they noticed any change in the orchard, which finally petered out only to be replaced by unattractive trees that had neither blooms nor fruit, and were rather spindly. This added to the mood of desolation that descended over them like a dense cloud, thickening with each step they took. The silence around them was almost absolute – no bird or insect stirred, with the only sound being a subtle creaking emanating from the trees themselves. Daghva became agitated, flicking his head from side to side and moaning. The three younger hyfnuks tried to calm him but he only became more panicky.

Mirrortac turned in time to see Daghva collapse to the ground. He was writhing and moaning, holding his ears with his hands as if deafened by a sound no-one else heard.

'*What in the Netherworld possesses you Daghva ... be you in some pain?*' Mirrortac asked, genuinely concerned for the hyfnuk.

'*It be the wooded things, master!*' Daghva agonised, adopting untypical affection in his tone with the erfin. '*I vow you will all hear it soon. Save us, master!*'

Daghva had no sooner said this when Ameece's breath quickened, and she grabbed the erfin's arm. He looked at her pale face and saw the panic in her eyes.

'*I am in fear ... The noise! It consumes my head!*' She was squinting as tears flowed freely down her soft facial fur and down her cheeks. She clutched her ears, frantically scratching at them as though invaded by annoying insects.

He looked back at the trees. Were they multiplying? They crowded in as though attacking, yet no movement was detected. Soon the others were similarly affected. Fervik fell into a ball and began screaming while all around him the roznoghs moaned and scratched at their ears. And now it was Mirrortac's turn.

The subtle creaking of the trees quickly altered into a sinister cackling that echoed inside his head, emerging from everywhere yet nowhere. The crazy cackling became louder at each passing moment, until it registered pain, forcing the erfin to also clutch and scratch at his ears.

'Screech of Gakar! Stop it! Stop it!' he yelled.

Mirrortac found it hard to concentrate enough to communicate with the tree essence, resorting instead to the Werdstone which warmed under his touch. He fought off the compulsion to clutch at his ears again while regarding the stone through the pain in his head. His focus was feeble but enough. The stone glowed softly, communicating the words he needed to say.

Through quivering lips he rasped, 'Shalabash ung destrum, lumuk om zestra neeve!'

The pressure and pain in his head eased instantly. The cackling stopped. The moans of the roznoghs gave way to relieved sighs. The disheveled party rose wearily, dusting themselves off. Shaduk the elder was distraught. '*Yidu be displeased with us … but why punish his loyal subjects … punish the erfin demon and the renegades. Why us?*'

'*Because he cares for naught,*' Mirrortac replied.

Daghva got up and came to the erfin with bended knee. His eyes were still streaming with tears. '*I be sorry, master. My concern be only for you. I am much afeared for you.*'

Mirrortac patted the hyfnuk reassuringly. '*It be safe for now, my friend.*' There was weariness in his voice.

Rimerelle the elder had noticed the erfin's spellcraft, yet again saving them from harm. '*These be unknown spells that pass your lips, erfin. You consulted the Werdstone … be it Yidu, after all, who directs your steps?*'

'*In my first life I was the roznogh Browagh who was given the Werdstone to take to the roznogh people … it was Browagh who was the father of the first daughter of the Werd. Yidu had told him to return with the stone when in his last life. This erfin be his last life.*'

'*But now he no longer trusts this erfin. Yet he leads you to him … perhaps to punish you himself,*' Rimerelle observed. '*And these renegades of yours …*'

'*He be naught a god!*' Daghva interrupted. '*We have all been misled, wise elder.*' Daghva scowled at the elder.

'*Yea, I be wise … listen to me. The erfin be a demon. Indeed, how should he suddenly appear in Yidrogh, if naught by a demon's magic?*' Rimerelle smiled smugly, regarding Daghva with disdain.

Daghva had no answer but grunted his displeasure. '*I may be a lowly hyfnuk, but I know I trust the word of the Skye-clan who spoke of Yidu showing his creature-ness. Mirrortac comes from the true master … and we shall know who that be in time.*'

Rimerelle and Shaduk both shook their heads in dismay. '*Foolish hyfnuk!*' Rimerelle concluded.

Ameece comforted Fervik who was still quaking with sobs. The younger hyfnuks were as bewildered as the others. Mirrortac gave out a long sigh before facing them.

'*I am filled with regret that I should have dragged you all to this demon place. Even as I address you, ancient ones speak to me from the stone.*'

Ameece and the elders looked quizzical. Mirrortac continued.

'*Yidu be testing us all and wishes us to fail in our mission. The screaming trees be but the beginning of these tests.*' He scanned the faces of the roznoghs, catching the despair in Ameece's eyes. The roznoghs wore haunted expressions.

'*Each of you must summon up all your will to come together in this great task – the greatest ever asked of any roznogh since Browagh walked the earth. Are you sworn to this? Do you still wish to go on?*'

Daghva looked around to his comrades and exchanged mind mutterings. Then he turned to face the erfin again. '*We be with you to the end, master. Where else can we go?*' he said, and the others nodded agreement.

The elder Rimerelle tugged at his greying beard. '*We be sworn to service to the maja-tak of the Werd and the Werdstone. Although we be cursed for it.*'

Then Mirrortac looked upon Ameece, and his heart tugged at him. '*And you, rainbow-child ... what be your feelings on this?*'

She wrung her pawed hands together, peering up to him and screwed up her mouth. '*It be madness, but I would follow you to the Netherworld if need be.*' She was looking down as she said this but lifted her eyes up at him with a hint of a smile.

Mirrortac's eyes twinkled at the remark. This surely was his Yenic.

The trees stood silent as though chastised. Finally, he gave the sign for them to move on and summoned Daghva to walk with him. The elder hyfnuk was slightly hunched so as not to appear too bold alongside his master. His manner was nervous. Mirrortac was quiet for a short time before communicating his concerns.

'*You have the right to worry of this task. But I feel that you are not telling all. Speak up.*'

Daghva's breathing was unsteady. '*Oh master, you must naught take heed of this silly hyfnuk.*'

Mirrortac looked at him sharply. '*If you do naught wish to tell me then I can leave you alone with the trees to consider your life.*'

Daghva let out a sigh and after a few long moments answered. '*I do naught peer into the stone as you do, master. For a hyfnuk I give matters a little too much thought. It be in my nature to be wary of all that belongs to spellcraft and I can naught help but observe things beyond the notice of others.*' He paused and looked back darkly. '*I fear the Werdstone be taking possession of you, master. Yidu gives you some power only to control you. He will corrupt you ...*'

A tear fell down the hyfnuk's face as he turned his face away again. Mirrortac was not perturbed. He merely gave Daghva a friendly pat on the shoulder.

'*Do naught be afeared. I have control of the knowledge of the ancient ones. I believe Yidu has use of the stone only ... it be naught his. It be the ancients who give me the words ...*'

they be of maja our sacred tongue.' He gave a quick check of the others then turned his attention back to Daghva. 'Confide in no-one what I had just told you. I feel more will come to the light. Go now and join your friends.'

Daghva fell back and rejoined his comrades. Ameece, Evarngar and Fervik increased their pace until they were alongside the erfin. Overhead, the strange white birds were again circling, this time gliding downwards towards them. Fervik tensed up when he saw the birds, eyeing them with trepidation. Ameece felt his small body tense and gave him a hug. 'Be brave little one. We shall come to naught harm.'

The birds quickly dropped out of the sky as they all watched and halted their march along the path. As they came closer, the birds took on more of the appearance of alien beings with intelligent unreadable eyes glaring down at them along elongated beaks. They were gigantic, at least two-erfin lengths high. They alighted on the path with a flurry of wings which quickly folded out of sight. The hyfnuks assumed a defensive stance, taking up position to either side of the erfin and Ameece in a protective huddle.

The alien birds stepped up to them on tri-toed feet and Mirrortac answered by stepping forward as he kept a wary eye on them. They scrutinised each other for what seemed ages before the alien birds' voices sounded in perfect unison in all their minds.

'Go no farther, Mirrortac. Yidu has sent us to take the stone.'

The erfin's mottled green and blue fur fluffed in the breeze as he stood boldly, his head held up and the Werdstone clutched firmly in his paws.

'I can naught yield to your suggestion, bird-ones. I must give the stone to Yidu in person so that we may receive his blessing.'

The three alien birds were unfazed. *'We are the sacred chuffs who serve the great god, Yidu. Do you challenge the wishes of your god?'*

Mirrortac replied with all the cleverness he could muster. *'It be you who claim service to Yidu but how can I be certain of this?'*

The chuffs gazed at the erfin with cold unblinking eyes.

'The sacred chuffs of Yidu need no answer to a traitor. Give up your stone and save yourselves the torment of the Pathway Forever.'

Gasps rumbled through the party as Mirrortac remained steadfast. *'No servant of Yidu would call this erfin traitor,'* he tested.

'You flatter yourself, erfin. Yidu sees your purpose. We challenge you to vow upon the Werdstone that you naught seek to keep the stone for yourself!'

For the first time, the erfin hesitated. Tense moments passed tediously as Mirrortac considered his next course of action. At last, the eyes that rose up to meet the glare of the chuffs were filled with rebellion.

'If Yidu knows so much of me and my purpose, it be clear that his eyes watch me through another such stone as the one I possess. But you be slaves ... he be naught god. His

powers be great, yea, but such trickery I have also seen from those who rule the Netherworld of Hopocus. I shall seek him out and take his all-seeing eyes from him, and he will be blind!'

A vocal cry of dismay rose up from the elders, and even the hyfnuks were taken aback by the erfin's boldness. The chuffs remained unmoved, their eyes glazed and cold.

'You have chosen death, erfin. Yidu reveals all truth in Skye. He who curses the Skyemaster is dead already! And all who choose to follow this erfin is likewise cursed.'

The elder Shaduk raised an anxious arm in protest. *'We do naught support this erfin's plans. We be prisoners ... we must follow our mistress, and she must remain with the Werdstone.'*

'Then Yidu will send you to the Otherworld. You should have returned to Yidrogh when the erfin gave you the option.' There was no hint of compassion in the chuffs' reply.

Ameece came up to Mirrortac's side and placed an arm around his waist, startling the erfin.

'I am slow to accept the truth, but here it be. I shall stand by this erfin.' Her eyes turned to him. *'I shall stand by Mirrortac.'*

The elders frowned in distress. Evarngar tried to pull her away from the erfin's side but she resisted.

'She be demonised ... she knows naught of what she says,' Shaduk blurted in a vain effort to excuse his mistress. Rimerelle agreed, nodding.

The chuffs stared down the elder. *'She has made her nest. It be already fouled.'*

Daghva now stepped forward also. *'I shall trust my master in this though it may mean my death.'*

'Aye!' the other loyal hyfnuks chorused. But Rimerelle and Shaduk were shaking their shaggy heads, and Evarngar sighed and looked down at the ground in despair. *'We be all dead,'* he said.

Young Fervik was close to tears. He pawed his head with agitation. *'This be all too much for this roznogh to bear. Mirrortac master, you granted me sight and my life ... and for this I am very happy ... at least, I was happy. I do naught wish to die. I wish to return to my father and mother in Erga and be with my friends.'*

The erfin's heart dropped but he bore no malice against the young roznogh. Indeed, he knew it was foolish to bring the youngling along on such a dangerous mission. *He has so much life to give, and his parents must miss him badly.* Mirrortac shoved his hand under the cloth and placed his palm over the Werdstone, seeking its aid.

'Be this your chosen wish, little one?' he asked, and Fervik nodded, his head bowed, unable to look up at the erfin.

'Then I release you from Skye and its demons and return you this moment to your kin.' Mirrortac shut his eyes and began muttering maja under his breath. Fervik stole a quizzical look at him, but as the erfin's mutterings continued, they all watched with

incredulity as the young roznogh faded from their sight. In just moments Fervik had vanished entirely.

Mirrortac opened his eyes and looked around at the others. '*Do any of you wish to return to Yidrogh? I can end this nightmare for you now ... but you must tell me now. Yidu will naught make the path easy, as you have already seen.*'

The erfin particularly regarded the elders and Evarngar, who were still open-mouthed at his latest trick.

Rimerelle sighed. '*We can naught leave our mistress, though she be demonised. We are sworn to her service.*'

Daghva reiterated his last reply. '*You know we be with you unto death.*'

The chuffs, which had been silent and had witnessed everything with dispassion, tested their wings before saying, '*Your choice has been made.*'

Mirrortac scowled at them. '*Return to your master, you gakar droppings,*' he said, referring to the predatory bird of his homeland. '*Tell your master that we be on our way to see him and I will settle this matter with him in his temple.*'

The sacred chuffs spread out their wings and took flight, quickly gaining height and disappearing into tiny white dots in the sky above. A final message was communicated from them before they had completely disappeared from sight. '*You may search for Yidu for all the rest of your days, but it will be in vain. Madness will overcome you and even when you call upon him to rescue you, he will naught hear you.*'

MASTER OF SKYE

An updraft lifted the chuffs above the steep stone walls of the mesa and through a thin layer of cloud where they leveled out and circled. Beneath their wingtips was the large clustered crystal shape of a palace; its many crystalline pencils poking up at them at every angle. The sacred chuffs curved their wings in unison, and fell downward, taking them around in a wide arc towards the hexagonal clusters. Flashes of refracted sunlight projected up at them in rainbows and the sound of trickling water drifted up on the breeze. They banked in a tight formation around the side of one of the higher crystal spears, passing near its smooth rounded peak which wept a spring of clear water. The water streamed down its sides and meandered through a jagged crystal forest, finally collecting in a deep pool at the centre of the courtyard. The chuffs homed in on a glazed crystal platform and an opening which led down a hollowed-out crystal cylinder into the heart of the palace beneath. Their gangling legs alighted in turn on the platform as their wings folded to their sides. The platform was also streaming with water and slippery, but the chuffs allowed their legs to collapse beneath them as they slid in one smooth action into the crystal cylinder.

The three slid expertly to their feet again into a great hall where others of their kind stood sentinel alongside two rows of gemstone columns that girded the high crystalline ceiling. Hallways led off from either side, and at the head of the great hall was a high-backed marblelite throne adorned with a generous scattering of gems, inlaid in abstract patterns and rich in colour and lustre. Marblelite steps led down from the throne into the expanse of the great hall itself, with its floor made up of myriads of grains of gemstones formed together in flexible matting that was soft underfoot.

The figure of the demi-god stood half bent over a marblelite pedestal at the centre of the great hall; his three sapphire hued eyes gleaning information from the large clear stone cupped within the circle of marblelite perched atop the pedestal. He barely acknowledged the arrival of the three chuffs as he remained fully concentrated on the stone; its smooth hemisphere spoilt by a flaw at the top where a portion of stone had been broken off. The tiny black pupils at the centre of his eyes expanded along with his grin. Yidu snickered as he stared into the stone where he could clearly see Mirrortac and his entourage wearily resume their journey along the Pathway Forever.

At last Yidu pushed himself up from the pedestal and revolved his head around to address the newly arrived chuffs.

'You have given me satisfaction, oh holy ones. I shall enjoy the play with this erfin. He is clever, but the knowledge of the ancients will soon make him swoon with just enough power to corrupt his mission. I will slowly wear down the spirit of his "clan" and throw them into a confusion of lies. This will prove to my brother Wa-ku that Yidu has absolute power and will beat all the gods in the Great Game.'

The sacred chuffs bowed without changing their expressions. *'Oh mighty Yidu, but this Mirrortac seems to know you. There is naught in the discerning to reveal this.'*

Yidu swirled around in his glistening robe until he faced them. *'How can he know me? Though the stone tells me of some anomaly in his journey. He was taken to a beach north of the Islands of the Meretees then disappeared for some time. When he reappeared, he was suddenly in Yidrogh, many leagues from that beach. Perhaps someone who knows me ... my brother ... got to him, to thwart my plans in the Great Game.'* Yidu rubbed his hands together in contemplation. *'The supreme Werdstone may yet hide some things from my sight, but when the times of the triad of the worlds is again aligned, I shall be able to activate the Three Stones of Destiny on each of the worlds and the Great Game will be mine!'*

Yidu turned back to the stone on the pedestal and peered at the vision depicted within it. *'Walk onward oh Mirrortac!'* he said, mocking the image. *'What a fur-balled fool you are! Bring back the stone to me if you will ... I will send another to Yidrogh. The roznoghs are already mine, anyway. You only have a fragment of the Werdstone, stupid erfin! The remainder is here before me. I can make other eyes now that I have learnt how ...'* He grinned but there was a hint of a frown. The erfin was a mystery, even though his nine souls were tied to the Werdstone. Why had he disappeared? Where had he disappeared to, and how did he come to appear in Yidrogh? The stone would not reveal this. Did not the Werdstone see all?

Yidu was lost in his own thoughts when the stone before him clouded over and sparkled. Yidu knew this was prelude to a communication, and sure enough the image coalesced of another demi-god whose long golden locks of hair fell to shoulders a hands-breadth broader than Yidu's own. He reacted by folding his arms when he recognised his brother Wa-ku.

'So you finally worked out how to transmit with those greenstones of yours,' he said, startling the chuffs with the sound of his voice.

Wa-ku smiled but his expression was steeped in irony. A pair of sky-blue eyes studied Yidu through the medium of the stone. 'You should use your voice more often, my brother,' Wa-ku smirked. 'And not only when you need to address your subjects through the stone.'

'Nay, I have no need to speak, unless through this.' Yidu indicated the stone. 'Besides, your petros did enough talking for all the worlds. It is good that you are finished with them. That multi-coloured furball of an erfin of yours saw to that!' Yidu half chuckled. 'What is it that you want from me, anyway? Have you finally decided to join me in the Great Game, brother?'

The eyes in the image grew cold and any semblance of Wa-ku's former civility vanished. 'You play in a dangerous field, Yidu. The knowledge of the ancients needs the wisdom of great spirits. You saw what happened on Nerthule ... the temples of the Utlontees and all the priests and priestesses were all destroyed ... and the Universal Master will destroy you too ... or perhaps you will do that yourself.'

Yidu laughed. 'Hah! They were foolish students in the Game. They deserved to be drowned ... in any case the clever ones survived and will be reunited at the alignment of the triad. And I will lead them. Let any god try to stop us!' Yidu raised a fist and glared wildly.

Wa-ku's face paled. 'You are worse than I had feared. This is madness, brother! You may know enough to believe you know everything, but all your knowledge will be scattered like feathers in a great wind when you are recalled to face the Universal Master.'

Yidu turned his nose up at his brother's image. 'The knowledge of the ancients is the knowledge of the Universal Master ... but he did not wish us to have it because he knew it would make us as powerful as he is. It is all part of the Great Game, brother. If you only knew what great knowledge this is, you would realise then that you are limitless! You are the Universal Master!'

Wa-ku shook his head. 'I did once also think as you do, but I realised that I knew too much yet far from enough. I thirsted for more and became drunk in its embrace; like the lips of a loose woman, it is treachery. We may be worshipped as gods but our souls are forfeit ... we are as leaves upon a tree – we are the tree only as long as we are joined to it.'

'You have spent too much of your time listening to those philosopher Nerthulians, brother,' Yidu sneered. 'If you wish to use symbols then I will tell you that I am not the leaf but the seed that separates itself from the tree and grows into a tree as large as and mightier than its mother ...'

'A seed that carries all the heredity of its mother and therefore only gives the appearance of separation,' Wa-ku quickly cut in.

'And thus we are at one with the mother/father ... we are they and they are us ... we are the Universal Master!' Yidu shouted.

'Precisely,' Wa-ku said, then added. 'Except you do not have the wisdom to understand one very fine difference.'

'I'm sure you are going to enlighten me, brother.' Yidu smugly offered.

'That you are not the source of your own creation,' Wa-ku finished.

Yidu dismissed his brother's statement with a wave of his hand. 'Maybe not ... but I am the source of my creations. It is all in the Game, my brother. Those of us who have the knowledge of the ancients realise we have the right to be gods and our many subjects will fall down at our feet and worship us ... instead of us worshipping someone else of no real substance.'

Wa-ku sighed deeply. 'I should have known that I was wasting my time trying to persuade you to give up your foolish plans and accept the universal Truth ... "The first will be last and the last shall be first" – no truer words were spoken.'

Yidu gripped the marblelite lip surrounding the stone as he hung over the image of his brother. 'More Nerthulian philosophy, no doubt,' he said. He was losing patience with Wa-ku. 'Don't waste your sentiments on me, brother. In a hundred more orbits of Nerthule, all three worlds in the triad will come under my power ... and I will reign over all the "Master's" so-called "children". The Great Game will be mine!'

The pallor of Wa-ku's face became tinged with the ruddiness of his barely controlled anger. 'You will be stopped!'

Yidu's eyebrows lifted. 'Oh, by that furball I suppose. I don't know how you hid him, but it will do you no good. He's as good as dead already.'

Wa-ku looked confused. 'Mirrortac? He's alive? I thought he was killed by Beeble-zub. He is of no consequence ... but now that you mention him.' He raised his hand to his face thoughtfully. 'Perhaps I should help him ... though it seems he is on an errand for the Universal Master already.'

Yidu sneered. 'It's of no matter. Perhaps it is someone else in the Game who wishes to challenge me. I'll take care of him ... good and proper!'

Wa-ku was silent, now considering this new information. There was a slight hint of a smirk as he signed off. His face abruptly vanished from the stone, leaving Yidu staring into its cold opaqueness. He too was now uncertain of this latest development, adding to the mystery of the erfin's inexplicable absence from the stone's knowledge. The only way he knew that the soul-link to the stone could break would be if the erfin had died and gone to the Otherworld. But as he was clearly alive, that was impossible. There was some powerful magic going on here, which made the erfin a greater threat than he first reckoned.

Yidu cursed out loud then walked towards the throne, muttering more curses as he went. The chuffs inclined their heads in unison at him. '*Do you know that this Mirrortac intends to confront you here ... in your temple?*' they said.

Yidu laughed but it was tempered with doubt. '*When that fat-headed erfin wakes up to the riddle of the Pathway Forever, I shall lure him to his death at Wergaen. Whoever is conspiring against me will not win. I am the all powerful Yidu!*'

'Wergaen is the shield of Oashu ... the stone that links this world to the Werdstone. Do you think it wise for the erfin to get so close to that stone of destiny?'

Yidu waved his dismissal of their suggestion. *'You give wise advice, oh sacred chuffs. But I will not let him near Oashu. He cannot cross the molten lake. He and his "clan" will all die before that ...'*

The chuffs nodded. *'Yea, you speak rightly. There is no way across the lake.'*

Yidu was about to sit down on the throne when the chuffs posed another question.

'Nonetheless, should this erfin find a way across ... and it is impossible certainly ... but should someone come to his aid ... an enemy ... then what then? You need to be prepared.'

Yidu found their questioning unnerving and frowned. He went quiet for a few moments before he arrived at a solution to their hypothetical problem.

'Then even if he should pass over the lake somehow, aided as you say, and even if the web wraiths are not enough to discourage his advance, and he manages to gain a hold of Oashu, somehow ... then I will instruct the stone to bring him immediately here, and you will take Oashu from him, and I will send him to Thenigmas. He can make no trouble there ... he will no longer have access to Oashu nor the Werdstone. Problem solved!'

The chuffs turned to each other then faced Yidu again.

'And that shall leave the erfin trapped in Thenigmas forever. He cannot escape that world ... and its vicious natives will have their way with him. But as you say, he will not even cross to Wergaen. You have nothing to fear.'

Yidu smiled weakly. But he felt sure that the sacred chuffs were not fully convinced. However, as he realised the cleverness of his solution to all hypothetical possibilities, he grinned, showing perfect teeth between thin lips. The slowed magical construct of Skye made him still young although the planet Mareos had done more than a thousand rotations around its sun Luma. He sent the chuffs away to refresh themselves while he called on others to bring him cups of his own created beverage. Though he had no need for drink or food, the taste of a few of his favourites still brought him satisfaction.

The occult knowledge brought to him through thousands of seasons of studying the Werdstone had taught him to survive on air. Skye was his own proud creation. The intricacy of the many spells needed to create such a world in miniature had taken numerous seasons to complete. He had made it so time almost stood still while in Yidrogh and all over Mareos, life continued at a normal pace. Browagh turning up when he did was a master stroke of luck. He simply gave him a fragment of the supreme Werdstone and sent him on his way, allowing him to completely enslave the roznoghs and control their lives in detail. Although at the time he naively believed he was guiding and protecting their lives and would get the stone back on Browagh's ninth life. But the stone taught him otherwise, and he soon discovered what he could do with its powerful knowledge. He couldn't let Browagh ... now Mirrortac, return and spoil his plan. What he did not plan was that the roznoghs would split and form other tribes that would journey farther afield on Mareos. Yet still, this erfin returned from the other side of Mareos to upset his well laid plans. Not for long, he thought.

Long before he had come to Mareos, Yidu had been a student of the Werd and was instructed to place the specially inscribed Stones of Destiny on each of the planets of Mareos, Thenigmas and Nerthule. At a certain point in cosmic time, the three planets would be powerfully linked in a triad, and it occurred to Yidu later that this was an opportunity for him to control the destinies of the three greater worlds and all the peoples in them. The Werdstone had initially been a simple tool of enlightenment, but Yidu realised he could link it directly to the Three Stones of Destiny, which he did later after creating Skye and after many daughters of the Werd had already passed on the fragment. He went to Thenigmas and Nerthule again, this time with the Werdstone, and performed the links with the stones. He had opponents in the Game who were working to enslave other planets/worlds ... there were so many to go around. Yet someone clearly had their eyes on his prize – jealous of the power he would hold.

Yidu stirred from his reverie to notice the arrival of a servant delivering a frothy liquid served in a silver goblet encrusted with gemstones. Yidu accepted the goblet eagerly, lifting it to his lips. Since he had no specific need to drink it, he took a mouthful and allowed it to swill around over his tongue, bringing to his senses every nuance of the liquid's special flavour. He kept on savouring the flavour for some time without swallowing. The liquid would simply be absorbed through the soft tissue of his mouth. Yidu shut his eyes for a few brief moments of micro-sleep; inducing a state of total relaxation worth a full night's sleep. He 'awoke' refreshed and alert, urged again to consult the polished hemisphere of stone on the pedestal.

He was bewildered and annoyed at the arrogant erfin who now had the gall to confront him in his own land. Who told the erfin about the stones, if not Wa-ku? He must be lying, Yidu thought. He watched, waiting.

Wa-ku watched the vision of his brother dissolve from the greenstone crystal bowl. He swiveled in his hoverchair and pressed a button on the side that made it float across the room to an array of instruments on the other side. His paralysed legs dangled over the side of the chair that contained a crystalline base with anti-gravity boosters to allow the chair to hover and be propelled anywhere he wished it to go. He winced with pain as his hand muscles struggled to manipulate the instrument controls.

He frowned deeply at his handicap. It had not always been this way, and had he been fully able, he would have stopped Yidu himself, but his brother now scared him. He was more capable of overpowering this cripple.

The accident had occurred after he had created Petrosium, which was also the source of the greenstones and the other useful gem crystals used in the operation of the cosmo-ship. The Petrosium mine was the richest source of power crystals in this sector of the universe, but before he could mine it, he had initially to gain the trust of the inhabitants there, the Petros, who had a rather dangerous means of disabling any creature, or man, with their sub-sonic horns. Gaining their trust was far easier than he had at first expected. The Petros were dazzled by him; they saw him as a god, so it was just a matter of instilling in them a ritual system of worship and constructing a device that allowed him to transmit his vision to them. The cosmo-ship worked on universal time, which like Yidu's Skye world, allowed a thousand cycles of Mareos to pass while only a few cycles passed in universal time. Transmissions, of course, had to be equalised to local time. It was all quite amusing for a time ... Wa-ku joined in the Great Game in his enslavement of the Petros, but certain cosmic events made him realise his error. He was truly not a god, which was only made too painfully clear by the accident. It was ironic that the evil underworld creature Beeble-Zub was no more corrupt than himself. Mirrortac had not only destroyed Beeble-Zub, but the godhood of Wa-ku in one fell swoop. Now, what remained of the Petros, were again free to pursue their own ways, though some will continue to practise their useless rituals.

Wa-ku recalled the scenario that led up to the accident. The cosmo-ship had been descending for a routine mining expedition at Petrosium when there was a failure in the crystal instrument array, causing the ship to descend too quickly and crash into the ground. The landing restraints broke, sending him careering into the ceiling with a painful thud. The next thing he remembered was waking up in a ward at the healing station. He had lost all feeling below his waist and his arms were also partly numb. The medical attendants had done all they could, but it was to no avail. The ship too, was badly damaged, and had been retrieved from the Wastes of Nug to undergo repair.

Wa-ku tuned in the crystal screen to the Werdstone portion that the erfin held. 'Now, who are you Mirrortac? Who is informing you, my friend?' Wa-ku stared at the fuzzy image. The clever erfin was consulting the stone about what he should do next.

'Careful, erfin ... the knowledge of the ancients is mesmerising,' he whispered. But Mirrortac could not hear him, as Wa-ku had no control over the Werdstone portion except to listen and watch the erfin's progress.

Wa-ku absently scratched at his chin. 'What can I do to help ... I cannot go to Skye as long as my brother sees. Too risky.'

Mirrortac consulted the stone, fully aware now that Yidu might be watching him. But it was not to Yidu that he addressed his question. He formed a question in his mind and asked the stone how to escape the never-ending path they were now on and go about locating the first Stone of Destiny. As he closed his eyes, his hands clutching at the now warm Werdstone, he could feel the archaic energies of the ancients filtering into his mind. He saw an image of a long and spiraling pathway, leading nowhere but into itself, while across from the path was a varied landscape with no marked trails but pointing the way to Oashu.

Mirrortac opened his eyes and wrapped up the stone in its protective hide. Ameece and the others stood by in anticipation.

'*We shall now be leaving this pathway and crossing there.*' He pointed through the trees.

There was a note of hesitation amongst the group, but Daghva stepped forward with confidence, following close behind the erfin as he led them away from the path and through the trees. The other hyfnuks eyed the trees suspiciously; afraid the cackling would begin again. But all remained calm. Ameece left Evarngar's side and caught up with the erfin, clearly eager to be going somewhere, anywhere. However, as she regarded him with a growing admiration, she couldn't help but feel afraid for him.

The clan made its way through the grove of trees until they returned to the path. Mirrortac ignored their bewildered expressions as he continued to lead them back across the path and onward through more trees.

'*The path turns upon itself. We can only defeat it by moving across it,*' he explained.

The others nodded without truly understanding, as the path seemed to be straight, yet the erfin said that it turned upon itself. But they reluctantly followed and crossed the path many more times before there was any noticeable change to the landscape. The maddening monotony of ordered rows of trees thinned out finally, giving way to rolling hill country covered with verdant pastures of grasses resembling the nif-grass of Mirrortac's homeland Eol. Thick hedges of low bushes grew along the gullies, populated by tiny birds that were perpetually moving about and whistling in short abrupt notes. The ground became alive with the activity of insects: the common sooz like those of the desert Petrosium, and many bugs and beetles and flying insects. Indeed, there were so many of them, that they flew up in waves at the group's approach. Karn snatched up a handful of insects and tentatively tasted them. His nod of approval prompted the others to do likewise, and soon the hyfnuks and the elders were dumping clusters of insects into their mouths with abandon.

Ameece grabbed some herself and chewed noisily, then proffered some to Mirrortac. '*These be tasty. Try some.*'

The erfin's lips curled up in disgust as he regarded the handful of crushed, stinking insects. '*Nay. I find birds more to my liking.*' He stopped near a hedge and looked back with a cheeky smile. '*Just watch!*'

Remembering his lesson from the Islands of the Meretees, he casually reached in and invoked a blessing on the spirit of the bird before withdrawing his arm and clutching a feathered lump in his grip. He tossed the bird into his mouth with a self-satisfied grin, eyeing the roznogh with a smirk.

'*I will never forget the lesson of the yone,*' he said. But Ameece did not know what he was talking about.

She glared back with a scowl, but the corners of her mouth inched upwards.

'*I suppose you will be telling me of this lesson of the ... yone.*'

Mirrortac proceeded to tell her about the journey with the islander Twx on the islands of the Meretees, and how Twx had come upon the lizards, killing them with such ease that dismayed the erfin as his own attempts failed one after another. Twx was able to grab the yones every time, while the erfin snatched frantically, only to find the yones escaping his grasp. The islander finally revealed his secret – to approach the yones with the frame of mind that they were nothing more than pretty flowers to be admired, and for that impression to be transmitted to the lizards. It was then quite simple to casually pick up the yones, accompanied by the necessary ritual blessing.

Ameece communicated a cautious '*Interesting*' while she continued her noisy munching as the insects crunched in her mouth.

'*What wonders that you know ... and strange peoples.*' She smiled at him, their eyes meeting.

Now safely away from the Pathway Forever, the group relaxed, and the erfin decided to make camp on a level area of meadow near a small stream. Evarngar kept a wary eye out for any danger to his mistress, while the hyfnuks amused themselves trying to catch fish which were present in large shoals in the stream. Daghva was not with them, but sat, sullen faced, alongside the stream, lost in his own thoughts. A travel-weary Ameece curled up in the shade of a bush and went to sleep while the elders conversed, exchanging worried glances.

The sky darkened.

The change in the light was so unexpected that it caused everyone to look up at once. Evarngar's eyes grew wide and Daghva leapt to his feet.

'*What be this? A moving cloud. Save us master Mirrortac!*' he shouted in their minds.

Mirrortac spun around to see an enormous cloud of insects descending towards them from the rise of the hill. An angry humming preceded their flight as the insects massed so thickly they cast a dark shadow on the low meadow. The hyfnuks turned from their fishing exploits with hands dripping, and their mouths gaped with horror. Rusk's gaze fell to a spot on the ground ahead.

'*The hyfnu-stuff is moving!*'

There was an outcry of alarm as everyone instantly realised that the grass was also a crawling mass of insects.

Evarngar took command. '*Move now – to the stream!*'

The hyfnuks were first to duck into the water, and the others quickly followed. But it was shallow and afforded limited protection. Evarngar awakened his mistress and hastened her to the stream where they prostrate themselves. Mirrortac searched around for the Werdstone, his eyes darting from place to place as he tried to recall where he had left it. Valuable time was lost as he tramped back and forth, his eyes straining to see into the knee-high grass.

The black flood of insects drowned out the sky; the sound of their humming rising as they approached the meadow. Mirrortac looked around anxiously. Ameece looked up and saw his frantic search. '*Forget the stone. You must save yourself!*' she told him. But he knew that the water offered scarce protection once the hoard was upon them. And then he saw the hide enfolded stone a moment before it was overrun by the scuttling insects.

He felt the first sting then his body erupted with pain. A wall of flying insects attacked; their pulsing abdomens stinging and snapping jaws biting as they crawled over him. He squinted and brushed frantically at the mass of insects on his head, while his legs felt fat and heavy with zooz. He stumbled towards the Werdstone as he continued to fend off the swarm. Through clouded vision he glimpsed the others dunk their heads under the water while the insects buzzed above them. Ameece and her elders suffered the worst as they could not hold their breath as long as the hyfnuks, and when they were forced to surface for air, they screamed in pain as the insects attacked.

Mirrortac collapsed, writhing in pain from all parts of his body. His nose bled where some insects had entered his nostrils to bite at the tender flesh inside. He opened his mouth in brief, desperate gasps, each time swallowing clusters of acrid insects that stung as they went down his throat. He gathered his waning energy and crawled in throbbing, slow movements towards the Werdstone, which was now invisible under a moving mass of insects. He stifled the urge to scream as that would let in more insects. He focused his mind on blocking out the severe aches all over his body, until gradually a glorious numbness inebriated his senses.

Then, with an effort of immense will, he summoned up all his reserves and stood up. Oblivious to the thick matting of insects covering him, he lumbered up to the spot where he had seen the stone and thrust his hand deep into the wild mass of zooz. There was little left of the wooil hide but bits of fluff, revealing the glowing form of the stone beneath. He picked up the stone and let out a hoarse invocation.

It took only moments before the insects flocked off him and fled back up the hill and into the air. He followed with an invocation of healing for all the blistering sores covering him and the roznoghs. Swollen faces, too many times exposed to the waspish stings, settled and smoothed over as though nothing had happened. Ameece wept and rushed up to the erfin, throwing her arms around him. '*I thought you were dead! It was horrible!*' she uttered.

Mirrortac hugged her tightly to him, feeling the rapid beat of her heart against his chest. Rimerelle's expression said everything about how he felt. He was displeased and disturbed. However, it was Daghva who spoke up, or rather it was his mind who met theirs.

'*This be Yidu's doing. He means to do us great harm,*' and turning to the elder he glared at him. '*Do you still wish to follow this imposter or our master Mirrortac?*'

Rimerelle scowled. '*We have offended the great Yidu … we deserve death. The erfin consorts with demons.*'

The loyal hyfnuks growled and began arguing with the elder, but Mirrortac called for silence.

'*Division be what Yidu wants, though we be ne'er united. We be safe now. Rest and have something to eat.*'

However, the tragedy had just begun. Ameece wiped her tears with the back of her furred hand and looked around for her elders. Rimerelle had emerged from the water but Shaduk remained prostrate in the stream, unmoving. Ameece gasped and cried out when she suddenly noticed him still there. He had not emerged for a breath.

'*No! Shaduk! My dear one!*' she shouted as she again burst into tears.

She let go of Mirrortac and rushed to where Shaduk lay in the stream. Mirrortac hastened after her, while the others looked on in shock. Ameece reached him and sunk down beside his body. She lifted his head, now wet and still, like a soggy rag, and placed his head in her lap. She rocked him gently, moaning and sobbing in mighty gasps. Shaduk's neck and face were still swollen from the insect stings, and a sludge of blood and water leaked out of his mouth. Rimerelle began muttering and rocking, adding his own grief to that of Ameece's. She stared back up at Mirrortac with pleading eyes. '*Bring him back … you have performed such magic before … do it for me, now …*' But he shrugged. '*There be no words for this … e'en the Ancients can naught bring back those who have already entered the Otherworld.*'

Rimerelle grabbed the erfin by the arm and tugged him away. '*You be the bringer of death, unblessed one! You have brought the wrath of the almighty Sky-master upon us, and we all shall die as the talking birds have warned.*'

Again, it was Daghva who came to Mirrortac's defence. '*You old fool! Who do you call unblessed? It be Yidu … naught master Mirrortac. He has shown us the truth of this demon Sky-master!*'

Rimerelle shook with anger. '*You and your renegades have already earned death. Shaduk be now in the great temple court of the Otherworld at the side of Yidu. Blessed be Shaduk!*'

The normally jovial faces of Iyaji, Ruck and Karn were downcast and solemn. Ameece sighed and rocked, moaning all the more.

Mirrortac took a deep breath and let it out in a long sigh. '*Come now Rimerelle … be no words to see Shaduk on his way? Shall we argue while his spirit looks back at us from the Otherworld?*'

Rimerelle gathered his senses and began to mutter some words for Shaduk's safe passage to the Otherworld, while the others remained silent in respect. When he had finished, Mirrortac called on them to leave Ameece alone with Shaduk's body to grieve properly. Rimerelle remained behind to console Ameece and say his own farewells to his fellow elder.

Mirrortac sat down a respectable distance away to eat while he watched them carry the body to the stream's edge to continue their dirge. Rimerelle clutched his fellow's body with shaking hands. He now seemed suddenly old and frail, his greying fur flustered and wild. He shut his eyes, quaking with his own grief. It was his turn now. Ameece rubbed her head up against Shaduk's and nuzzled him with her flat nose.

Rimerelle stirred and reached up a hand to her face. '*My little Ameece, why be you here? Renounce this journey and leave the erfin and his renegades with the demons. Let us return to Yidrogh before it be too late …*'

Ameece sniffed as she beheld the elder who had been with her throughout her life. She beheld Shaduk's solemn face, remembering how he too had played with her when she was just a child. Both elders had been her joy and source of sage advice. They had steered her course through her life as Maja-tak of the Werd. Now, as Rimerelle sought to again save her from a course that in all her upbringing could only mean death, she hesitated. The erfin that she for some bewildering and mysterious reason gave her heart to beyond question had tested all that she believed in. Yidu had been there for all time ... or so it seemed. Now, she wondered what the Sky-master truly was – god or some incredible fake. She looked back into Rimerelle's kindly eyes with her own innocence, with the question hanging pregnant.

'*I must do what I must do,*' is all she could say.

They covered Shaduk's body with stones and sand from the stream, until all that marked his grave was a mound of ground. No-one said anything. A brooding mood of sadness covered the group while time passed without a leaf stirring or any sign of insects or birds. They all slept and rested, though it was a troubled sleep for everyone. Finally, Mirrortac called them together and led them away into the rolling green hills beyond. Insects and all kinds of creatures fled from them as they approached, and tree fruits rotted at their approach. Another curse was upon them.

Mirrortac realised it was now Yidu's intention for them all to slowly starve to death but having the Werdstone again gave him an advantage. He was able to invoke food out of the air, and these proved tasty and nourishing to the hyfnuks who eagerly accepted the morsels of meat. Rimerelle refused to eat the invoked food, calling it '*food of the demons to poison sober minds*'. Instead, he pleaded to Yidu to spare him, but nothing came of it.

The group crossed over many streams, all bubbling with cool, sweet water. Mirrortac guessed that Yidu did not want them to die quickly, and so the waters of the streams kept them refreshed while the lack of food would weaken and taunt them. Ameece tried to make Rimerelle eat the conjured food but he refused every time and was steadily losing his fat. The fur on his body fell out in clumps and his step was wandering and uncertain. They slowed their pace to allow Rimerelle to rest but he was becoming dangerously gaunt.

The landscape changed gradually in the days ahead – though the sun of Luma moved imperceptibly. Rusk and Iyaji now carried a haggard Rimerelle on a makeshift litter. The elder's eyes were grey but his hatred for the erfin still burned fiercely in their hollow, sunken pits. For the first time since they had come to Skye, they saw clouds; small at first but later growing in number and size, bundled together and dark brown beneath. They rose out of the horizon ahead like smoke while the air carried a faint pungent odour, like something burning.

The hills flattened out into plains covered only in low shrubs and ratty dry grasses, gathered in clumps with a pale-yellow earth between. The shrubs were blackened with the marks of previous fires. Evarngar inspected the burnt shrubs and turned up his nose at the pungent odour.

'*We be surely at the gates of the Netherworld,*' Rimerelle said, raising his head slightly before slumping back with the effort.

Mirrortac too was disquieted at the unfamiliar stench and questioned the Werdstone to verify his course. He was answered with the image of a castle set up on a knoll above a steaming plain. The stone flashed brightly; pulling him in the direction they were headed. '*Oashu is well protected,*' he said.

Ameece regarded the erfin with a feeling of unease. There was nothing left now of his former green fur; it had changed completely to a brilliant blue. Her soul knew him, yet he was still a stranger. The Werdstone now never left his grasp and had grown more active as they neared the first Stone of Destiny. Mirrortac's powers had also grown with it, until she could barely distinguish between the energies of the erfin and the stone. She was frightened for him.

They continued through the plain, resting little. The shrubs petered out into withered grassland where the ground was covered with a layer of yellowy powder and was hot as though a fire burned beneath the earth. Wisps of smoke issued out of cracks here and there, while ahead, the earth was blanketed in rising whorls of smoke merging into cloud. Ameece complained of feeling ill but insisted on continuing on. The odour was now unmistakable and most unpleasant.

Finally, Rimerelle ordered a stop.

'*I can go naught further,*' he said, his breathing shallow.

The hyfnuks laid down the litter and Ameece moved to his side. Rimerelle's eyes rose up and rested on his mistress. '*I wish but I could change your mind ... however, your heart be naught yours, oh She of the Werd. Your intentions be clear. I have failed.*'

He sucked in a breath and coughed. What little fur left was folded over skin-taut bones. '*You must leave me now at the edge of this Netherworld. Death beckons to me and I have naught the strength to resist it.*'

Ameece shook her head in denial. '*Nay ... dare naught leave me! My dear Rimerelle. Will you naught eat. It is good. There is still ...*'

Rimerelle stayed her thoughts. '*I hear my brothers calling me ... I see ...*'

Ameece drew her nose to his and nuzzled him fondly. '*I love you my dear elder. You shall always be in my heart, dear ...*' Her lips parted. 'Rimmy', she blurted in a broken voice. It was the name she had called him when she was a child.

The memory forced a dim smile from the elder. He rasped a breath and his throat rattled as the last air left his lungs.

Tears burst forth again as she cried anew for her second elder.

GATEWAY OF THENIGMAS

Steam issued out of fissures in the desert plain ahead of them as the group halted at the end of the vegetation zone. The hyfnuks found it uncomfortably hot in their shaggy coats; suited more to the freezing climate of Yidrogh. Ameece was haggard and distant. The death of Rimerelle had deeply affected her, turning her inward and brooding.

Mirrortac frowned as he inspected the ground. The earth was so hot that any attempt at crossing the plain could only result in severe burns to the feet. He inclined his head towards Ameece and asked her whether she knew any spell to protect their feet from being burnt. She shook her head gravely.

'*You be the great caster of spells now. In sureness you can find such a spell,*' and pointing at the Werdstone in his hand, she added, '*Why not ask the stone!*'

Mirrortac winced inwardly at her acrimony. '*Then I shall ask the stone and find my answer.*'

He stared into the stone as he formed his question. It flickered into life and created another image in the erfin's mind. He was perplexed as all he could get was the form of some giant creature covered all over with spines. And when he asked for clarification, the image simply repeated itself.

'*The stone fails me.*' He settled back on his haunches to consider the problem further.

Daghva squinted through the clouds of smoke that issued up from the plain like steam from a cauldron. Cupping a hand above his eyes, he struggled to see something in the distance. '*There be something out there, and it is moving!*' he claimed.

Karn was unconvinced. '*Your eyes deceive you. No animal can live in that Netherworld!*'

'*Unless it is one of the darkness,*' Iyaji said; his eyes widening as he realised the implications of his remark. He dawdled up to Daghva's side and squinted towards the vague dark blotch in the distance. '*... You are right! It moves! I think it be coming this way!*' He looked to the erfin for reassurance but Mirrortac only sat, head in hands, frowning.

Ameece regarded the distant object with dispassion. The lustre in her eyes had gone, replaced with a tone of grey that reflected the mixed emotions within her. She got a whiff of the pungent smoke and sneezed. Evarngar, who was standing nearby, strained to identify the moving object, which was steadily growing larger as it made its way towards them. He edged away from the plain, directing his thoughts at the erfin privately.

'*I fear there is danger in staying here,*' he said, his eyes locked on the moving object.

Mirrortac glanced up and was silent for awhile before answering. '*I am afraid there can be no turning back, there be danger everywhere now. Without my protection you will all perish quickly, but with my help, we will live.*'

He surveyed the form now taking shape. '*I have spoken with it ... that which is named Tordwin and comes to meet us to carry us across the plain to the place called Wergaen.*'

Evarngar shuddered. '*Then this animal or whatever thing it be, offers naught harm but help?*'

The erfin nodded. '*Yea, but it is help that will bring much distress to you all, I fear. Its back is covered with spines of poison.*'

'*That WILL bring much distress!*' Evarngar said.

'*I have naught told you all.*' The erfin waved his palms up in protest. '*We can naught be carried among the spines. The poison would kill us. Nay, we must all allow ourselves to be ... err ... eaten up. Then when the Tordwin reaches Wergaen, it will vomit us out again.*'

The colour drained from the hyfnuk's face.

'*Eat us up!*'

The others jolted as though they had been physically attacked, and stared across at the two. Evarngar threw up his arms. '*I forgot to exclude the others. You are crazy. I can find many better ways to die. This is madness!*'

Mirrortac shrugged. '*This is the only way to live. We must do this or truly perish.*'

A barrage of voices besieged the erfin's mind. '*Eat us! What do you mean by EAT US?*' they demanded.

'*He means that he wants us all to be eaten by that thing out there!*' Ameece volunteered, screwing up her lips and glaring straight at the erfin.

'*Does she speak the truth, master?*' Daghva asked, expecting a plausible clarification of what he thought must clearly be a misunderstanding. Everyone's eyes were now on the erfin.

'*It may be something like what she says,*' Mirrortac said, avoiding the question.

'*Ah, you mean that we shall naught be eaten, but something like that?*' Daghva scratched his head in confusion.

'*Nay, exactly like that ... only we will naught die,*' he sighed.

They were all horrified. Nobody, including Ameece, would agree to what he was suggesting. He knew that he would have to resort to drastic action to enforce the solution. The form of the Tordwin was more than a vague blob now, revealing the shape of a giant spiny creature with reptilian eyes on a head protected by flat bony plates. Its legs were not visible, giving it the illusion of floating across the cracked and steaming earth. Ameece turned her back on it and assumed command.

'*Come! Let us leave this madness behind us! We must leave the erfin to his fate. He is under the power of the dark one now.*'

Evarngar was eager to join her but the others were hesitant. However, the thought of being swallowed up and disgorged was too much even for Daghva, who squirmed at the thought. Reluctantly, they all joined Ameece as she started to walk away.

Mirrortac swung up to his feet and stretched his arms in the air towards them.

'*Sorry, but you can naught go. It be with great regret that I must do this ...*' he shouted into their minds.

Ameece caught her breath as she glanced back over her shoulder at the Mirrortac she loved. His deep blue fur was bristling with sparks as the being that was this erfin wielded his tremendous power. He shouted aloud in maja and suddenly the whole world went black. And when she awoke, she found herself lying at the foot of a mountainous boulder with a stairway leading around its side and disappearing into the glare of Luma above. She felt dazed and disoriented as well as properly angry. He had used his spells to force her to go where she had not wanted to go. She raised her head and gazed with shock at her body. It was covered in a sticky slime that stunk terribly. She looked around for the others and found them all recovering nearby; their bodies also covered with the obnoxious slime.

'*There you are, I have saved your lives!*' she heard Mirrortac's voice in her mind. She twisted her head around and spotted the erfin standing behind her with a smile on his face.

'*Why did you take us here? What kinds of demons have possessed you?*' Ameece forced her words at him with all the strength of her anger.

Mirrortac ignored her temper and squatted beside her. He took her hand and spoke aloud. '*I can naught leave she, who I love, to die.*'

She snatched her hand away. '*Then if you love me send us all back to Yidrogh, like you did for Fervik.*'

Mirrortac brushed slime and sweat from his brow and shook his head. '*This be naught possible. We have passed through five zones of Yidu's magic. If I try the returning spell now, it would kill you.*'

Ameece frowned. '*Zones of magic? ... kill us? This be all too vexing!*'

Mirrortac felt her pain. '*We can naught allow Yidu to succeed in his trickery. I know that it be your grief that speaks, and ... in time, I hope, you shall discern the truth of all this.*'

Noting the discomfort everyone had with the slime, he invoked another spell that immediately lifted the slime from their bodies, leaving their fur dry and clean again. The hyfnuks were relieved but Evarngar was alert, staring back across the steaming plain for signs of the Tordwin or anything that could be a threat. Satisfied for the time being, he looked to the erfin. '*You have brought us here, now feed us,*' he said simply.

Mirrortac conjured up the food they needed, and they ate in silence. Above them, the great boulder cast its shadow over the plain, showing up the rough silhouette of a castle with three turrets topped by irregular shaped poles. The boulder and the castle stood on a flat platform of stone which was at least two erfin-lengths above the level of the plain. The earth of the plain at this spot was molten hot, flowing out in streams of fire and acrid smoke. The air around the platform itself was surprisingly cool. There was also something odd about the boulder which seemed to split into two when one shifted one's eyes at particular angles. This mirage provided some amusement for Daghva, who was twisting his head every which way and squinting at the boulder.

'*We are on the edge of a magic zone,*' the erfin ventured. '*You have noticed the weak point where the zones connect,*' he said.

Daghva was disturbed at this but continued to turn his head back and forth. Evarngar tried to ignore the image, alternatively shutting and opening his eyes in the hope of cancelling out the effect, but finally he resorted to adopting an awkward angle. Karn began kicking the side of the boulder as though it had come alive.

When everyone had finished eating, Mirrortac ordered them to begin their march up the narrow stairway. Ameece mooched along at the tail of the party, accompanied by her ever-present and loyal guardian, Evarngar. She was sullen and even less impressed now than before. Her despair hung thickly in the atmosphere.

In next to no time they were able to peer up and make out the brilliant yellow walls of the castle with its inscriptions in some unknown tongue. Twenty steps on, they could see the blue spires spearing upwards from each of the three towers, and above them the looped, diamond shaped pinnacles and poles. Aquamarine flags fluttered on the poles, bearing an alien symbol. Enormous webs were strung between the spires, hinting of some oversized arachnid. Mirrortac knew this did not bode well, and the hyfnuks shuddered when they beheld the ominous webbing. Each step was also marked with alien symbols which Mirrortac examined as he crept up each one.

As they ascended around a sharp curve, the steps leveled out, stopping short of a high arched gateway. A portcullis blocked the entrance. It bore a central metal plate marked with the symbol Delta and below it an inscription that Mirrortac translated to mean 'Protectorate of Oashu'. The first Stone of Destiny was somewhere beyond that gate and in the castle. And obtaining it would be no mean task, the erfin judged.

The hyfnuks inspected the gate and the castle with something close to awe. Karn ran his palms over the stonework and the metal bars of the portcullis, feeling the solidity and hardness of these alien materials. Ameece lifted her eyes with cautious scrutiny, taking in the wall of the castle beyond the gateway. High above them the twin green flags hung limp from the pole on the central tower; ominous in the still air.

Mirrortac lifted the Werdstone up to the central plate of the portcullis and uttered a few brief words of maja. The aged metal squeaked into life, groaning as the gate lifted into the stone arch above. He stepped forward into the courtyard with Ameece behind and their retinue of hyfnuks. Around them the ground was just dust with no ornaments or fountains to please the eye. A shadowy archway yawned at them from the base of the central tower, revealing a wide internal stairway as they approached. A fragment of giant web, like rope, was strung out from a nearby balcony to the perimeter wall. The Werdstone pulsed brightly like a guiding beacon, showing the way. Mirrortac let it pull him into the darkened stairway of the central tower and up its spiral to the level above them. They struggled up the stairs which were covered in a sticky substance that threatened to bind their feet to the stone if they tended to linger too long in any one spot. Daghva became gloomy as his sensitivity picked up the imminent danger ahead. His eyes were wide spheres, searching every hidden corner for threat.

Webbed silhouettes played over one wall as the light from torches in a nearby room fluttered with their yellow flames. Mirrortac reached the top of the stairs. He approached the doorway to the room then stopped abruptly. But the sticky floor forced him to march on the spot so as to avoid being glued to the floor. A thick web barred the way to the room where a number of torches were held in containers affixed to the wall.

Karn sidled past the erfin and was about to attempt to clear the web with his arm when Mirrortac forestalled him. '*You must naught touch the web. It will pull you in and entangle you!*' he warned.

'*Then what shall we do, master?*' Karn asked.

'*We need do naught. The stone shall be my gate breaker,*' Mirrortac boasted.

Then he lifted up the stone and muttered a few quick words.

The web disintegrated and oozed into sticky heaps on the floor. Mirrortac strode over the threshold and into a room that was empty except for a single wood table in its centre. A lancet window let in a meagre light. A smaller stairway led up from a narrow doorway at one end of the room, marked by a trailing rope of web set like a trap to catch anyone foolish enough to enter the room. The rope now terminated in what remained of the web on the floor.

Daghva backed away as Mirrortac turned toward the stair. '*You will naught lure me up there.*'

'*We shall naught return this way, I suspect.*' Mirrortac was matter-of-fact. '*When I have found Oashu, little time shall pass before Wergaen will be no more.*'

Evarngar frowned as he regarded the stairs. Ameece was sullen, looking away whenever Mirrortac glanced over to her. '*She-folk!*' he thought.

With reluctance the others followed Mirrortac up the stairs, preferring to be together than left behind. A slight rustling sound issued from the top of the stairs, adding to the air of uneasiness, yet Mirrortac forged on with no hint of nervousness.

A piercing scream froze everyone in their tracks. It was an unearthly sound, mournful and filled with pain. The hackles rose up on the hyfnuks' necks. Daghva shouted aloud. 'That's it! I'm out of here!' He turned and there was a panic of arms and legs as the hyfnuks fell over each other to escape. But they soon turned tail again when they saw what was waiting for them downstairs.

A black shapeless mass rose up from out of the floor, and Mirrortac glanced back as it crept up at them. Glowing violet eyes peered up with malice while in the blackness beneath them appeared a gaping mouth that continued opening until it almost reached the floor. The wraith let go another terrible scream, unleashing more panic among the hyfnuks who jostled over one another to try to reach the top.

'*Ignore it! The wraith has naught authority over fleshness,*' Mirrortac attempted, but found himself being flung down as the terrified hyfnuks scrambled to escape.

The wraith oozed up the stairway, crackling as threads of silvan web were ejected from elongated arm shapes. Ripples of what looked like stars emanated out from its eyes. Mirrortac gripped onto the Werdstone and lifted it up at the wraith, muttering in maja. However, this only served to accelerate the wraith's approach, forcing the erfin to withdraw the stone in shock.

The wraith screamed again; this time even louder and more horrible as it sucked towards the Werdstone. Mirrortac regained his composure and held out shaking hands grasping the stone in front of him. His fur prickled up as he now watched while the wraith was fully absorbed into the stone. A spray of sparks rose up within the crystalline depths then died away. He wiped droplets of sweat from his brow, and as his eyes rose, they met Ameece's who was still staring into the stone, mesmerised.

'*Of course! The Werdstone was used to create everything here. There is naught to fear! All is illusion!*' Mirrortac proclaimed.

Suddenly coming to her senses, Ameece looked up from the stone and into the eyes of the erfin, staring in silence at him for a few moments before she broke off her gaze and walked past him. Mirrortac shook his head then continued up only to meet the others hurrying down.

'*It be another of those wretched Vyndroolsh!*' Evarngar scowled, referring to the ghosts of the greevuns. '*But where be my mistress?*'

The old hyfnuk twisted around in alarm, and gasped when he looked back up the stairway. Ameece had continued to lumber up the stairs towards another wraith.

'*My one of the Werd! The Vyndroolsh!*' Evarngar warned.

Ameece ignored the warning and walked on as though in a dream. Mirrortac struggled past the hyfnuks and fought the stickiness of the stair to get to her with the Werdstone. The wraith floated down to envelope her in its web; its violet eyes glowing and sparkling with stars. A second and third wraith emerged out of the walls, and all of them converged on the white furred roznogh.

'A-kesh ta sar-deedwa!' Mirrortac shouted, desperately proffering the stone towards the assembled wraiths. The wraiths turned towards the erfin for a moment and screamed in unison. The hyfnuks cowered, covering their ears with their hands. Ameece checked in her step and turned to face Mirrortac who was still holding the stone. She gave him a sly smile before turning back up the stairs where the wraiths waited, as though expecting her. Mirrortac repeated his command but the wraiths were fixed on the roznogh.

Ameece was unhesitant as she approached the spectres. The wraiths floated in on her as everyone watched on helpless. She gently pushed her way through as though the wraiths were nothing but froth in a stream. With no fear to feed out their webs, they moaned in chorus, shuddering and manoeuvring in vain attempts to menace her. Mirrortac broke into a grin as he watched her.

'*You have challenged the illusion and won, wonder of my heart,*' he said, and was rewarded with a curt '*Interesting!*' as Ameece stepped into the room above.

Deprived of victory, the wraiths changed their attentions to the hyfnuks still shuddering on the stairs below. Mirrortac again raised the stone and uttered the appropriate words. The wraiths swooped into the walls and disappeared only to reappear beneath the hyfnuks. The erfin did not have to encourage the hyfnuks to move past him; they hastened before being stopped again by three more wraiths that appeared out of the ceiling above.

'*The wraiths feed off your fear,*' Mirrortac warned. '*You must stay close to me if you are afraid. But they will all go if you do as She of the Werd has just demonstrated to you.*'

The hyfnuks remained unconvinced. Daghva ventured. '*She of the Werd knows the ways of spirits but we know only how to fight things of the flesh. Show us a Wooil and we shall overcome it.*'

The hyfnuks clustered around the erfin as he again lifted the stone and cried out the words. The stone glowed a deep violet, and as before, lured the wraiths into it, absorbing their existence. The echoes of their screams bounced through the corridors of the castle, providing an eerie requiem to their passing.

The hyfnuks were still trembling as they clung to Mirrortac and entered the chamber room above. This room was large and circular with a single window shaped like an inverted triangle. Ameece stood framed by the window where she stared out in her contemplation. They found the room bare. Mirrortac tuned in to the Werdstone which had brightened considerably since entering the room. There was no ceiling, so they could clearly see the spire of the roof leading up to a point high above their heads. The floor was presented in an intricate pattern of concentric circles that played on the eye if stared at for too long. Mirrortac could see no clue of Oashu's whereabouts but knew that it had to be in that room. Ameece turned from the window and regarded the erfin with a little more of her old warmth. She even managed a slight smile. Mirrortac relaxed at the sight of her. '*I had hoped you would return to my heart, shining eyes. I shall need your strength and support.*'

Ameece came to him and nuzzled him. '*I was lost in my grief. And in the darkness of my tears I could only feel the heartache you had brought my people. When you spoke of the illusion of the wraiths, I realised that all that Yidu has given us has been an illusion. You, my erfin, have always spoken and acted truly. I must trust you ...*' She broke into deep sobs, resting her head on Mirrortac's chest.

The erfin enfolded her in his arms, speaking to her in soothing tones. Meanwhile, the hyfnuks inspected the room, but were distracted in their manner, glancing back at the doorway and walls anxiously. Evarngar fidgeted near his distraught mistress, turning his back out of respect while he too kept his eyes peeled for danger.

Mirrortac looked down absently as he patted Ameece. Then he saw it. There, beneath their feet was the first Stone of Destiny neatly disguised into the floor pattern. He recognised the stone's own strange patterning, but thoughts jammed on how to extract it. He tapped Ameece on the shoulder and bent down to the floor.

'*Oashu!*' she proclaimed as she saw the stone that Mirrortac now touched with his fingers. When he put down the Werdstone, the glow was extinguished, but the patterning on the Oashu stone started to pulse with a red light. Mirrortac cupped his hands around the stone and slid it across the floor towards Oashu. Ameece sniffled and bent down opposite him. She gazed into his eyes, put out her own hands, and asked, '*May I?*'

Mirrortac smiled and nodded.

'*And the others too?*' she added. The lustre in her eyes had returned along with a cheeky smile.

'*I love your perception.*'

She beckoned to the others to add their own hands to hers and Mirrortac's already cupped around the Werdstone. Evarngar shook his head with a hint of amusement. *'More of these magic games,'* he said, complying with her request as a matter of duty to his mistress. The Werdstone had all but disappeared under a dozen hairy paws.

Guided by Mirrortac, they slid the stone nearer to Oashu, which brightened with every move closer of the Werdstone. Ameece locked her gaze on Mirrortac, looking deep into his emerald eyes as he concentrated on the movement of the stone. The room shuddered and a whoosh of air blew in and whirled around them. The light from the window darkened, plunging the room into shadow. They found it harder to push the Werdstone, but with the combined effort, it inched its way forward. The room shuddered again, but with more violence. The atmosphere snapped with energy. A sound like thunder struck outside the castle walls; the floor heaved and shook, roof girders rattled. They exerted another thrust on the stone. Its edge overlapped that of Oashu. Another volley of shudders, quakes and crashing thunder struck simultaneously. The hyfnuks were trembling but persevered. Sweat dripped from brows fully concentrated on the effort. They pushed the stone a last time. It slid into place directly over Oashu. There was a blinding flash then something like an explosion, which sent them all spinning into a violet coloured void with streaks of lightning surrounding them in a tunnel of darkness.

There was a gradual lightening that coalesced into an azure blue then into a conglomeration of colours that shifted as the spinning sensation eased. When their eyes finally adjusted, they found themselves lying on a floor composed of myriads of grains of gemstones inlaid like soft matting. They raised still dizzy heads to behold a great hall flanked by rows of columns. Only Mirrortac and Ameece had managed to maintain their grasp on the Werdstone along with Oashu which clung on underneath like a youngling to its mother. Standing over a marblelite pedestal at the centre of the great hall was the one who the roznoghs called their Sky-master. He scrutinised them with his three sapphire eyes and let out a slow chuckle.

'You are most clever, one called Mirrortac, but naught as wise as the great master, Yidu,' the demi-god boasted.

The hyfnuks abandoned all bravery as they fidgeted in the presence of the mighty Yidu. However, Mirrortac looked the demi-god in the eye (or should one say three eyes!) with defiance. Ameece too was curious as she appraised the one who had been god to her people for a thousand seasons or more.

'Where be your wisdom strange one? I have beaten your magic!' Mirrortac straightened, grasping the two stones close to him.

Yidu was not fazed. *'Fools see nothing but their own reflection, furball. Do you truly think you can come here and claim the master Werdstone from me? Do you think you are greater than the god, Yidu? ... Show us now, before these roznoghs, that you can overwhelm me.'*

'*I have met ones such as you,*' Mirrortac said. '*You be like the Nerthulians ... mere men who be full of trickery.*'

Yidu's brows rose. '*You know of Nerthule? How can that be? Did Wa-ku tell you this?*'

Now it was Mirrortac's turn to be surprised. '*Wa-ku? God of the Petros ... be he your kin? I have only seen his vision in the deep pool, now destroyed. I learned of Nerthule with the Meretees ... and met one in Hopocus ... a wizard.*'

Yidu frowned. '*Wizard! Hopocus! What is this wizard's name? Where be this Hopocus?*'

Mirrortac's eyes widened as he beamed. '*It seems that you do naught know all, mighty Yidu! Be it that gods should know all? You be no god ... this be the proof!*'

This angered Yidu. His face blushed red as his eyes screwed up like arrow points spearing the erfin in his place. '*You are insolent, erfin! I was here in your first life ... and now this be your last. You will soon be thrown into the Netherworld forever!*'

'*Yidu be many thousands of seasons in age ... he is always our Sky-master,*' Evarngar interjected.

'*T'is all a conjured world that defies time,*' Mirrortac explained. '*His magic be strong, yea, but this I have seen too in Hopocus where all be lies ... though no more, thanks to the Staff of Thaum and Roderick.*'

Evarngar was about to question further when Mirrortac cut in. '*You have naught been to such places as I have seen ... worlds beyond worlds.*'

Yidu looked curious. '*The stone has no record of this Hopocus. Perhaps you have been dreaming ... your mind has tricked you, Mirrortac.*'

Mirrortac realised he had an upper hand. '*Much would seem like a dream ... even this palace of yours. It be all illusion ...*'

The Sky-master chuckled but his laugh was hollow. Why would this erfin challenge him when it was so easy to get rid of him? Or so he had thought. It was true that the Werdstone had no master but that of the mysterious ancients who first created it. Its power belonged to anyone who learned how to use it. And even a small slice of it made an ordinary erfin drunk with its magic. Nevertheless, there was more to this Mirrortac than met the eye. What had made him travel so far on a fool's errand?

Yidu leaned forward, pressing his hands onto the pedestal as he addressed the erfin. '*Tell me erfin, where be this Hopocus? Who be this wizard of whom you speak?*'

Mirrortac grinned with mischief. '*Hopocus be nowhere ... and the wizard be called Roderick. He be there yet with the Nerthulian female Beth helping the lost ones ... but naught so lost now.*'

Yidu frowned and scowled at him. '*You think you are so clever. I do not care where Hopocus is ... it is just that I have never heard of it. It cannot be anywhere in this world.*'

'*It be naught in any world. It belongs to the dead … yet some who still lived were there also … such as the wizard and his helper. Both be Nerthulians. And all the dead there be Nerthulians also.*'

Yidu nodded. '*I see. That is why the stone did not pick it up … you were in a place of the dead. Curious.*'

The hyfnuks gaped at the erfin at this revelation, while Yidu seemed deep in thought. Many sacred chuffs were standing silent alongside the borders of the hall, at the beck and call of their master. Yidu paced around with his head down; his luminescent robe sweeping across the floor.

'*I must pose a question, my almighty Yidu,*' Ameece ventured.

Startled, Yidu swiveled around to behold the daughter of the Werd.

'*Of course! My mind opens to your query, daughter.*'

'*It vexes me that you changed your mind. You told Browagh to return the stone in his last life, yet when I queried you through the stone, you did not wish it anymore.*'

'*I saw that the stone was needed in Yidrogh, and the carrier … this Mirrortac.*' Yidu pointed. '*… had been corrupted.*'

Then Yidu pursed his lips and his eyes flashed wide. '*Yes, corrupted! He has consorted with the dead in that forbidden place, Hopocus. Where no living being is permitted to walk. The dead have revealed sacred secrets … those demons. They have sent him back to the land of the living to lead you astray. And to challenge your god … the great, the Skyemaster … Yidu!*'

Ameece considered for a moment then communicated again. '*Indeed, it be as you say, oh great one. But this erfin be of no use to you. Vanquish him to Yidrogh and return your loyal servants to their homes. We will return Oashu to you, and I shall return home with the Werdstone.*'

Mirrortac looked sideways at her but caught the gleam in her eye. Yidu shook his head and shrugged at Ameece.

'*No-one who enters this sacred place may be permitted to leave. You must remain here, and your companion hyfnuk … and these others, who sought also to challenge me, but now stand as cowards before me.*' The hyfnuks shrunk to the floor, quivering, but remained quiet.

'*But as for the erfin,*' Yidu said with a hard edge to his voice. '*There is no redemption for him. I will vanquish him, yes, but not to Yidrogh. He will go to the Netherworld where demons will torment him.*'

Yidu turned to the chuffs. '*Take Oashu back from the erfin. And place him on the transporter.*'

Several chuffs stepped toward the erfin who was still clutching the two stones.

Mirrortac reacted, muttering maja as he held up the Werdstone. He repeated some spell words over and over, but there was no life in the stone. Nothing happened.

Ameece screamed. 'No!' She ran to his side and held him, but she was no match for the chuffs. They thrust her aside, snatched the Oashu stone out of his grasp and grabbed him. Mirrortac struggled against them but they were too strong. They took him to a spot in the hall where they locked his feet to the floor with something metallic. Mirrortac still had the Werdstone in his hand but realised he could do nothing with it.

Yidu grinned as he moved something on the Werdstone pedestal. A circle of stone moved and clicked into place on the pedestal. Mirrortac tried lifting his feet but was held fast. He turned back at Ameece and the hyfnuks, and they could see that his cheeks were streaked with tears.

'*I be out of answers, rainbow of my heart. It be up to you now. You must discern what to do.*'

Ameece wanted to run over to his side but the chuffs barred the way. It felt like her heart was breaking all over again. She knew that she loved him more than life itself.

In moments the air in the hall shuddered, then from above came a churning funnel that roared like a thousand storms. It descended towards the erfin who now was standing on a rising column that was coming up to meet it. Ameece screamed but her voice was drowned out by the howl of this strange storm. The erfin returned her gaze, tears running freely down his cheeks. The footholds released, sending the erfin floating up into the air. The funnel reached down further, swallowing him up until he was a mere gusting shadow in the twisting vortex. The piece of Werdstone could be seen now freely flying around in a wide circle while the erfin was no more than a shapeless thing writhing within. Ameece slumped down and cried out loud. 'I remember!' she cried. 'I remember my dear Mirrortac ... I was Yenic.' She broke into deep sobs, banging her arms on the floor and tearing at her fur.

'*You remember me now, rainbow of my heart. Find a way ... Find a way ... Find ...*' His thoughts faded away as the wind-form retreated towards the high ceiling; its haunting moan whistling back to a whisper before ceasing altogether.

The slice of Werdstone still flew about the hall until it too descended towards the pedestal, rejoining the master stone with a decisive click as it merged with it.

The hyfnuks stared blankly at the spot where the erfin had been. They were too stunned to react, and even Evarngar was astounded. Yidu was calm as he surveyed them.

'*You have now witnessed the penalty of folly against your god, Yidu.*' He motioned for two of the sacred chuffs to join him. The equally impassionate bird-beings obeyed to stand either side of him.

'*Now, what to do with you all. Since you are servants of mine, then you will be servants of my servants. You must be loyal to their every whim and be prepared to serve at any moment, even if they should disturb your sleep time.*'

The hyfnuks appeared sickly as they bowed to Yidu. Evarngar attended to his mistress as she lay still weeping on the floor. Yidu dismissed them to the sacred chuffs who took them to another part of the palace where they were given tasks to perform.

PART 2

A MEETING IN THE FOREST

A soft breeze ruffled the leaves of the great forest. Immense trees rose up almost to the clouds, while spearing up through them stood the giant of giants that was wide enough to house the royal halls and chambers of Greenfaug, the royal community of the faugs. The gibbon-like people who lived there possessed wings like bats that enabled them to glide up on the updrafts above the Faug Forest. This was the final refuge of the erfins who escaped with Mirrortac before the great battle that exterminated the giant serpents known as the snerks. Since the end of the age of darkness, most erfins had returned to their native Eol across the mountains and re-established their community there. These included Mirrortac's child-fins Wynper and Fentil who were effectively orphans after the death of their mother, Yenic, and the disappearance of their father. However, the triplets born in Greenfaug – Treetam, Mitac and Ezof – preferred to stay with the faugs to enjoy the freedom of the trees and their fun-loving adopted faug uncles and aunts.

Treetam hung upside-down from one of the smaller branches that spread out over the platform of Yu-wood. Her brothers Mitac and Ezof were standing on a nearby bough practising their archery skills on a wood target about 50 erfin-lengths away. Ezof nocked his arrow and pulled back slowly on the bow. His emerald eyes fixed the target in his sights before he let go. The rainbow hued cock-feather fluttered as the arrow shot true, piercing the carved form of a snerk and shuddering the target that was held fast to a bough above the opposite side of the platform.

'You missed its mouth,' Mitac mocked, his one green, one blue eye full of cheek.

'Was not aiming at the mouth, muddle-eye. Back of the head is where you will kill the nasty thing,' Ezof retorted.

'Nah ... you kill it like dada did ... up inside the mouth,' Mitac grinned.

'You just watch me. I know what I'm doing.' Mitac lifted his bow and nocked.

'Okay muddle-eye … show me how good you are.'

Mitac concentrated on the target, and just as he was about to shoot, Ezof shoved into him. 'Oh, something bit me,' he said, winking back at Treetam.

The arrow wavered off at a tangent to bounce off a nearby bough before dropping to the platform below.

Mitac punched his brother sharply and scowled. 'Nothing bit you … you just don't want to bow to the better archer!'

Ezof crossed his arms and looked at this brother smugly. 'Okay, you show me. I won't do anything.'

'Better not,' Mitac warned, nocking another arrow to his bow.

This time Ezof kept his word as Mitac focused on the target, keeping one wary eye on his brother. The arrow flew with a swish and a thunk of wood as it entered the mouth of the carved snerk.

Ezof gave a grunt of approval while slapping Mitac on the back. 'Maybe it's time for a goblet of merma-mead to drink to our champion archery.'

'Aye bro. I will drink to that!' Mitac laughed.

'Not without me … your champ sis,' Treetam shouted across to them, which spurred a burst of laughter from the two brothers.

'We are the three champs!' Ezof boasted, prompting more laughter.

Treetam swung with deft movements from one branch to another before dropping to her feet on the platform in front of her brothers.

'Race you to the fruit chamber,' she dared. And in a flash the three were bounding across the platform towards the entrance to Greenfaug Halls, their silvan fur glistening as they charged for the door. They were slim and agile and full of energy. But it was Treetam who reached the door ahead of her brothers. She turned and poked her tongue at them before attempting to shut the carved timber door in their faces. The brothers rammed their full weight into the door, struggling against the strength of their sister before forcing their way in.

The trio emerged some time later, full of mirth and a little unsteady on their feet. A faug servant smiled at them as they stumbled together across the platform. The three were muttering incoherent grunts in faugish with arms wrapped around shoulders. The sun of Luma was near to the western horizon where a thin line of yellow barely distinguished the far Wastes of Nug beyond the melded hues of green that could be seen through breaks in the clouds. A little to the north of Luma was a star that brightened and moved slightly.

The romantic among the three, Treetam, stopped to look at the star, causing them all to topple in a heap on the platform. She pointed. 'I think I have refreshed myself with too much merma-mead. I fancy that wonderful moondrop has moved from its place in the greater sky.'

'Indeed, your eyes must be rolling, Treet. Moondrops do not move,' Ezof blurted.

'Sheez right … or my eyes must be rolling too,' Mitac managed to say.

All three were now watching the star that continued to grow in size and visibly move across the sky as it seemed to make its way towards them.

Ezof's jaw dropped. 'I vow not to drink too much merma-mead again. I am seeing a vision of light!'

Some faugs who were out on the platform also looked up. The glowing star was taking form, like a shining stone suspended in the air, and they all could hear a low humming that was alien to the ear. The faugs quickened their pace towards the platform and the entrance to Greenfaug, casting up nervous glances at the shining object that whirred ever nearer. The triplets were too drunk and awe-struck to move and lay with mouths agape at the spectacle.

The object grew larger as it flew rapidly over the forest towards them. Its hum pulsed along with the lights that flickered around it as it revolved. The erfins could only stare at it in amazement, then looked at each other to confirm that they all could see it. This was not how the goddess Yu had been described. She had no shining throne that flew through the sky. She was in the air, and in the great tree that was home to the royals of Greenfaug. She was the tree and spirit. But this … thing … this flying stone of light was not anything they had ever been told about.

The huge object was now hovering above them, and they could see that it was circular with a smaller circle marked underneath. Something came out of the smaller circle – a ray like sunshine – that shone down on them with a cool glow. They all felt suddenly giddy for a few moments, and the platform around them dimmed before vanishing into a white void. In no time the void coalesced into a chamber filled with crystal arrays and screens, and a material that was neither wood nor stone. Seated in a throne that floated around inside this chamber was a being as alien and strange as the chamber and the object they now found themselves within. He was not furry like erfins, but he did have long locks of golden hair on his head. He was robed like a god, resplendent in green with a sash tied around his waist.

The triplets all felt as though they were hallucinating under a bad batch of merma-mead and peered with pale faces at the man. He swiveled around to face them, giving them his best smile while his blue eyes were mesmerising.

'You must surely be Treetam, Mitac and Ezof, though I do not know who is who. Since you were the only erfins I could see there, and all three together, I hope my assumption is correct.'

The trio nodded, too stunned to talk.

'I apologise for taking you like this. There are not any places to land my ship in the forest, and I'm afraid I would have damaged the decking of your community had I tried to land there.'

More nods were accompanied by some head scratching.

'My name is Wa-ku, and I am afraid I have come with grave responsibility and news for you three. You must have a lot of questions for me, and they will be answered in time. You see, your mother, or should I say the reincarnation of your mother Yenic, has made contact with me ... though she was not really seeking me at first,' he said, pausing. 'She was reunited with your father ... err ... that's before my brother Yidu sent him to that terrible place Thenigmas. It may as well be the Netherworld. Close enough to it.' Wa-ku struggled with his words, frowning deeply. 'Your father Mirrortac is in big trouble and it is all because of my brother. He is an evil and powerful man who is corrupted...'

Treetam abruptly found her voice, and her senses. 'You say our father and mother be alive? My mother died here giving birth to us, and our father went into the desert never to return. They are lost to us. How can what you say be true?'

'Yea, are you some demon come to taunt us?' Ezof said, quickly sobering.

'My head hurts,' Mitac cried, staring at the floor. 'This vision will go away soon. Go away!' He shouted.

Wa-ku sighed with sympathy. 'I know that I must seem very strange and frightening to you, but you three are the only ones I can turn to for help. I need you to rescue your father Mirrortac and to help him complete his mission. A mission that his guiding spirit gave him and one that I share.'

'A mission? Guiding spirit?' Treetam quizzed. She shrugged. 'What can we do that a god like you cannot do better. You can take us up into the air and put us here in this ...' She looked around but words escaped her.

Wa-ku manoeuvred his chair closer to them and flicked a switch, which made the chair drop to the floor. 'Without this,' he gestured at the chair. 'I am useless. I cannot walk, nor run. I cannot go outside and roam in the forest or on the plain. And therefore, I cannot search for your Mirrortac, and even if I did find him, I could not help him complete his mission. I must stay here in this ship, a prisoner of my own disability. I found you because I was told exactly where you are, but with Mirrortac, he could by now have gone a long way in Thenigmas.'

Mitac stole a glance from his bowed position on the floor. 'Then how is it that our dead mother could talk to you? Did she appear to you?'

Wa-ku looked up and paused, thinking. 'This is not simple. Your mother Yenic is dead, yes. But she is now in another body of another race closely related to the erfins. Her name now is Ameece, and she can speak with her mind over great distances. But this time she could not, as she is a prisoner of my brother, where the magic in place will not allow it. This time she spoke to me through what is called the

Werdstone ...' Wa-ku continued his explanation, telling them about the abilities of the Werdstone and the crystal stones like the ones in his ship. She had won the trust of one of the sacred chuffs who organised for her to secretly access the Werdstone to communicate with Wa-ku and tell him about their predicament. Wa-ku realised then that he had an ally in the roznogh and a way to perhaps stop his brother from going through with his plan to gain complete power over the three planets of Mareos, Thenigmas and Nerthule. This, of course, was overwhelming for the three erfins who with still groggy heads had to decipher all this strange information about other worlds, their parents, and alien magic.

Finally, Wa-ku decided they had heard enough and needed time to digest it all. In the meantime, he had a ship to fly, as it was still hovering over Greenfaug, closely watched by the many faugs who had witnessed the disappearance of the erfin youths. The braver ones were venturing out with their bows and trying to shoot at the ship; which was about as effective as hitting a tree with a leaf. Wa-ku smiled at their attempts as he moved back to the instrument array to arrange the crystals to put the ship on a path away from Greenfaug and up into the sky, and beyond. The cosmo-ship accelerated at a phenomenal rate, rapidly disappearing to a tiny point of light from the viewpoint of Greenfaug. The faugs rushed out with expressions of astonishment and shock. The children of their greatest hero had been stolen away from them.

The triplets awoke after some time. They were now resting in comfortable bedding in a separate chamber in the ship. Wa-ku was busy manipulating various crystals shapes as the ship sped across space at lightning velocity. There were no windows, but screens gave views and representations of the exterior, which now only revealed abstract diagrams and elongated flashes of light.

Mitac rose with a grimace. 'We be not dreaming, or I am lost in my mind.' He glanced around fearfully, wishing away the foreign surroundings.

Treetam was curiously calm. 'I have never believed that my dada was dead. I heard such wondrous stories about him. I want to meet him!' Her aquamarine eyes glinted.

Ezof stared at nothing. 'I do not remember anything of him. But I want to be like him. Afraid of no-one!'

'Then you believe this Wa-ku, Treet?' Mitac quizzed.

Treetam mused for a moment. 'I do not know. I want to believe.'

'And you Ezzie?' Mitac asked, still frowning with uncertainty.

'Right now, I have no choice. If it be true, then we are about to join in a quest of heroes.'

Mitac shut his eyes and opened them again. 'We will see,' he said.

They heard Wa-ku shout from the control chamber. 'Treetam, Ezof, Mitac, come here. Speak to your mother!'

The three exchanged puzzled glances. They rose and walked through to the control chamber where Wa-ku was at the centre console gazing down into a clear gemstone bowl that glowed up into his face. He smiled up at them. 'Look here. This is your mother reincarnated!' He indicated the bowl.

Treetam stepped up to stand beside Wa-ku and looked down at the bowl. She gasped when she saw the live image of an erfin-like being looking back at her.

'Is that you Treetam? You have grown into a fine she-erfin,' the being said.

Treetam thought Ameece had kind blue eyes and a gentle manner. If she were her mother, then she was certainly worthy of the title.

'Is that truly you, mumma? Can you remember your life with us?'

Ameece sighed. 'I did not know you because I died giving birth to you, but Mirrortac told me everything about you. I came to remember my life as Yenic when the storm took him away.' A tear escaped her eye and rolled down her furry cheek.

Treetam felt her mother's sorrow as her own. 'Do not cry mumma. We will find him and bring him back to you.'

Ezof had moved into position to see, and now was pushing Treetam out of the way. 'Mumma! We will fight the snerks, anything to get our dada back.' His emerald eyes flared with his passion.

Ameece managed a smile. 'You must be Ezof. You be most like your father. Brave and foolhardy. And you have his eyes.'

Ezof puffed out his chest at this. Mitac glanced over his shoulder at the image, still tentative.

'And there you be, Mitac ... the clever one,' she observed.

Mitac blushed and tried to look away, but he was transfixed.

'Kind words are like Merma ... sweet to the taste but it can make you foolish,' he ventured.

Ameece's eyes teared up as she beheld the three of them, her children in a former life. 'Wa-ku thought you will perhaps believe more if you were to see me, and speak to me,' she said.

Treetam shoved Ezof back out of view. 'Mumma, tell us about our dada.' She was so excited; she wanted to hear everything about her father and what he had done since leaving the Faug Forest.

Ameece told them then of what was related to her and revealed in the discerning – of his journey to Petrosium and the battle against Beeble-Zub, the voyage to the islands of the Meretees and onwards to Hopocus and Yidrogh. The threesome reveled in the amazing stories of Mirrortac's exploits, even Mitac, who tried to hide his interest in a stern expression. Finally, Ameece looked away from the screen for a moment before saying, 'I must go now. Yidu will be returning.'

The greenstone bowl faded back to its natural colour, leaving only the memory of their mother among the triplets. All three agreed the evidence seemed more convincing but Mitac still erred on the side of caution. He would know the truth when he saw the erfin that was his father Mirrortac. If they could find him.

It was impossible to gauge how much time had passed in the enormous space between planets as Wa-ku's cosmo-ship sped onwards, but it was long enough to make the triplets restless. The brothers wanted to be out in the forest with their quivers and their bows, while Treetam just wanted to swing freely from branch to branch like her adopted cousins the faugs. Except for some slight movements and giddy feelings, they had no inkling that they were travelling at all. Wa-ku gave them chewy pieces of material that he described as his food. It tasted a little like fruit but without the juices and the full flavour they were used to. Their toiletry had to be performed in a strange sunken bowl in its own private chamber, which curiously never stank. Wa-ku was modest about his status, preferring not to be regarded as a god despite all the magical appliances and abilities he possessed. Treetam and Ezof built up a modicum of trust for Wa-ku, while Mitac remained slightly aloof and cautious.

The time eventually arrived when they felt the ship slow down, and the former streaks of light in the crystal screens resolved into stars, while one object was observed to be suspended like a giant ball, with curious shapes and colours – blues, greens, browns and striking reds that shone. The triplets were curious that this planet called Thenigmas could sustain any life as surely the ones on the bottom and sides would fall off. When Wa-ku assured them that they also lived on such a giant ball, they all thought it rather funny until they realised he was serious.

Thenigmas rapidly took up the whole view in the screen until its spherical shape was less obvious, and they noted there was a zone of blue-green embracing the planet in an aura of light. Dark clouds could be seen rising up, and beneath them mountains and snake-like valleys, hills and plains. There were greenish patches and a blue-green expanse wrapping around a huge land mass with a few islands and two white caps at the top and bottom. The southern cap soon disappeared as the ship homed in on the northern area of land.

'The portal ends near the mouth of Grorl,' Wa-ku said, and pointing at the screen, 'The mountain of fire in the north of Thenigmas.'

The triplets now saw the smoke issuing from out of the volcano along with a searing seam of molten material leaking down one side.

'What be this portal? Another device of magic?' Mitac frowned.

'It is like a doorway, a gate joining one world with another. It is how my brother sent your father to this forsaken place.'

'Then it be some kind of magic?' Treetam mused.

'To your mind, yes,' Wa-ku said.

He adjusted the crystals, causing the ship to veer in towards the volcano. The mouth of Grorl gaped up at them, and beyond it loomed a small mountain range and a forest. Tiny dots like insects could be barely discerned moving across the land. Soon all they could see was Grorl and an area of plain around it. Then they could see vegetation, like shrubs and plants unknown to them. The ground was stony, cluttered with the litter of volcanic ash. The ship homed in on a patch of flat ground covered in withering grasses, and then with a slight thud, they felt the ship make contact with the land.

Wa-ku pivoted around to a panel in the wall, which he opened. He withdrew three moulded objects containing an arrangement of crystals and handed one to each of the erfins.

'You must not lose these,' he said, then withdrawing a fourth one from the panel, he held the object in his hand with the crystal arrangement pointing outward, so that the smooth curved side fit into the palm of his hand.

'You do not have your primitive weapons, but these are far more effective.' Wa-ku extended his hand and pointed the object towards a goblet that was sitting on a raised ledge on the other side of the chamber. He then clenched his hand into a fist over the weapon before opening his palm again. A narrow beam of brilliant light flashed out of the crystals and struck the goblet, which was flung off the shelf to crash onto the floor in pieces.

The three gaped in amazement.

'The strength of the solar-bite is controlled by the length of time that you keep your fist closed before opening it again,' Wa-ku explained. 'The longer you keep your fist closed, the more power it has. A short fist will stun an enemy while a longer hold will kill him.' Wa-ku narrowed his gaze at them. 'Do you understand what I am saying?'

They all nodded.

Treetam screwed up her mouth. 'Will there be enemies here like snerks?' she ventured.

'Worse than serpents. There are savage men here who will kill you without notice.'

'I will splatter their blood and leave them for the snerks to eat!' Ezof proclaimed.

'I have not killed any thinking being. But I will not let harm come to my brother and sister,' Mitac frowned.

Wa-ku chuckled softly. 'There are no snerks here, though there be other creatures to fear. But the men are the most to be feared. There are many warriors and many tribes, and each hates the other. Even with these weapons you must take care. If a warrior should get hold of one of these, they will be most dangerous indeed.'

Wa-ku twisted around again and took some pouches from the panel where he had gotten the weapons. 'Here,' he said, handing them each a pouch. 'Put your solar-bites in these and sling the straps around your shoulders ... there is also another purpose for these.'

He took his own solar-bite and pressed a small button on the side with his finger. The crystals immediately began to pulse with a green glow which was echoed in one of the crystal screen arrays on the wall. 'You can call me by pressing the small button here on the side, and I will find you wherever you are.'

They all nodded while Treetam tried the button on hers to see it work. The crystals responded, and another pulsing spot appeared on the screen.

Wa-ku pressed the button on his again, and the pulsing ceased. Ezof and Mitac also tried theirs, creating three pulsing dots on the screen before they each switched them off.

'When you go out, try to practise with the solar-bites first before going to look for your father.'

'How can we find him?' Treetam asked.

'Try to look for signs of him – blue fur, leftover fruit, perhaps. It will not be easy. You must creep around with quiet feet and not be seen by the savages.'

'An impossible task,' Mitac frowned.

'We will find him muddle-eye.' Ezof placed his hand on the other's shoulder to reassure him. 'We will be heroes like our dada!'

After some further instructions about surviving on Thenigmas, and locating the Darm stone, Wa-ku surveyed the three of them soberly. 'Are you ready to find your father?'

There were some reluctant nods before Wa-ku pulled a nearby lever. A hatch opened on a far wall, revealing the exterior surface of the planet they had previously only seen on the screen display. A flush of smoky cool air entered the chamber, causing Mitac to cough.

The three tentatively ventured outside onto the grassed area and were confronted by the enormous volcano in front of them. It rumbled ominously, and they could feel the ground shaking beneath them. They felt vulnerable out in the open, especially as the hatch on the ship shut, and it whirred back into life, soon disappearing into the sky above.

The three looked up at where the ship had gone. It was early afternoon and the sky had a tinge of green to the blue. There was a peculiar pungent smell in the air that made them want to gag and cough. Mitac was despondent as he regarded the surrounds of yellowed clumps of grass and shrubbery. It was so totally unlike the Faug Forest that he knew. Curiously, everything had two shadows as there were two suns in the sky, barely an arm's width apart when looking up at them.

Ezof withdrew his solar-bite and aimed it at a nearby shrub, closing and opening his fist as instructed. A sharp bright beam struck the shrub, burning some of its leaves. He tried again, this time holding for a stronger charge. The beam struck again, this time with spectacular effect, causing the whole shrub to burst into flames.

'Whoa!' Ezof shouted, grinning.

'Come on muddle-eye, you must try this.'

Mitac reached into his pouch and withdrew his solar-bite. He examined it for a few moments before trying it out on a shrub some distance away. The result was the same. The greater distance had not diminished its effectiveness. Treetam tried her solar-bite but aimed hers at some of the large rocky structures littering the ground to the south of their position. The beams exploded chunks of stone that scattered around like a spray of sand.

They continued practising with their solar-bites, quickly mastering the power of the weapons to have the desired effect on their targets. By the time they had finished their practice, there were several burnt out bushes and stone rubble within a radius of them.

Treetam led the way, marching off in the direction of the faraway hills where larger trees could be seen.

'Wait for us, Treet,' Ezof shouted, running in behind her with Mitac trying to keep pace with his brother.

'Yea, find the forest. It will be easier to hide there,' Mitac puffed.

'Look for signs of dada,' Treetam cried back at her brothers.

They travelled west towards the hills and the forest, stopping occasionally to examine the ground for any signs of Mirrortac. They struggled over mounds of stone rubble, keeping a wary eye on Grorl as it thundered, pouring out big clouds of ash and smoke. The ash rained down to the south-west, covering the earth.

Ahead of them the hills loomed larger, and the edge of the forest could be discerned. Small timid animals scampered in among the shrubs, disappearing into holes beneath. Treetam yearned to go into the tree tops but there were none. The plants here did not have the depth of green present in the Faug Forest, and everything was stunted. The trio found the walking tedious and the air hard to breathe. The earth groaned beneath them, shuddering every time Grorl exploded with a renewed outpouring of ash. The two suns descended towards the west, glowing yellow and red through a haze of acrid air.

Mitac suddenly called a halt. Ezof and Treetam turned around to see their brother waving at them to get down.

'What is it, muddle-eye?' Ezof shouted.

Mitac pointed to a spot near a thicket of bushes. 'Something there! It shines!'

Ezof and Treetam followed Mitac's outstretched finger until their eyes rested on the spot he indicated. There was something reflecting in the sunlight. The three approached with caution, crouching down as they crept closer. As they neared the object, they saw it was metallic like many of the alien-created things. It had the shape of a torso; indeed, it appeared to be some kind of metal clothing. It comprised metal threads knitted together in an elaborate pattern but torn. There was a gash in the chest area of the mail shirt, with a large patch of dried blood around the hole. The shirt was sleeveless. There was a leather skirt nearby and as they surveyed the area, they found broken pieces off swords and spears.

Then there were the bodies.

Mitac retched when he saw the headless and badly mauled body of a man behind a clump of wild grasses. He was dark skinned and almost naked except for a skirt of leather covering his midriff. There was a huge hole in his chest corresponding to the gash in the mail shirt. His heart had been removed and it seemed that his head had been taken as a trophy of war. Worms and maggots now infested the open flesh where wild animals had taken their fill.

Treetam covered her nose and mouth, muttering. 'They do not entomb their dead. They are left for the creatures to eat.'

Ezof grabbed the end of a spear and prodded the body. 'The softness is gone … dead maybe a half moon. That be if they have any moons here.' He sneered at the body then threw the spear end away.

Mitac retreated from the scene. 'Let us be away from this before these beings add our bodies to the pile.'

The other two acquiesced, leaving the body to whatever scavengers inhabited the area.

However, the march ahead was strewn with more bodies, broken armour and weapons. Some of the bodies were nearly black, contrasting with the lighter shades of brown skinned warriors. Clearly, there had been a great battle with much loss of life on both sides. They began to encounter squabbling flocks of ugly birds that feasted on the carcasses, and other larger creatures with jaws armed with flesh-tearing teeth and greedy yellow eyes.

Ezof used the solar-bite on one of the more thickset creatures, which died instantly with barely a yelp and a frizzle of burning skin. This disturbed the other scavengers which ran off at astounding speed into the scrub.

They left the field of death behind and marched onward towards the hills. The acrid air stung their eyes and breathing was difficult. The first sun had already set when they reached the first stand of trees under the shadow of some foothills. They had killed enough small animals on the way to quell their hunger, although the meat was unfamiliar and chewier than what they were used to.

'We can sleep up there.' Mitac pointed up into one of the bushier trees. 'It has big branches … and it will shield us from the wild ones.'

'I'll beat you up!' Treetam dared, already clawing her way up to the first branch.

'No you don't!' Ezof shouted after her, leaping onto the trunk after her.

Mitac just smiled. 'I'm last … I close the door.' He followed them up, quickly gaining on Ezof.

Treetam laughed as she swung deftly up the branches, leaping and hopping from one to another, all the time rising higher and well beyond the two brothers.

Ezof struggled upwards, kicking back at Mitac who was about to overtake him.

'You close the door muddle-eye … that's what you said! Stay behind.'

Mitac swung around him to another branch, and then leapt up a few, giggling as he looked back at the scowling face of his brother. 'You close the door now, bro.'

Ezof screwed up his mouth and crossed his eyes. 'Your day will come, muddle-eye.'

Treetam laughed at both of them as she settled herself down on a large high branch.

'Hurry up you two. It will be dawn before you get here,' she teased.

Mitac made it to the branch with another giant leap and swung himself up onto it.

'Oh, there you are Treet … sorry to keep you waiting sis.'

Treetam smiled. 'So good to be up here away from that … hot ground.'

Ezof finally clawed up to the branch and sat down beside them.

'Door closed … now where is that merma-mead?'

Mitac nodded. 'Yea, could do with some of that right now.'

He looked out through the branches and into the nearby foothills. The second sun was now glowing gold and red through a gap in the hills with the ground below already in shadow.

Grorl boomed in the distance, causing the tree to sway as though some giant had shaken it. The three lost their mirth and exchanged frightened glances.

Treetam stared at her brothers. 'What are we doing here?'

Ezof shrugged. 'Saving our dada, I suppose.'

Mitac sighed. 'Yu knows … it's all misty to me.'

Treetam shuddered as she looked around her. 'I hope this Wa-ku is not just a demon full of trickery. He seems all right. And mumma … her tales seem … real.'

They all went silent, haunted by their own fears. Here they were in a place as far from their home as one could get, on a mission to find a father they hardly knew.

One sun had already risen in the east when Mitac awoke to the sound of voices in the forest.

'Ezof, Treet ... wake up! Someone is coming,' he whispered while prodding Treetam.

'Uh ... go back to your bed chamber, Misha,' came the groggy reply.

Treetam slowly opened her eyes, suddenly realising that she wasn't back in Greenfaug. Ezof yawned, forcing his eyes to open.

'Wha ...?'

'Shush! There are men in the forest,' Mitac warned.

The voices were coming closer, forcing the other two awake and alert.

There were a few deep grunts before the Yu-essence kicked in, turning their tongue into something intelligible that the three could understand.

'The blue bear is a great warrior. He is stronger than 10 men,' they heard one say.

'Yeth, it is by the great god Zarv that we have been sent this beast. With him we make the Bluves eat dirt,' said the other.

The other laughed heartily, slapping his colleague on the back.

They passed nearby, with the three watching warily. The two wore mail shirts with animal hide skirts that barely covered their manhood. Their black waxy hair fell over broad dark shoulders and they both wore woven headbands and spiked anklets. One of them had a scraggly beard and was carrying a crossbow, which Ezof eyed with envy. It would be far deadlier and more accurate than a bow and arrow, he thought, but nothing to the solar-bites Wa-ku gave them. Yet, he preferred the primitive weapon, which felt more like you were armed than with some small magical item.

When the men were some way off, the three decided to climb back down to the ground.

'We must follow the wild ones,' Treetam suggested.

'I wonder if the blue bear is our dada,' Mitac mused.

'That is what I am thinking,' Treetam replied.

Ezof frowned. 'Blue? Why is our dada blue, anyway? It be most strange that his fur changes colour. We are always grey.'

Treetam shrugged. 'He does not care to stay the same.' There was a hint of a smile on her face as she said this.

Ezof grinned. 'Yea, good one Treet.'

'It bores him to remain grey. I wish I could change colour sometimes,' Mitac added.

Treetam examined the ground and started following the direction of the two men.

'Come on, we must take care. There may be others about.'

'Sure to be many where they are going,' Mitac said.

Suddenly, there was a rumbling sound and the ground started swaying beneath them. The three staggered and were showered with leaves. Ezof dodged a falling branch that slumped down beside him.

'Surely, we are in the Netherworld,' Mitac observed, frowning.

The rumbling quieted along with the swaying, allowing them to proceed normally again.

'Seems like there is a giant beneath us.' Treetam looked around anxiously.

The trail of the men led them through the forest and into the foothills and onto a well-worn pathway. The larger trees gave way to shrubs and clumped grasses that grew out of small patches of earth between boulders and bald stone hills. The path became more regular and was ridged with a line of bones, mostly human, then as they reached the peak of a hill, there were eerie skulls placed at the top of poles on both sides of the path. There was still hair on the skulls which were painted red with streaks of black falling away from the eye sockets, giving them a menacing look, which was no doubt aimed at scaring enemies away.

Mitac motioned to his siblings to leave the path and hide among the boulders, as it was clear that the village of these people was not far away. No sooner had they crawled in amongst the rocks then a small group of men could be seen walking up the path fully armed. There were perhaps half a dozen warriors carrying crossbows, long swords and daggers. One of them halted opposite the three and was examining the ground. The others also stopped, which caused the triplets to gasp and hold their breath.

'More beasts here!' the first man said, indicating the footprints. 'They be like the blue bear, it seemeth,' he mused, and his eyes followed the prints off the path.

'Great gakar's claw!' Mitac cried. 'We are found!'

Treetam and Ezof paled as they realised that they had done nothing to cover their tracks. It was not something they ever had to do in the Faug Forest, being always above the ground.

The men were all looking towards them now, with the first man arming his crossbow and starting to make his way towards where the three lay partially hidden.

The men were stealthy in their movements – experienced hunters – and all now making their way towards them in deadly earnest.

Ezof sucked in a breath as his heart beat fast in his chest. Without consulting the others, he pulled out his solar-bite and stepped out into the open. There was an outcry among the men who were about to rush him when Ezof opened his palm. The ground in front of the men exploded as the beam struck, forestalling their advance with a chorus of alarm and wide frightened stares. Treetam and Mitac now joined Ezof out in the open and were also armed and ready to shoot at any provocation. Ezof was still breathing heavily as he looked upon the men with as much fear as they now had of him.

Treetam shot at a boulder near the men, showering them in a spray of stones and dust. This proved too much for them as they fled back down the path in a clutter of voices.

'So much for surprise. The whole village will know we are here now,' Treetam frowned.

'They found us anyway,' Ezof said. 'I nearly lost a package.'

'You be not the only one,' Mitac observed. 'I never thought of our footprints. Thank Matcote for these solar-bites!'

'We cannot sneak up on them now. We must go on the path again, in plain view.' Treetam had already made her decision and was walking ahead to the path again.

'I don't know,' Mitac said, scratching his chin. 'Perhaps we can still sneak up close to the village since the wild ones are too afraid to seek us out again.'

'Yea, Treet ... Mitac is right. We must see if our dada is there without them seeing us,' Ezof nodded.

Treetam halted and turned around to face her brothers. 'Very well then. Whatever.'

The three set off again, skirting the path to not be seen, but it soon became obvious that they would have to climb up high as they found themselves in a narrow junction between a canyon of steep cliffs. This was a relatively easy task for the erfins who had been brought up in a forest, but the sharp, hard rock was unforgiving on the claws. After a lot of scrabbling up steep inclines and overhangs, the three finally were on top where the bare rock provided no cover. The village could now be clearly seen below in an area where the canyon widened out again, but any chance of them not been seen was again foiled. It was evident from the commotion that could be heard in the village and the crowd that assembled outside that they had again been sighted.

'Shriek of gakar!' Ezof shouted. 'What do we do now?'

Mitac was examining the line of cliffs to see where they could skirt around further to descend away from the village, but it seemed hopeless.

'I can't see any way down where we will not be seen,' he admitted, shaking his head.

Treetam was calm in her assessment. 'We have solar-bites; they do not. We go back to the path. Simple!'

The brothers found no argument so the three decided they had no choice but to confront the tribe or leave without their father.

They made the painful way back down to the pathway, took out their solar-bites, and began the march towards the village. It was still some time before they again sighted the stone walls of the village dwellings where a crowd of women and men awaited them. Some of the men were armed, but they did not ready their weapons even when the triplets were in plain sight and only a hundred erfin-lengths away from them. There was no sign of children, who had obviously been kept away from the "dangerous strangers". But a murmur had risen among the people who eyed the three with a mixture of awe and controlled fear.

When they were within just 20 erfin-lengths of the crowd, there was a jostling from behind the centre of the group, and out stepped an erfin with the darkest hue of blue, and himself heavily armoured in a large shirt of mail that fell to near his knees. He stepped out in front without any sign of fear, and his green eyes narrowed down on them. There was no hint of a smile, just a scowl.

'Halt! Who be you who dares to enter the place of the Clunuks? Who be you who threatens my kinfolk with a sorcerer's fire? Speak up now or leave this place!' the erfin commanded.

The three looked at each other in confusion. But it was Treetam who replied.

'Dada, it is your childfins Treetam, Ezof and Mitac. Do you not recognise us? We came to rescue you, but it seems you don't need rescuing. What are you doing here with these wild ones?'

The erfin frowned at them. 'Childfins? I never heard of you. I am Clunuk. The hills belong to us!'

Treetam approached slowly but stopped when the erfin shouted to her again.

'Don't you see that you are erfin? You are the same as us. Look at yourself … you are furry like us and not naked such as these.'

The erfin was uneasy but maintained his menacing stance. 'I know only Clunuk. I am Clunuk.'

Mitac pulled Treetam to him and whispered something to her. She then looked up again to address the erfin.

'We wish to be Clunuk too. Can we join you?'

The erfin screwed up his face and turned towards a man in the crowd nearby. 'What of these? They wish to be Clunuk,' he asked the man.

The two engaged in a strained conversation before the man stepped forward. The man was differently dressed to the others. He wore a robe of animal hide and had on several necklaces with various stones hanging from them.

'Why did you attack my kinsmen? What are these magic stones that you carry?'

Treetam was about to speak when Mitac stayed her and spoke instead.

'I do not know why our father remembers naught of us. But you can clearly see that we are of the same blood. Your men surprised us, and we shot at the ground to protect ourselves. Nothing more. Had we been an enemy, all your men would be dead now. You have seen what our weapons can do … it be better if we are in your service than that of your enemy. Accept us as friends and we will grant you aid to defeat your enemies.'

The chief man called others to him and engaged in a brief discussion before he turned towards them, smiling.

'We accept you as friends of Clunuk. You must come and join with us in treaty.'

The triplets put away their solar-bites, which made the crowd more relaxed. The blue erfin stood staring at them with confused eyes. Treetam was now free to approach him without fear, closely followed by her brothers who looked him over, eager to meet their father the hero.

The erfin brushed away tears. 'I wish I could remember ... you are my ... childfins?'

Treetam bounced up to him and hugged him hard. 'Dada! What has happened to you? We have heard so many wondrous tales about you.'

Mirrortac hung his head sadly. 'You have? You are such brave ones! Tell me these wondrous tales. I have but confused dreams of my life.'

Ezof and Mitac also hugged him but were more reserved.

'Come, join me at Clunuk hall!' the chief called out to them.

Children now appeared from the dwellings, snatching curious peeks at the three erfins. Some dared reach out to touch their fur as they passed, dashing back to their friends full of giggles and cheek.

The three and their father were carried along with the crowd to a larger stone building at the centre of the village, where the chief bid them to enter along with a small group of chosen men and women. Inside was arranged in a circle with a small fire on a flat low boulder in the middle. Smoke rose up and escaped through an opening at the apex of the roof, which comprised heavily thatched hay set down on girders of roughly hewn tree trunks. The triplets observed that it was nowhere near as elaborate as the Royal Halls of Greenfaug, perhaps more consistent with that of the lesser communities of the Faug Forest itself.

The chief made them all sit down near him on the floor surrounding the fire while the elders took their places in the circle. A man child entered bearing a plate with small bowls of a steamy liquid which he gave out to the erfins and the chief. He quickly left the building, leaving them with the chief and elders. The triplets eyed the bowls expectantly, and then surveyed the chief as he made himself comfortable on the floor at their side.

'Zarv has been gracious!' he began. 'He has sent three new warriors to join the blue bear. Now, we have three grey bears as well to smash our enemies!'

The elders nodded their pleasure and murmured loudly. 'Yeth! Zarv is well pleased ... Clunuks forever!'

The chief motioned to them to pick up their bowls as he took his with large thick fingers.

'Zarv is the great one! Warrior Who Eats the Sky! Hail to the almighty Zarv!' he proclaimed, lifting up his wooden bowl and lifting it to his lips. 'Drink!' he commanded.

Mirrortac did not hesitate as he took a big draught of the steaming concoction.

The triplets were less keen but obeyed. Mitac breathed in the aroma of the tea that reminded him of some of the pungent smells of the forest. He took a sip and tasted the liquid in his mouth before swallowing. Treetam did likewise while Ezof simply slurped the tea without regard for its taste.

'Zarv is greater than Eam ... Zarv leads her across to their bed and is first to wake in the dawn! Eam is Mother of All Fire but bows to the great warrior. Hail to Zarv!' Again, the chief drank, and again the erfins followed his lead.

'Grorl is the son of Zarv. Grorl is the Warrior of The Great Thunder! Grorl keeps watch on the earth. He is the angry one! The loud one! He stomps his feet and the ground shakes. His breath is fire. He vomits out the fire on the earth. But Grorl is but the son. Zarv is the great one! Hail to Zarv!'

Another taste of tea. The ceremony continued.

'Somok is the second son of Zarm and Eam. He is Warrior of The Burning Stones! In his anger he hurls burning stones all around, to destroy our enemy, the Bluves. Hail the sons of Zarv! Hail Zarv!'

Another toast, and by now the triplets were feeling the effects of the tea. Indeed, it was no ordinary brew, although its effect was quite unlike that of merma-mead. The trio was not only feeling strangely but was seeing visions of ghostly warriors and creatures that breathed fire and flew. These flying lizards menaced them with their bright yellow eyes and snerk-like tongues but vanished like reflections disturbed in a stream.

Ezof sprang up and challenged the spectres, drawing his solar-bite. The chief just laughed and pulled Ezof down. 'You will make a great warrior, my friend! But do not be afraid of what you see. They will not harm you.'

Ezof grunted and sat down again, frowning and disturbed by the visions.

Treetam preferred to snuggle close to her father while Mitac also cried out at the visions.

The chief nodded knowingly at them all. 'Our ancestor warriors and their creature totems are here with us. They are here to join us in welcoming the grey bears. Our new warriors!' He finished his bowl of narcotic tea and the others followed. Mirrortac was not disturbed as he was used to the spectres. Or it seemed that they spoke to him of his dreams and other life.

The strange tea had also made the erfins feel rather floaty and disconnected from their bodies. The three all wished they could feel normal again and be rid of the spectres that haunted the hall. But none of them spoke of their fears, trying instead to hold it all together in the presence of the men, who were taller than them.

A woman then entered the hall. She was dressed in a robe which had the feathers of all kinds of birds stuck to it. She wore a headdress which was partly the head hide of some creature, with its rounded ears still attached. Her face was painted with black eye-drops such as the skulls they had seen on the approach to the village, and her teeth were stained red from berries she had been eating. The woman circled the triplets, holding a stick with a hollow seed pod that rattled as she shook it. She was chanting something unintelligible and doing a little dance. She shook the pod over each erfin except Mirrortac, chanting and dancing as though out of her mind. Indeed, the triplets weren't sure if she wasn't crazy as her eyes rolled up to show the whites. Mitac saw some of the warrior spectres enter the woman, and as they did, she shook and convulsed before collapsing on the matting of the floor.

The woman rose up from the floor again and started to levitate, which quite unnerved the triplets. Her eyes opened with pupils that were so large that her whole eyes seemed black. Her mouth quivered before she spoke with a deep male voice.

'We hail the great Zarv and chief Ngarr of our kin the Clunuks! We hail the blue bear and the grey bears who have come to us from the sky tribes. We honour Darm – the stone that sleeps with the great warrior of fire, which the great Zarv brought to us to protect us. May our warriors, the bears, aid us in wiping out our enemies ... may their stones of flashing fire strike them and burn their flesh ... that they may roast under the face of Zarv and be feed for the worms and death birds, and all the creatures of the long tooth. All hail the mighty Zarv!'

The woman again slumped to the floor and the spectres were seen to leave her body. The triplets looked at each other, acknowledging what they had heard. Mirrortac gave them an awkward grin before bowing his head.

Chief Ngarr shouted out for food, and again children of the men entered bearing plates and bowls, this time containing unknown vegetables and fruits, and much raw meat. The erfins were each presented with the food, which they ate with gusto. They were also given a green juice which thankfully had no narcotic properties, just refreshment. The feast was not like that presented in Greenfaug, but although the tastes were different, it was not disagreeable.

In the morning, the triplets awoke feeling groggy. They had been bedded in a stone hut with straw on the floor for sleeping. Mirrortac was already chewing at some meat from a shallow bowl that was loaded with meat and some fruits. There was also a jug of the green juice with clay mugs. He eyed them curiously.

'You waste the day, childfins. Zarv and Eam have already begun their march across the sky,' he said, chewing busily.

The triplets answered with muffled groans. Mitac sat up while Treetam and Ezof lay squinting with sore heads.

'Dada, you talk in your sleep ... and snore loudly.'

'I talk in my sleep? ... what do I say?'

'You keep asking "where is Oashu?" What be Oashu, dada?'

The old erfin shrugged. 'I know naught. It must be important ... something I forgot. But then I have forgotten everything.'

'Perhaps your dreams hold the answer,' Mitac mused.

Mirrortac stopped chewing. His forehead crimped up with his concentration while he paused, searching his mind for some clue.

'Sometimes I dream of others such as ourselves but somehow not the same. And a cold place ... there is ice. Everything is cold. Then there are the giant birds that talk ... and,' he paused again. '... no, it be impossible."

'What be impossible?' Treetam asked. She was now sitting up also as she reached for the bowl of food.

Mirrortac waved his hand in dismissal. 'Just dreams childfins. Just dreams.'

'Tell us, dada. They be not dreams, I fear,' Treetam beseeched.

'The weirdness is too much. How can such things be true?'

'We have had our own share of weirdness, dada ... try us,' Mitac said.

The old erfin began to wander around the room with his head down.

'I saw a spiny creature that swallowed me up ... and others ... and it spat us out again. There was a wondrous place ... but it was haunted with spectres ... and my she-one ... although she was not my she-one. I could make things happen like a sorcerer. Can you believe such things?'

Mirrortac stopped and stared back into the faces of his three children. They were all wide-eyed with incredulous expressions. Mitac shook his head. 'Maybe they be just dreams. I do not know.'

'But what we saw last night was like a dream, muddle-eye,' Ezof ventured.

'Yea, and the wild woman hanging above the ground. I was scared,' Treetam added.

Ezof brightened. 'The creature that swallowed you ... mumma said something about it ... and the magic. Do you remember?' He was addressing his siblings.

They both thought for a few moments before Treetam nodded, smiling. 'Yea, she did speak of it ... she was angry with dada. But it was the only way across the burning ground ...'

Mitac acknowledged the truth of it. 'Then these be not dreams, but memories dada.'

Mirrortac stared at them in disbelief. 'Me, a sorcerer?' The old erfin shook his head gravely.

THE SEARCH FOR DARM

Wa-ku had not prepared them for the consequence of Mirrortac losing his memory, which made the prospect of seeking out the stone and bringing their father back with them that more daunting. It was now several days later. The siblings had gone on several scouting forays with the chief and Mirrortac and were able to demonstrate the power of their solar-bites to Ngarr's astonishment. Ezof had tested the tribe's crossbow and found it more to his liking than the solar-bite, as did Mitac, but Treetam was happy with the less cumbersome and more powerful device. She had become adept at its use and knew just how much energy she needed in any given circumstance. They had killed enough animals to feed everyone for days, which pleased the chief mightily. He grinned as he sat in Clunuk hall with the elders and the erfins chewing greedily at the meat.

'You serve the Clunuks well!' he said, clutching a thigh bone. 'This night we will wipe the Bluves from the face of Thenigmas!'

The three young erfins exchanged nervous glances. 'These be your enemies?' Mitac queried.

Ngarr nodded. 'Aye! With your magic stones, we can destroy them!'

Treetam looked sheepish. 'All of them? ... how many be there that we can destroy?'

The chief laughed deeply. 'You have nothing to worry about. With such magic stones it is an easy task ...' He crossed his throat with a hand. 'Dead!'

'But how many?' Treetam repeated, anxious.

'We do not count how many,' Ngarr dismissed. 'Their village is more than ours ... but no matter, the magic stones ... boom!' He made an explosive sound.

Mitac paled. 'Excuse us chief Ngarr. I must confer with my brother and sister. We will find the best way to destroy your enemy, the Bluves ... boom!' he ended, imitating the chief's sound.

Ngarr burst into a hearty laugh. 'Aye, boom! You talk ... find the best way!'

Mitac stood and signaled to Ezof and Treetam to follow him a short distance away out of earshot of the chief and his elders.

The other two looked just as concerned as he did, but they tried not to let on to the chief who was still chuckling and making 'boom' sounds.

Ezof and Treetam leant their heads towards Mitac as he whispered to them. 'They want us to eliminate their enemy. These are men such as they ... not snerks or dark creatures. We must go along with them, but try not to kill anyone, unless we must.'

Ezof frowned. 'How can we do that? Kill or be killed, I say.'

'He's right bro. We are not killers of people, whatever they may be. Unless we have to ...' Treetam added.

'But we be warriors! Like dada." Ezof's eyes widened.

'And what of Darm?' Mitac reminded. 'It is with the Warrior of Fire. We must be about finding it.'

Treetam nodded. 'And taking it and dada back to Wa-ku.'

Mitac paused in thought then brightened. 'That's it! We will pretend to go on this battle with the Bluves but seek Darm instead. Tell the chief we need the power of Darm to power up our solar-bites!'

Treetam grinned. 'You be most clever brother!'

'And we can destroy the Bluve village while we do it!' Ezof chimed in, still keen for a fight.

Mitac and Treetam both shook their heads, saying nothing.

Mitac gestured for the other two to follow him. 'Let me speak with Ngarr. I know what to say.'

The three returned to the chief with Mitac in the lead.

Ngarr looked at them eagerly, grinning widely. 'Boom!'

Mitac smiled graciously at the chief. 'We need something first so our magic stones can be filled with enough power to wipe out your enemy. We need the Darm stone energy ...'

Ngarr's toothy grin faded as he stroked thoughtfully at his chin. 'You ask much ... but we expect much. It shall be done. It is with the Warrior of Fire who is buried in the hills, under the rocks. You will need many strong warriors to lift them.'

'Then give us these warriors, and show us where he lay,' Mitac said.

'We must hurry. The Bluves are a half day's march.' Ngarr called out a list of names, and a group of the strongest warriors were summoned into the hall. 'Take the bears to the Warrior of Fire and lift the rocks from him. They must use the Darm stone.'

The warriors muttered among themselves, and one man, whose face was disfigured by large scars, spoke up. 'But mighty one ... this is the sacred stone. It must not be disturbed.'

'The bears come from the place of the gods. They have come to destroy our enemy. You will do as I say!' Ngarr growled.

The warrior was still not convinced but bowed in obeisance. 'As you will,' he said through gritted teeth.

The group of warriors promptly left with the erfins, leading back up the path then off to a rocky overhang where there was a cave. They entered a short way until they reached a cairn of large rocks which was marked with several spears driven into the ground and topped with skulls such as the ones seen on the path. However, these also included tassels of bird feathers and an assortment of armour in honour of the one buried beneath the cairn.

'Forgive us, oh Warrior of Fire for this disrespect,' the scar-faced warrior said, as he turned and glared at the erfins with his dark eyes.

'Ngarr has much trust in you, grey bears. But if you betray him, I will tear out your hairy bellies and feed you to the gizzard birds.'

'You will do naught such thing!' Mirrortac, who had also accompanied them, growled. 'My child-fins will naught betray Ngarr. Control your anger, Ming!'

The warrior scowled back. 'Don't think you be safe, blue bear.'

Mirrortac was taken aback but was unafraid.

Mitac cleared his throat nervously. 'Darm will defeat the Bluves ... you will have to trust us.'

Ming grunted but said nothing more. The other warriors were silent but were also clearly disturbed. However, they knew they would be punished if they did not obey. They approached the cairn and began to lift off the heavy rocks, struggling and sweating as they moved each one aside.

Ezof scratched his head before removing his solar-bite. 'Will it not be easier to blast the stones with this?' He proffered the solar-bite.

Ming turned on Ezof and had his thick fingers around his throat before the erfin could react. 'We can't protect the warrior with rubble you crazy bear!'

Ezof choked a gargled reply. 'Just an idea ...'

Ming loosened his grip to return to the job at hand.

Treetam came to Ezof's aid as he stroked his sore neck.

'No time for heroics here. Just stay quiet,' she advised.

Soon, the last rock was removed, revealing a skeleton that was still dressed in mail armour and richly decorated with tassels and circlets. Mitac stared down into the shallow grave, searching for the stone with its specific pattern as described by Waku. The air was musty, but the odour of death had long gone.

'There!' Treetam pronounced, pointing at a small stone that hung from a necklet around the dead warrior's neck.

Mitac reached down but Ming stayed his hand. 'I will take it off.'

Ming handled the necklet, carefully moving it over the back of the skull until he held it up like a sacred thing. Mitac put up his palm to receive it but Ming snatched it away.

'Do what you need with Darm, but do not touch it,' he warned.

Mitac frowned. 'I must have it, or I cannot power the magic stones.

Ming and Mitac's eyes met. Ming narrowed his eyes and glared at the erfin long and hard. But Mitac only pushed his hand out more, with silent insistence. They stood eye to eye for what seemed forever until the warrior finally relented, slowly handing over the necklet with the Darm stone.

The siblings examined the stone with some interest, fingering the pattern while the clunuk warriors stood by expectantly. Treetam had a look of consternation as she regarded the stone. 'It is smaller than I expected,' she mused.

Mitac moved over to his father and held him. 'It is time, dada, for us to return home.'

Mirrortac's ears twitched at this while Mitac drew out the solar-bite and pressed the tracking button. The other two did the same while the warriors became more agitated at their strange actions. Ezof was quick to point his solar-bite at the warriors, while the other two soon followed. This time it was Ezof's turn to speak.

'Don't try anything or we will turn you all into dust and ashes!' he proclaimed, adopting his most aggressive stance.

Ming growled loudly. 'We have been tricked! Get them!'

The scarred warrior moved swiftly but Treetam was quicker, firing her solar-bite at the ground just in front of his feet with a blast that was strong enough to throw the warrior backwards into the rocks behind him. The other warriors were hesitant, choosing instead not to challenge the might of the solar-bites.

Mirrotac regarded them with mouth agape. 'Why do you betray your own tribe?'

Mitac pulled his father along with him as they all backed slowly out of the cave. Ming gathered himself up out of the dust cloud created from the solar-bite, and scurried towards the entrance.

'Run! We must run!' Mitac cried, urging his father along as they hastened out into the open.

Ming emerged behind them, shouting a warrior's curse after them. Ezof aimed at the rock overhang and fired his solar-bite. A bright stream of light tore into the stone, dislodging large chunks and sending it raining down on Ming and the other warriors now also giving chase.

'Can I kill him? I want to kill him,' Ezof shouted back at Mitac and Treetam.

'NO!' they chorused, prompting a smirk of disappointment from the battle hungry young erfin.

The rock fall was enough to send the clunuks diving for cover, giving the erfins enough time to put sufficient ground between them to await Wa-ku's arrival.

Within moments they could hear the distinct humming of Wa-ku's cosmo-ship as it rapidly closed in on them from above.

Mitac turned to his father and pulled him down to the ground. 'You may want to sit down for this,' he said, a sly smile escaping his lips.

Mirrortac was in total bewilderment, not knowing what to do, but complying nonetheless. The others also sat down as the ship hovered overhead, and its beam passed over them.

The smell of the dust and the feel of the hot sun was soon a memory as the erfins all vanished from the ground, soon to find themselves in the confines of the cosmo-ship. The clunuk warriors looked up in stunned silence, except for Ming who threw curses at the departing erfins.

Mirrortac clutched desperately at the floor of the cosmo-ship as he glanced around in horror. 'I am taken up with the gods. Who be you my child-fins that you do this to us?'

He felt dizzy and nauseous as the ship accelerated, displaying the mass of the earth beneath quickly receding and turning into a giant ball in a black void. He could see Wa-ku seated in his hoverchair in front of a crystal array of screens and controls. His blond locks fell over his shoulders and he was pale ... but he was a man like the clunuks.

'It is weirdness, dada, but you will get used to it,' Treetam assured him, moving over to him to hug him close to her.

Wa-ku swiveled around to face them. 'Welcome Mirrortac! I am Wa-ku. We have work to do. Where is the Darm stone?'

Mirrortac looked at the blue-eyed man with a mixture of awe and uncertainty. 'Wa-ku? I think I know such a name ... but my memory fails me.'

Wa-ku looked over to the triplets. 'Darm?'

He was looking around expecting to see the stone immediately. Mitac lifted up the necklet to him. 'Here it is?'

Wa-ku frowned. 'What is that? Where is Darm?'

Mitac fingered the stone on the necklet. 'Here!'

Wa-ku sighed, swung back to the controls and suddenly changed the ship's course back towards Thenigmas.

Turning back again he wrung his hands through his golden locks and stared at them with a smirk. 'I don't understand. Mirrortac, you know Darm must lock into Oashu. You know how big Oashu is, don't you?

Mirrortac just returned a quizzical expression. 'Oashu? Yes, I know something of Oashu ... the dreams ...' the old erfin shook his head to himself, searching his mind for some semblance of memory.

Mitac spoke up. 'He remembers nothing. Only in his dreams does he remember anything.'

Wa-ku clawed his face as though he wanted to gouge out his cheeks. He let out a long sigh. 'I did not think of the effect of the portal. My friends, we must go back. This is not Darm.'

'But ...' Mitac tried to answer.

'No. It is a small version, yes, but Darm is a much larger stone. This is not the true stone. We must go back and find it. What did the tribe's people say about it?

'The chief Ngarr said it was with the Warrior of ...' Mitac stopped himself as he came to a realisation. 'Fire! Warrior of Fire ... how stupid I was ... it is at the mountain of fire. It is with Grorl! They thought it was with the dead man they called the warrior of fire, but it was not him, it is the mountain – Warrior of Great Thunder!'

'I told you it looked too small,' Treetam said, almost accusingly, as if she had known all along.

'Then we can go back and fight the clunuks!' Ezof grinned.

'NO!' Mitac and Treetam chorused.

Wa-ku betrayed a hint of a smile. 'We don't need to fight any savages. I will take you to Grorl where we must look for it.'

Mirrortac shook his head. 'I be befuddled. I wish I could remember.'

Wa-ku steered a course for Grorl and set them down again at the foot of the volcano, this time on the southern border. As night was falling, they spent the night in the ship until Zarv peeped up from the horizon, shedding light again on the land. The erfins watched as the ship again ascended into the sky and disappeared from view. Now, they had to begin the search for Darm in earnest.

Mitac sneezed as the acrid air assaulted his nostrils once more.

'Where do we start? The mountain is angry,' Treetam asked.

'Perhaps there is a cave leading under the mountain where it rests. The fire guards it,' Mitac replied, staring in the direction of the peak that rose above them, billowing ash and dark clouds.

As though in warning, the ground shook as the volcano rumbled, spewing cinders into the sky.

'Then to the mountain!' Treetam cried, already falling into a stride towards it.

Mirrortac's ears slumped back on his head as he surveyed the volcano with fear in his eyes. 'Grorl is angry with us. We must not go there,' he pleaded.

'C'mon dada. It is your mission. We must find Darm.'

The old erfin dug his feet in and crossed his arms over his chest. 'You go. I will wait for you here. I will naught anger the mighty Grorl, Warrior of Great Thunder.'

'We cannot leave you here. The naked ones will kill you,' Mitac urged.

'I am Clunuk. They will naught hurt me.'

'You are not Clunuk. You are erfin … we have betrayed them … you have betrayed them.'

Mirrortac stood his ground. 'I will naught go there.'

Mitac sighed but Ezof waved him away. 'I will stay with dada and protect him. I can destroy any enemy with my solar-bite.'

Mitac scrunched up his mouth and frowned, hesitating. 'So it will be. You stay with dada but try not to kill anyone. We will return before the suns take rest.'

There was little shade here as it was open plain, but Ezof and Mirrortac were able to shelter under a large shrub a short distance away. Meanwhile, Mitac and Treetam set off towards Grorl, striding across the sparse grassed plain and into a field of ash that covered the ground for the remaining distance to the foot of the volcano. A rain of ash now shrouded their path as they trudged onwards, forced to cover their mouths and noses with their hands against the choking grey dust. The two suns were angry red balls peering through the ash cloud. The erfins coughed and gagged as their breathing became laboured.

Treetam gave Mitac a pained look. 'I don't know how much longer I can go on …' she hacked violently.

'We must find shelter near if we can …' Mitac rasped.

The gloom of ash was thick and acrid, making it difficult to judge what direction they were headed. But thankfully, it began to clear and they found themselves emerging out of the rain of ash. Finally, they looked up at the crater almost directly overhead, still streaming black clouds that now thundered loud like a storm. Streaks of lightning flashed inside the cloud, filling the erfins with trepidation.

'We will follow the base. See if there is an opening somewhere,' Mitac said, and Treetam nodded.

They began skirting the volcano after resting for a time to gather their breath and cough out the bad air.

'It is sense that Darm is here … the portal leads here … and the mountain will protect it,' Mitac said.

'And Wa-ku's brother kept it secret from the naked ones … telling them it was the small stone,' Treetam mused.

The two continued their discussion until they reached an impasse – a stream of fire running down the side of the volcano and across the plain in front of them. It steamed and belched with molten rock as it congealed and cooled beyond their sight. They followed alongside the lava stream until they had reached an area where it was no longer a ferocious red but a black yet still very hot rock. Yet still further revealed a field of stone that was set and cool enough to support some sparse plant growth. And then they discovered it.

The opening was disguised amid stony outcrops that shielded the entrance until you were almost on top of it. They might have walked right past it had Treetam not looked back towards the volcano.

Inside was a hollow tube that traversed some distance back towards the volcano. It was soon dark and hot as they moved cautiously onward. A superheated steam issued from far into the cavern, causing the erfins to break out in a sweat as they made their way through. This thwarted progress as the heat became close to unbearable. The cavern widened into a huge space where they could hear dripping water and steam bubbling up from a subterranean watercourse. Mitac and Treetam abruptly stopped as their feet touched hot water. Their eyes adjusted to the blackness until they could barely make out a pool in front of them.

'What now?' Treetam asked, turning towards the luminescent orbs of Mitac's eyes.

'We need more light,' Mitac replied in a matter-of-fact way.

He felt for his pouch and withdrew his solar-bite. He immediately fired it without drawing up energy and was rewarded with a soft beam of light that illuminated the cavern.

'A little trick I learned,' he said, showing a smile reflected in the mild light.

They glanced around the pool and noticed something resting on a raised rock platform in the centre. The light from the solar-bite quickly faded, forcing Mitac to repeat the procedure several times to reveal a path to the stone in the centre of the pool. There was a shallow way across to the centre, but the water was scorching hot, and it would burn their feet before they could reach the platform.

'I am sure that it is Darm ... but the way is too hot,' Mitac said.

Treetam thought for a few moments then suggested, 'Perhaps we need something to wrap our feet in, or ...'

'Put under our feet,' Mitac finished for her.

'There is nothing here. We must go outside and find something to suit,' he said.

They emerged out in the sunshine to discover it was already after midday, with both suns hiding behind the cloud of the volcano.

Mitac motioned to Treetam with his arms, indicating the surrounding area. 'Help me look for two flat deep stones that I can put on my feet, sis. I will tie it to them with some of these grasses.' He bent down and uprooted a bunch of thick grass growing nearby.

There was no shortage of stones littered about, but it took some time to find suitable flat ones with the right depth to keep his feet out of the scorching water. Finally, Mitac had to make do with two reasonably flat stones that had uneven bottoms. He tied some of the grass to them and around his feet and tried them out. They wobbled under his feet, making any attempt at walking difficult, but it was enough.

They re-entered the cavern carrying the stones and soon were back at the pool where Darm rested. Mitac put on the rock shoes.

'Here goes,' he said, setting off through the pool. Treetam fired light beams intermittently to show the way for Mitac, who struggled to maintain his balance as he stepped slowly towards the centre.

He reached the centre after a while and bent over to grab hold of the stone resting on the platform.

Mitac grunted as he lifted the stone. 'Snerk's curse! This is heavy. My stones are getting hot, sis. I must hurry.'

'Don't fall. You will boil to death!' Treetam warned.

Mitac let out anguished cries as he clomped his way back along the shallow path. The stones under his feet were heating up, and combined with the incredible weight of Darm, made progress that more risky and painful.

He wobbled forward and had just made it half way when one of the grass ties snapped, sending the makeshift stone shoe splashing into the water and Mitac left balancing on one leg. He could not retrieve the shoe without letting go of Darm, and his leg trembled as he struggled to stay up. Mitac felt himself losing balance, with the boiling water waiting to embrace him.

The next moment was a blur as he swung with all the energy he had left and released Darm into the air and towards the shore. He instinctively struck out with his free leg, forced to let it plunge into the seething water, bracing for the inevitable rush of burning heat. It came like a piercing shot of fire up his leg as he forced out his other still shoed foot forward, pulling his burning foot out as he did so. Another step forward and another piercing pain up his leg, then released as the other foot again stumbled forward. He felt his consciousness wavering as each time he was eclipsed in pain as his free foot plunged into the water. The steps became a jumble of movements while his chest exploded with pain and the darkness grew foggier.

Mitac awoke to bright light and surrounded by tall grasses. Treetam was staring down at him with concern on her face. His foot felt as if it was on fire, and painful spasms radiated up his left leg.

'Darm ... is it ...' he gasped.

'Yes, we have it. You must rest. Your foot is badly swollen and boiled. I don't know how you were able to keep walking. You threw Darm to the shore. I have it here. I had to make a separate trip to pick it up. I had to get you out first.'

Mitac glanced back at the volcano, which was now casting a long shadow over them. It was late in the day. Too late to return to Mirrortac and Ezof.

'We must sleep here near the cavern where the rocks will hide us from enemies,' Treetam said.

Mitac was in no position to argue. He could hardly collect his thoughts as he dealt with spasm after spasm of pain. It was a long night in which he drifted in and out of consciousness. Treetam tendered to his foot, wrapping it in grass and leaves to try to relieve the pain even just a little. She slept little, and worried about her brother surviving.

Dawn found Mitac much weakened and moaning with pain. Treetam killed a few night rodents and boiled them in the water of the cave, returning to feed them both. However, Mitac refused the food.

'You must eat, bro. It will help you live.' Treetam regarded his pale eyes – the one blue, the one green – now glassy with tears as he fought the pain. He begrudgingly accepted the boiled meat to chew at it with tentative bites.

It was now up to her to get them back to Mirrortac and Ezof. Then she thought of the solar-bite tracker and slapped herself on the face. 'We will be safe in a moment ... I wish I had thought of this earlier.'

Treetam pushed the tracking button, grabbed hold of Darm and sat down next to her brother. They were soon back on the cosmo-ship with Wa-ku grinning back at them when he spied the stone.

'That is Darm,' he said. 'But where are the other two now?'

'We left them where you dropped us. Dada would not come with us. He feared the mountain,' Treetam replied.

'Mitac needs help. His foot was boiled in the hot water. I fear he will die.'

Wa-ku hovered over to where Mitac lay and examined his foot.

'Hmm, bad ... very bad,' he muttered. 'There is some burn cream, but it will be of little help I'm afraid.'

Wa-ku rummaged around under the screen array and pulled out a tube made of an alien substance. He handed it to Treetam after removing its cap. 'Here. You must squeeze this tube to gather the cream, then rub it over his foot.'

Treetam accepted the tube before clearing Mitac's foot of the grass and leaf wrap. His foot was bulging and swollen, and she could see the red raw skin beneath his fur. She squeezed the tube, which spurted a liberal dose of yellow coloured cream, which she gently applied on the foot. Mitac cried out as she touched his foot with her hands. She winced at his pain, trying her hardest not to aggravate it. She had never seen him like this. Never had he been in such pain.

Wa-ku turned his attention to the controls again, quickly flying them to the point where they had left Mirrortac and Ezof. They were there in seconds but were not prepared for what awaited them. There was a group of clunuk tribesmen holding Mirrortac and Ezof captive, and one of them was pointing Ezof's solar-bite at them.

Wa-ku cursed aloud in some unknown tongue, at the same time reaching for the controls to try to steer the ship away.

A flash of light could be seen issuing up from the solar-bite followed instantly by a violent jolt that shook the ship and threatened to bring it down.

Wa-ku cursed again as he took the ship up and away from the solar-bite's range. The screen's view of the tribesmen rapidly diminished before another view of the ground some distance away came into vision.

'This is not a war ship. It is not equipped for battle,' Wa-ku gasped. 'I shall have to drop you out of range so you can catch them. But I don't know how you will do that.'

Treetam paled as she realised. 'Can't you do something?' she pleaded.

Wa-ku shrugged. 'We have the Darm stone. We can leave them behind and complete the mission ourselves.'

Treetam shook her head. 'No! I will have to do this alone.'

Mitac tried to talk but his voice was barely a rasping whisper. 'Get dada and our bro, sis ... you can do it.'

She was close to tears as she looked into her brother's eyes. 'I will do this bro ... or die in the effort.'

'Then it be settled. We are depending on you. Take your brother's solar-bite. You may be able to succeed with two.' Wa-ku nodded to her sympathetically.

Treetam was on the ground before she knew it. Her mind was racing. 'What to do, what to do,' she was saying to herself. She had always depended on Mitac for all the strategy and planning. Now it was only her. She tried to think what he would do if faced with this situation. First, get out of the open and try to sneak up behind the cover of the shrubs, such as there were. How had Ezof been relieved of his solar-bite? He was always such a fighter. The thought was just improbable.

The erfin used her stealth to skirt towards the tribesmen and their captives. She crept up behind shrubs and rocks, all the time keeping a lookout for any surprises. Her senses keened as she put her total focus into the task, finding a strange pleasure in keeping out of sight and closing in on the enemy who were unaware she was anywhere nearby. Finally, she was behind a large boulder within earshot from the group and was able to observe them secretly.

The scar-faced clunuk Ming seemed to be leading a group of warriors, perhaps a dozen or more. Mirrortac and Ezof had their hands tied behind their backs and were prodded along by men wielding swords and cross-bows. Ming was armed with the solar-bite, which he aimed right and left and up as he strutted along, scowling.

'The sky demon has abandoned you, bears. You will both make good bedding when I have skinned you,' Ming boasted.

Ezof looked sullen and pale, defeated. But Mirrortac was struggling violently against several warriors who were manhandling him.

'How dare you kill Ngarr. You be naught but a traitor to the clunuks!' The erfin was furious.

Ming turned on him and snarled. 'He was weak minded. We are best rid of him. I never trusted you bears from the day I saw you. I am chief now.'

Ming motioned to one of the warriors who carried a spear with the head of man propped up on its end.

'We will plant his head here as a warning to the bluves and anyone who may think they can challenge the might of the clunuks,' Ming said, indicating the ground in front of him.

The warrior strutted forward and shoved the spear deep into the earth. Ngarr's head stared out of sightless eyes. Blood dripped down the spear shaft and congealed on the ground.

Treetam gasped in horror and revulsion. She remembered the many skulls on poles as they had made their way on the path to the clunuk village.

Then Ming sneered up at the erfin captives. 'And now it be your heads to join Ngarr's to show the sky demons we are afraid of no-one!'

Ezof whimpered at hearing this and began to struggle as the warriors brought him and Mirrortac forward. Three warriors were having a hard time moving the old erfin as he used all his strength to resist them. Treetam's heart began to pound as she knew the time had come to act, or watch her brother and father die in front of her.

Two warriors were wielding wide bladed swords, waiting with Ming to cut off the erfins' heads. The three were still separated from the rest of the group, giving Treetam an opening to use her solar-bite. It was now or never.

Treetam raised both solar-bites and energised them to full capacity. Abruptly she stepped out into full view and gave out a cry so loud it echoed across the plain. She opened her palms.

Two sharp beams erupted and slammed into Ming and the two warriors, disintegrating them on the spot. An explosion of red dust was all that remained. The warriors holding the two erfins immediately released them and ran off screaming, along with all the warriors present. Treetam ran after them with such fury that some warriors emptied their bowels on the ground as they made their escape. She was still screaming at them as she aimed the two solar-bites directly at them. Blinding twin streams of light erupted again, exploding into the group, and killing many instantly. Treetam energised the solar-bites yet again, and fired, killing the remaining warriors.

Ezof stared at his sister in disbelief as she glared wide-eyed after the now dead warriors lying in untidy heaps on the plain. She was growling like some wild creature and ranting curses. Mirrortac too, looked at her in horror, his mouth agape.

Treetam stood there for some time, growling and panting until the rage inside her subsided, leaving her slumped and crying.

Ezof approached her and put his arms around her shoulders.

'It's okay sis. It's all over. We're safe now.'

Treetam leant her head on his shoulder, still sobbing. 'I killed them, bro. I killed them all. I was so scared for you and dada ... I could not help ...'

Her body shook with shock. Ezof patted her gently, and began to cry too, out of sheer relief.

Mirrortac was also relieved but did not understand all that had transpired.

'You have saved us, my child-fin. I do naught wish to stay in this place any longer.'

Treetam let go of Ezof and ran over to her father. She hugged him hard and smiled up at him through her tears.

'We're going home dada.'

She pressed the tracking button on her solar-bite. Ezof looked around as though he just realised something.

'Where is Mitac? What happened that you did not return in the last sun's sleep?'

'He is badly hurt.' She explained what happened the day before as the whir of the cosmo-ship came overhead and took them on board.

Wa-ku smiled at the three as they appeared unharmed.

'You succeeded then?' he said, turning back to his controls and steering the ship into space.

Mitac was still in agony on his bunk. Treetam and Ezof came to his side, wearing looks of concern. Mirrortac too, entered the chamber and perused the swollen foot.

Without warning, the old erfin reached out with the palms of his hands and held them both over the weeping sores. Treetam and Ezof exchanged quizzical glances as Mirrortac began muttering in a tongue they had never heard and could not understand. His eyes glazed over, and his palms began to glow with a soft light that bathed the foot in its hue. They gasped with amazement as the sores congealed and then disappeared – the swelling subsiding. Mitac stopped moaning and fell into a deep sleep.

Mirrortac removed his hands. His eyes were normal again and he seemed surprised as he again perused the now healed foot.

Treetam's mouth was agape as she looked with awe at her father. 'You healed him! It is magic ... how did you ...?'

Mirrortac gave her a confused look and shrugged. 'I healed ...? Nay. How ...?'

'You just put your hands over his foot and said some strange words, then his foot was better.'

'I did?' Mirrortac's eyebrows rose.

Treetam just chuckled and hugged her father. 'I love you dada?'

Mirrortac smiled awkwardly, glancing sideways. 'I think I love you too my child-fin.'

Ezof joined in to hug his father and sister, saying nothing.

After the hugging, Treetam turned on her brother with a stern face. 'How did you get caught? And how on Yu did that nasty Ming get hold of your solar-bite.'

Ezof looked away. 'When you did not return, we had something to eat, then … I guess … we both fell asleep. When I woke up, Ming was standing over me with the solar-bite in his hand. He knows how to use it too. Must have watched us doing it.'

Treetam frowned.

'I was tired …' Ezof said, pouting.

'You could have hidden it somewhere.'

'And like that would help, sis, when there are a heap of strong warriors guarding me.'

Treetam paced around him, frowning. 'You could have both died. You should have stayed awake.'

'Enough!' Wa-ku shouted from the control room. 'You are all safe now, thanks to Treetam.'

'Yes, thanks to me!' she emphasised.

Sometime later, after they all had had a good nap, Mitac emerged from the bedchamber with a grin from ear to ear. He walked around as though he had a new foot and was chuckling to himself as he joined the others in the control room. Wa-ku was startled to see him out and about and pointed quizzically at Mitac's healed foot.

'I knew the cream might help, but I didn't know it was that good. That's amazing!' Wa-ku said.

Treetam and Ezof both smiled at each other, then at their father.

'It was not the cream, but dada that healed him,' Treetam grinned.

'What? You're telling me that this old erfin fixed him? How?'

Mirrortac shrugged. 'That be what they tell me, though I know naught of this.'

'He went all funny, like he was under a spell … then he said some strange words … put his hands over his foot like this …' she imitated the pose with her palms, 'and his foot just wasn't red and sore anymore.'

Wa-ku looked at the old erfin thoughtfully. 'Your mind remembers the magic … or a part of your mind. This is good. You are even more powerful than my brother. Well, in some ways … he never was able to heal like that.'

Mitac strode over to the food panel and reached in to rummage around among the sterile items Wa-ku had stored there.

'I am so hungry I could eat ten tarmuts!' he said, referring to the rodent from the Faug Forest. 'I wish there was meat here to eat, instead of this ...' He smirked at the unappetising packages that Wa-ku provided. Unwrapping one, he shrugged and popped it into his mouth, following it with several more.

Treetam smiled at her brother. 'It is good to have you back, bro. You worried me so.'

'Yea, I'd have to put up with her on my own,' Ezof grinned.

Treetam punched him in the shoulder. 'I know you love me Ez. I nearly lost you too, and dada.'

Wa-ku turned around and hovered over to the erfins.

'I am glad you are all hearty and much recovered from this little adventure. Perhaps now is the time to remind you of the mission and how we are to enter into my brother's domain.'

The erfins grew solemn at this, reminded of the Darm stone now sitting in a corner of the ship nearby. Except for its exceptional weight for size, and the curled question-mark pattern on its dark brown surface, it did not appear to be anything magical. There was no glowing or other outward manifestation of magic, but that was because it was separated from the other two stones and its powers remained hidden. It was roughly triangular in shape with the base curved to accommodate the curve of Oashu, which, according to Ameece's description imparted to them, was oval in shape with a slightly more elaborate pattern.

Ezof keened at the thought of another adventure; his dice with death now cast aside.

'So, we just fly there, hit him and those bird people with the solar-bites, and grab the Oashu stone,' he chimed in, struggling with the pronunciation.

Wa-ku smiled at him. 'Not so easy my little furry friend. Yidu has created a complex of magical zones that protect as well as sustain his domain of Skye. I cannot simply fly in and drop you all at the palace. If only it was that simple.'

'How is it that he has this magic and not you?' Mitac asked.

'The Werdstone gives him access to the knowledge of the ancient ones. Their spellcraft is the greatest in all the known cosmos. This has made my brother very powerful, and dangerous. The stones would give him complete control over the destiny of many peoples. He does not have the wisdom to wield such power.'

Mitac nodded. 'Then gathering these stones will stop him?'

'Not the mere gathering, but the joining of them. And then not the mere joining of the three stones of destiny but conjoined with the Werdstone to destroy them forever.'

'Will that also destroy the Werdstone?' Mitac ventured.

'No. It will remain, and its access to the ancients will remain, but without the three stones, it can only influence the user. Yidu's access to the Werdstone must also be prevented or he can use his spells again to create domains.'

'Then, must we kill him?' Ezof asked.

'Much as I despise my brother, I prefer to put him somewhere where he has no power. I will take him to the Council of Atlantis in the Halls of Ra where he will face justice and most likely put in prison for his great crimes.'

'You speak of things we know naught about. What be a prison?' Mitac frowned as he tried to make sense of all this information.

'It is a place where we place ones who commit crimes against the cosmos and endanger the wills of peoples everywhere. He will not be able to go out of such a place. He is held captive and guarded by ones such as the warriors who took Ezof and Mirrortac.'

The erfins all nodded. Mitac then posed another question.

'Then how are we to enter such a magical domain ... itself like a prison where no-one can enter instead of leave?'

'That is the right question.' Wa-ku turned to one of the crystal screens and manipulated some of the structures to show an image of a map of Yidrogh. He pointed to the area where Mirrortac had entered with Ameece and the others. 'This is a representation from the air of the entry point to Skye. Ameece tells me that he spoke in a sacred tongue which opened the way up a stairway to Skye. He also used this tongue to prevent an attack from tree people, such as your faugs.'

Wa-ku sighed as he looked around at the erfins. 'And there is the problem. Mirrortac, do you not recall the sacred words to open the gateway?'

Mirrortac shrugged. 'My memory of such things is in darkness yet.'

Wa-ku frowned. 'That is regrettable. My young friends, you can use your solar-bites to repel the faugs, but you still cannot open the gateway.'

He paused, reaching for a mug of liquid which he sipped.

'I have thoroughly questioned Ameece about this while you were all sleeping. She says there is one of the roznoghs who was sent back to his people after entering Skye. He was close to you Mirrortac when you spoke the words, and just maybe, he will recall them. In any case I know a trick to make him recall the words ... anyone can do this, but I prefer it if I do it. We must find this one called Fervik as he will hold the key to the way. Ameece was not within earshot and did not recall anything when I tried her ... so Fervik is our only hope.'

Wa-ku turned to the screen again and zoomed in on the map of Skye. 'That is not the only problem,' he said, facing them once more. 'You must make your way through Skye and to the place in Skye called Wergaen ... but before you reach it, there is a fiery wasteland to cross. You cannot go on foot ... you must learn how to mind talk to the Tordwin … the spiny creature of the wasteland and allow it to swallow you up … cross the wastes … then spit you all out again.'

The erfins were aghast. 'Yuck! Eaten up by a monster! Treetam paled. 'Is there no other way?'

Wa-ku shook his head. 'I'm afraid Yidu has protected himself well. But he will not expect you this time. You will not be carrying a fragment of the Werdstone, but his chuffs … they are the bird ones … may be on the lookout. You must move with care. Surprise him.'

Mitac's face was a study in concentration as he prepared to speak again. 'If we should reach his palace, how are we to take him captive … will he not use his spells on us?'

'You must surprise him away from the Werdstone that is situated near his throne. One of the chuffs is on our side. It will be waiting for you at Wergaen. It is the one that gave Ameece access to the Werdstone so she could contact me. It is risky so I warn you that you must not be seen before the right moment. The solar-bites will still operate in Skye … but you must take care … the spell web is delicate and must not be broken. It can only be disengaged.' Wa-ku took another sip from his mug. 'And the chuff's name is Seventeen.'

Ezof laughed. 'The bird is named after a number?'

'Yes. The chuffs only are called by their number.'

TO CAPTURE YIDU

Ice crunched underfoot as the four erfins approached Erga. Ezof rubbed his hands to try to keep warm while puffs of mist issued out of his mouth. The others, likewise, were feeling the cold.

'What is all this cold white stuff?' Treetam asked, massaging her arms.

'Snow ... I do remember this,' Mirrortac answered. 'The child-fins love to play with it. You can roll it up ...' He picked up a handful of snow and scrunched it into a ball, then threw it at Treetam. She yelped as the ice splattered on her chest.

'Dada!' she grinned, bending down to make her own snowball.

'Take that bro!' She slung it at Ezof with all her might. It connected his head with a splat.

Soon they were all engaged in a full-on snow fight, their laughter echoing over the icy plain and to the holloks of Erga. Mirrortac took delight in the mock battle, landing a few in sensitive spots, but prompting more laughter and retaliation.

'Thanks dada! I am warm now!' Treetam grinned, brushing off ice crystals.

They stopped playing when they noticed some roznoghs emerging from the Erga hollok. All four heard the angry voice in their heads as they faced the stern-faced bearded roznogh. Although Wa-ku had tried to prepare them for mind communication, it still startled them, except Mirrortac who was calm despite having no memory of his time spent here.

'*What brings you here with your fellow demons, Mirrortac? Is naught stealing the Werdstone enough! You have dishonoured the Father of the Werd ... the Sky-master!*'

Mirrortac's forehead furrowed with thought. '*I am told that I know you, but I have no memory. I wish you naught ill, roznogh. One calling himself Wa-ku says he is kin to Yidu ... this Sky-master of yours ... He is but a man from the many tribes of men.*'

The roznogh marched towards them, clenching his fists and gritting his teeth.

Mitac now interjected. '*We only wish to speak with the one called Fervik. Can you hear my mind?*'

The roznogh stopped walking. '*Fervik? What do you wish with him? He be with his kin. I will naught allow it.*'

'*He holds the key to Skye. We will talk with him.*' Mitac pressed his lips together although he was not speaking. He looked the roznogh in the eye, emphasising that he meant business.

The roznogh shook his head and grunted. '*Who be you that you challenge the clan-master of Erga? I will call my hyfnuks to throw you to the wooils!*'

Treetam and Ezof observed the interchange with curious glances. They could hear the clan-master but not who must have been addressing him. All they knew that whatever Mitac or Mirrortac was telling him, the clan-master was taking great exception to it.

Mitac drew his solar-bite and pointed it away from the roznoghs and at a point in the snow some distance from everyone.

'Perhaps this will persuade you clan-master!' he shouted out loud, discarding the mind-speak.

He fired the solar-bite, creating a small explosion in the snow at the target point.

The clan-master gasped along with the female roznogh with him. They both hurried back towards the hollok, whining as they went.

'*We will send Fervik out to you,*' the clan-master cried.

Wa-ku's cosmo-ship was parked about 100 erfin-lengths away, its metal shining under the cold sun of Luma. It was some time before they detected any movement from the holloks, but finally Fervik ran out grinning, his now sharp eyes opening wide when he saw Mirrortac.

'*This be your family?*' Fervik asked. He ran up to the old erfin and hugged him. '*They told me I would never see you again. Where is the one of the Werd and her elders and Evarngar?*' He looked around eagerly.

Mirrortac smiled awkwardly. '*The tale is long in the telling ... and I am afeared I have forgotten it ... or you little one.*'

Fervik inclined his head and looked into the old erfin's eyes.

'*Yidu has taken your mind ...?*'

Mitac patted the young roznogh on the shoulder. '*He has no memory of his time here, Fervik. I am his child-fin Mitac, and these be my brother and sister Ezof and Treetam. We need your memory to return to Skye.*'

Fervik shivered. '*I still have bad dreams of that place. There be many demons living there. Do naught ask of me to return.*'

'*No need for you to return. All we need are the words that Mirrortac spoke to open the gateway to Skye.*'

The young roznogh's eyes were downcast as he thought hard.

'*I beg your patience. I have naught clear memory of the words. They be of another tongue.*'

'*Epna ... petro ... sha ... Skye,*' he recalled, brightening. '*Yea, Epna petro sha Skye,*' he repeated with confidence.

Mitac nodded, smiling. '*We are grateful to you, Fervik. These words may save many, including your people.*'

Fervik frowned, shaking his head. '*I know naught of this. It will send you to the madness of Skye. Is that a good thing?*' His question was more rhetorical.

Mitac saw the fear in the young roznogh's expression. '*We are sorry to cause a problem with your people. We will take our leave now.*'

Mitac nodded to the others and turned towards the cosmo-ship. 'We can go now. I have the words to open the way to Skye.'

Fervik bowed to them before running up to Mirrortac again and clutching him in a hug. The elder erfin shivered as a memory flashed through his mind, and he reached down and patted the roznogh with affection. '*I just now recall something of you, Fervik. You were blind and to be sent to your death in the numbing season of the White Veil. Something has saved you.*'

Fervik teared up, sinking his head into Mirrortac's chest. '*It was naught some thing. It was you who saved me.*'

Mirrortac raised a dark furry brow. '*I? How could it be?*'

Fervik sniffled. '*You called on a great spirit who gave you the power to take away the darkness. And after you said the blessing, I felt warm ... and I could see sparkles ... then my eyes were opened.*'

The triplets, who could hear the conversation in their minds, were astounded, although they had already witnessed their father's powerful magic. Mirrortac too was equally astounded, as he still had no memory of it. He could feel his child-fins' eyes appraising him with awe but felt embarrassed and at a loss.

He patted Fervik on the shoulder and looked around in preparation to leave. 'It be time for us to continue the mission that I be told is mine, but of which I know naught. Take care, youngling.'

Fervik let go of him and stood watching as they all returned to the cosmo-ship. His crooked smile and tear-filled eyes said more than words.

It took almost no time to travel the distance from Erga to the fir forest and high stone walls that marked the entrance to Skye. Swirls of mist floated up through the trees, wrapping their transparent cold fingers around moist branches. Wa-ku stayed with his ship again but left instructions for them to follow and provided them with solar-bites should they be forced to use them. The group of four erfins followed the rose quartz pathway, marveling at the pink lustre of the stone. Luma shone dimly through the rifts of curling mist, adding nothing to the chill in the air around them.

Treetam gasped with wide eyes and smiled as she noticed familiar forms moving about in trees up ahead of them. 'There are faugs here!' She suddenly leapt up a nearby tree and swung up into the branches with the deftness of a life lived among the tree-dwelling race. She looked behind her and down at her brothers. 'Come on!' she called.

Mitac put up his hand to forestall her. 'Do you not remember what your mother told you of these faugs? They are not friendly as our faugs.'

Ezof took no notice of his brother's warning and also shot up a tree, making quick progress up into the branches.

Mirrortac screwed up his face and frowned as he witnessed their ascent. Only Mitac stayed with him. 'You can climb these trees?' The elder erfin quizzed.

Mitac turned to him. 'We were born in the Faug Forest ... there are faugs here but you used your magic on them when they tried to stop you going into Skye.'

Mirrortac's eyebrows rose. 'Did I hurt them?' he asked with deepening concern.

'Nay. You simply set their arrows on fire.' Mitac's eyes glistened with mirth as he imagined the scene.

The elder erfin only frowned all the more. 'Great Mateote! I be a sorcerer!'

'A good one, dada ...' Mitac reassured him.

Any further talk was immediately cut short as their attention turned to a mass of grunting activity in the trees ahead where Treetam and Ezof had now encountered the faugs, who were armed with bows and were menacing the two erfins.

Treetam was trying to be friendly. 'Greetings faugs, from your brothers and sisters in the Faug Forest. We mean you no menace. Please lower your bows.'

One of the faugs was busily slapping his lips and snarling at them. 'More of these fools come to enter into madness. Now you want us to forget what the dark one did with his wizardry. You look the same as he, though your fur be grey.'

There was a commotion among the faugs who were retreating further up into the branches. They were all looking at Mirrortac. Then the faug who was speaking with them also saw the elder erfin.

'He is here? He returned? We did not see him come out of Skye! And his fur is even darker now.'

Treetam was amused at their reaction. 'Our dada? He will not hurt you.'

'But how is it that he is here when we saw him go into Skye?'

The leader faug was perplexed. He gaped at Mirrortac then at Treetam and Ezof.

'Wizardry! No-one has ever returned from Skye before.'

The faugs were all agitated and afraid. Treetam sighed. 'Yea, wizardry ... but not of our father's making. Yidu sent him to ... to ...' She couldn't finish. 'Never mind. It is beyond all of us.'

The leader inclined his head, musing over what was said. 'Perhaps it be best not to tell us any more. We do not wish to have anything to do with wizards! Go ... we will not stop you.'

Treetam opened her mouth to speak but the faug just shouted at her. 'Go! Leave us!'

The erfin hung her head in defeat. Ezof turned and was already making his way back to the ground when his sister faced the faug once more.

'You are not like the faugs I know. If you had come to them, they would welcome you.'

The leader scowled. 'If you were faugs, we would also welcome you. But you are pretenders ... and you keep company with a wizard.'

'They welcomed us ... erfins,' she shot back. 'And our father who you call wizard.'

The faug did not say another word. Instead he signaled to the others to retreat back into the forest where their grunts followed them until the erfins heard them no more.

Crestfallen, Treetam fretted as she accompanied the others into the canyon and the same stone wall that Mirrortac had entered some time ago. Ezof looked more disappointed than anything.

'We didn't get to use our solar-bites. I'd like to have seen those green fellas jump,' he quipped, but Treetam answered him with dagger eyes.

Mitac decided to be more diplomatic. 'I am glad; at least we did not have to fight them. They are faugs, after all, and kin to our kin. We are now free to enter Skye without challenge.'

Mirrortac nodded. 'Yeah, there be naught to gain in a fight with such beings. They can naught decide whether to fly or swing from their long arms.'

Ezof chuckled. 'Faugs glide ... they do not fly.'

Treetam was shaking her head. 'They stink. Do they not clean themselves ... they be most unlike our fellow faugs.'

Soon they were at the boulder that blocked the entrance to Skye, and it was time to mutter the words of maja. Mitac invoked the words, feeling at once a shift in his being. The boulder moved with a loud grinding noise, revealing a long staircase leading upwards. They all moved forward and up the stairs, but Mirrortac needed help as he was limping badly after only negotiating a dozen steps. The elder erfin grimaced with pain as he took each step, and it was a long 3000 steps before they finally stepped out into the strange surroundings of Skye. The young erfins were at once aware of the different light and temperature, which was more to their liking, except for the orchard that spread out before them towards the horizon.

Although Luma was still high in the sky, they decided to make camp and rest for a time to regain their strength and catch up on sleep. When they each awoke, it seemed little time had passed, when in fact it was an equivalent of a whole night. Feeling refreshed, they each had their fill of the many fruit that festooned the trees, and that were quickly replaced as soon as they were picked. They walked across the orchard as instructed, therefore traversing the puzzle of never-ending trees. When they reached the grove of bare trees, they were all overcome with a depressing atmosphere that filled them with morose thoughts of death and tragedy.

Treetam fell to the ground first, clutching her ears as had Daghva on the first journey through this land. She was screaming for the noise to stop when the other erfins also were likewise affected. Ezof drew his solar-bite and began zapping trees around him, but the noise did not stop. Mitac was in agony but was trying not to show it, while Mirrortac was walking around trying to uproot the trees. Mitac knew there was no Werdstone this time for anyone to use to evoke a quietening spell. There was just one thing they could do – RUN!

Mitac shouted at them all to run as fast as they could through the trees. He tugged at Mirrortac, who struggled to amble at a rolling gait, held back by a sore leg and an ache in his thigh. Ezof and Treetam ran ahead of them, blasting trees to the left and right of them as they made their mad dash for peace. New trees rose up from burnt out hulks, rattling and creaking with menace. Finally, they passed the last of the trees and silence descended upon them. Mirrortac rasped, gulping air, holding his heaving chest and half bent over with exhaustion. Mitac bid him sit down on the ground, which they all did.

'That was the easy part,' Mitac said. 'Worse to come yet.'

Ezof snarled back. 'Thanks! That is all I need to be reminded of just now, after having a horde of demons crying in my head.'

Treetam did not look too happy either, preferring to blank out any knowledge of what was to come.

When Mirrortac got his breath back, he looked around at the verdant country ahead, and his mood lifted. 'I know something of this ... it be as Eol. The grass is like that of nif-grass.'

Mitac nodded to his father. 'Nif-grass is like this?' he waved his arm towards the lush field of grass. 'I have never seen it.'

Treetam and Ezof looked up from where they squatted, seeming to see the countryside for the first time. It was not menacing or confusing like the orchard and dead-tree grove. It was more normalised, if anything in Skye could be described in such a way. There were bushy hedges, gentle hills, and gullies, from which nondescript birds and hordes of insects busily flitted and buzzed about. But Mitac remembered what Ameece told them about the cloud of insects that had attacked the party and killed one of the elders. It was only through the magic of the Werdstone that the rest were saved. He wished against all hope that this would not happen to them, but perhaps their solar-bites could suffice to ward off any such attack this time around.

'Be ready to draw your solar-bites,' he warned. 'The insects may group together at any time.'

Mirrortac casually walked over to a bush and snatched a bird out of the air. 'I remember this ...' he said, throwing the creature into his mouth to munch on it noisily before spitting out feathers.

The triplets, having witnessed this, could only exchange bewildered expressions and shrugs.

'How did you do that dada?' Ezof ventured.

Mirrortac winked back. 'It be a little trick I learnt somewhere.'

'Some trick!' Ezof said.

They had not gone far before the inevitable happened – a huge cloud of insects was massing on the hill behind them, preparing to swarm down. Mitac was quick to react, letting out a shout to the others. 'Insect attack coming!' He drew his solar-bite followed in rapid succession by his siblings. Three streams of burning light shot out at the cloud, exploding it into a ball of fire and smoke.

The insect swarm disintegrated, leaving behind a haze of putrid ash that rained down on the ground.

Treetam turned up her nose and sneezed. 'Sure does stink.'

Ezof let out a yell of triumph. 'Is that the worst you can send us, Yidu! Bring it on!'

Mitac was not so confident. There were still more challenges ahead, including dealing with Yidu himself. He was sure not to submit without using some of his spells on them. And he wasn't looking forward to returning to Thenigmas any time soon or being killed for that matter.

Despite Mitac's reservations, the days ahead brought no further hazards. In fact, the country retained a pleasant demeanor, providing ample food and water for them to go on, and no sign of the sacred chuffs or any of Yidu's spies. Mitac knew that most of the chuffs were still loyal to Yidu, and it was only some that had sided with

Ameece against him. They crossed several streams and camped under shady wide trees where the triplets preferred to sleep at night within their branches. Some things in the landscape occasionally prodded Mirrortac's memory, opening a small chink from his time before, but mostly he remained oblivious of who he had been. But, as in Ameece's retelling of Mirrortac's first journey, there came a time and a place when the green fields gave way to brown earth and stubby grasses, and the smell of something pungent in the air. Hot clouds issued up from what they already knew was a burning landscape ahead where the only way across was to be swallowed by a large spiny creature, then vomited out on the other side. None of them were looking forward to such a prospect. Mitac recalled the volcanic streams under the earth in Thenigmas, and the immense pain of the searing heat on his feet. He would not try such a thing with a plain many times larger and just as boiling hot.

They reached the plain of fire after making their last camp before their assault on Yidu's prime domain. They all gasped as they saw the Tordwin, already there as though expecting them. Mitac glanced sideways at Mirrortac who returned his stare quizzically. 'What?' was all the erfin could say. When Mitac looked away, a tiny smile crept across the elder's face.

Mirrortac led the small party towards the Tordwin, which appeared to be dozing at the side of the steaming plain. The triplets slowed their pace as they regarded the huge creature and the prospect of spending some time inside its belly. When the elder erfin reached the Tordwin, he inexplicably walked on past it, following the line of the plain boundary.

Mitac called out to him. 'Dada! Where are you going? Are we naught travelling within this beast?'

Mirrortac stopped and turned to face them. 'It will naught lead us to Yidu. We must be at his palace.'

'But the Tordwin ... the beast. That be the way,' Mitac frowned back.

'The Tordwin will take us to Wergaen ... we have naught need of Wergaen now. Come! Do you truly wish to be swallowed up in that thing?'

The triplets exchanged confused glances, hesitant to go any further.

Treetam let out a breath in relief. 'Not me. I'm with you, dada.'

Ezof nodded his agreement. 'Phew! Let's get at this Yidu!' he cried.

Mitac screwed up his mouth then shook his head in realisation.

'Way to go, dada. You remember now ... you know what to do ... your mission.'

Mirrortac had already started walking again, but he threw a backwards glance, grinning widely. 'I be proud of you my child-fins. We must capture Yidu first ... then we can gain Oashu.'

Ezof became most excited as he too realised that the great warrior of legend had returned. He bounced up to his father's side closely followed by his siblings who were now eager to join the fray.

Purpose had replaced confusion in the elder erfin's bearing as he stumbled onward, undaunted by his aged limbs. The Tordwin remained in a deep slumber while the small party moved along the boundary of fire. They passed mud pools that were bubbling and puffing super-heated steam while the horizon ahead appeared strangely to move nearer. After some thousands of erfin-lengths, they found themselves channeled into a narrow corridor of land, like a bridge suspended in space. Each side faded into a vague indistinct rim while ahead was a mesa that rose up from the land in steep cliffs. They had left behind the fiery plain, and all that grew or had life. They were walking on sand that sparkled and squelched underfoot.

In another few thousand footfalls they found themselves craning their necks up at a massive crystal array that reflected sharp glints of rainbow above the huge cliffs. Mirrortac squinted up at the palace and the seemingly insurmountable sheer rock parapets rising up before them.

'How are we going to get up that?' Ezof asked, and his brother and sister nodded agreement.

Mirrortac sat down under the cliff's shadow. 'We wait.'

The triplets exchanged crazy glances. 'Wait?' they chorused.

The elder made himself comfortable. He was obviously undaunted but was not letting on as to the solution to their problem.

'It will naught be long,' he said, adding to the mystery.

The young erfins decided they had no choice but to trust their father and sat down with him.

'Hungry?' he asked them.

'Yeah ...' Ezof hesitated.

Mirrortac suddenly revealed some fruit out of nowhere and shared it with them.

'Where ...' Treetam mused, now totally mystified.

'I remember everything now ... the magic, or whatever you may call it.' Mirrortac returned an innocent look but his eyes shone with mischief.

They looked back at him with amazement and awe. Here was the stuff of tall tales.

While they were still eating Mitac was the first to hear something in the air above, then a quick flap of wings. They all looked up to see the dangling legs of a large white bird creature descending towards them. The chuff betrayed no emotion as it slowed its descent, and with a final flap of wings, folded them in and came to ground on its gangly legs. The young erfins were about to reach for their solar-bites when Mirrortac rose and stayed them with his hand.

'There be naught to fear from this one,' he assured them. Then it spoke in their heads.

'*Be at peace furry ones. I am not as my brethren. I see how you all have been wronged. I am here to take you into the palace. But you must be careful ... arm yourselves against the chuffadon. My brethren will unite against you once they know of your presence.*'

Mirrortac stepped up towards the sacred chuff, who dwarfed him at twice his height. '*I will go first,*' he communicated simply.

'You must be prepared now,' he said, addressing the three. 'Yidu will naught yield without a fight. We must prevent him from going anywhere near the large stone on the post near his throne. His magic lies there, and it be very powerful.'

The elder's stern expression prompted a shiver of fear in Mitac and Treetam, but Ezof warmed to the challenge, his eyes wide with excitement.

The chuff approached Mirrortac from behind, using its wings to push him into its legs which it wrapped tightly around the erfin. With a noisy flutter of wings, it launched into the air, bringing with it Mirrortac aloft. It strained upwards bearing the weight of the erfin. The two soon ascended up the cliff face and disappeared beyond the crystal dome of the palace. In a short time, it returned and took each of the triplets in turn up towards the precipice of the dome where they all met standing high on the roof that was composed of jutting clusters of clear crystals. The chuff bowed towards them out of respect then walked up to a crystal cylinder where it entered an opening and slid out of sight into the palace below.

Mirrortac crept up to the opening but did not go in. Instead he squatted down and motioned for them all to approach.

'We must wait until the chuff gives me the signal to go down. We want to go in without being seen, if possible. But it be best if you are ready with your light weapons. We must move quickly to the throne ... Yidu is on his throne ... and it be short steps for him to reach the master Werdstone. We can naught allow that. Understand!'

The three nodded dumbly, each trying to prepare for an unknown and dangerous adversary.

They waited for some time, and waited some more, but it seemed they had been forgotten. Mirrortac was starting to look concerned as he paced around the entrance.

'Something be wrong. The signal should have come by now.'

The elder erfin stroked his bearded face. His fur was now almost black with white streaks starting to appear. But in fact, it was the deepest hue of blue. He placed a pawed hand on Mitac's shoulder. 'You follow me ... then Treetam and Ezof. We can naught wait any longer.'

Mirrortac took a breath and threw himself into the cylinder. Mitac immediately followed, along with the other two. The tube flushed them into a large antechamber and headlong into the chuff that had taken them up the cliff. Seventeen was lying at an awkward angle spread out on the floor. Its eyes were shut and a congealing stream of blood massed over its chest and across the floor.

'Weapons out!' Mirrortac whispered between gritted teeth.

A large column and a wall hid them from the palace proper. The four sidled up to the wall. Mitac, Ezof and Treetam drew out their solar-bites. Their ears strained for sound, but none came.

Mirrortac glanced back at them. 'Try not to think too loud.'

They inched forward along the wall behind him as Mirrortac poked his head out gingerly to a gap between the column and the wall. He could see a long empty hallway with no sign of any chuffs. Something wasn't right.

The elder erfin edged out from the column, exposing himself to the hall. He waved his hand to the others to follow.

The four crept into the hall, each one nervously searching the various columns for any sign of danger. Their fur bristled as they moved in short steps through the hallway, but no danger yet presented itself. Mirrortac stopped abruptly then pushed them all back against one of the columns. They then 'heard' the voice of Ameece within their minds.

'*Why be the chuffs gathering. We be found out!*'

They realised she was not addressing them. Mirrortac pushed his face close to the others. 'Don't answer her in your mind. Yidu will know. We face a grave danger. Be ready to fight!' he warned.

'*We can naught escape now ... the chuffs have killed Seventeen.*' Ameece's voice intoned.

Mirrortac moved them on towards the great hall while he swept his hand over the crystalline face of the wall.

'*The chuffs will be one ... one!*'

They were nearing the end of the hallway and would soon be in the great hall to face the chuffs. Shadows played on the floor at the entrance. They could hear them now – a mass fluttering of wings and croaking. The shadows flickered and played over the floor, coalescing into one monstrous unit. The four moved over the threshold and looked up in time to witness the spectacle. The sight made them gasp in horror.

In front of them stood not a large group of chuffs, but the last of them was merging into the group ... into a single monstrous form that transformed the gangly beings into something beyond their kin. White folded into white, then into red. Soft feathers transformed into scales. Beaks and legs disappeared. The creature stood on two enormous feet with claws as long as an erfin each. Its body towered up to the ceiling while its wingspan was too large to unfold in the already large dimensions of the great hall. A tough serpentine neck terminated in a head much like a gigantic lizard. Its huge jaw opened to expose a slithering forked tongue while steam issued out of its mouth. Its eyes shone a stark crimson with elongate pupils that fell upon the erfins with evil delight.

The floor shuddered as the huge beast stamped towards the entrance where the four stood frozen. It slammed down a long tail, spraying up shards of crystal dust. Then it opened its jaw wide, swung its head and roared so loudly that it made the erfins' ears ring, deafening them temporarily.

'Oh, Gakar's excreta!' Mirrortac proclaimed.

Ezof's lips quivered. 'Were Snerks ever this big, dada?'

'Nay. I have naught fought anything this big before ... save Beeble-Zub, and it was only half this size.'

The dragon snorted and started to suck in its breath in spasms.

Mirrortac looked alarmed. 'Move to behind the next column now!'

The three obeyed instantly, diving for the large column just out from the entrance. The dragon jerked as though it were about to vomit, but instead of stale food, it breathed out fire. Flames licked at the column while everything around them shuddered violently in the roar that followed.

The young erfins' faces paled. They felt the heat of the dragon's fiery breath as wisps curved around the smooth faces of the column. The stench of something burnt wafted into the air, along with steam and smoke.

Mirrortac inclined his head towards the next column.

'We must move there while the monster gathers its fire again.'

Already the dragon was sucking up another volley of fire.

'Now!' Mirrortac dashed across the floor until he reached another column.

The triplets followed in trepidation, but Ezof stopped in the middle, aimed his solar-bite and shot at the body of the dragon. The beam singed a scale but caused no injury. The dragon swung around towards him, preparing to retch flames again. Treetam snuck out quickly from behind the column and dragged him to safety. Ezof grimaced. 'I used full power! Why did it naught destroy it?'

The palace shuddered once more as another blast licked at the column they were hiding behind. This time the roar was louder than before, shaking some crystal pieces loose from the ceiling and sending them crashing to the floor.

'I think it be angry,' Mitac quipped.

Treetam pulled on Mirrortac's ear. 'How are we to defeat it? It cannot be hurt even by these great weapons.'

Mirrortac answered while keeping an eye on the rampaging dragon. 'We must find its weak spot. It must have one. Scaled flesh is too hard, but naught all be scale.'

Mitac looked thoughtful. 'Weak spot … keep it busy. I will go around.'

The four dashed towards another column as the dragon danced and snorted, sucking in more breath. Ezof looked his brother in the eye. 'You go muddle-eye. I will keep this flying snerk busy.'

Ezof jumped out from the column and began shooting randomly at the dragon. Beams bounced off scales and some struck at the soft hide near its belly, causing it to swing violently and snap wildly at the annoying stings. 'Don't like it you flying snerk!' he shouted.

Mitac took the opportunity to advance towards the back of the hall, keeping out of sight of the dragon as it struck out at the stinging shots that Ezof was pelting it with. Its temper was not improving. It slammed down its tail and strode out towards the young erfin who chastised it. Suddenly, it roared again, and crashed down its feet, causing Ezof to lose his footing and fall over. Its gleaming eyes spied him in a moment of helplessness, and it took the opportunity.

The dragon thundered across the floor, lowering its jaws down to snap up Ezof before he could get up again. Treetam raced out and shot several beams at its head, diverting its attention long enough for Ezof to scramble out of the way. Meanwhile Mitac was closing in on a jagged section of crystals that led from the floor to the ceiling. He swung up to grasp one after another, climbing as though he would a tree. The dragon sucked in breath then quickly flamed in an arc towards the two taunting erfins. Ezof leapt up in pain as he was hit with a passing tongue of superheated air. He clambered around a column and reached behind to massage burnt fur on his back. Treetam ducked in time for a flame to pass over her head, but she had only moments to run before another stream of fire shot across the floor, only a hair's breadth away from her feet as she made cover just in time.

Mitac reached the ceiling and hung closely over the half-outspread wings. The dragon was still occupied chasing Ezof and Treetam who had both sought shelter behind separate columns. Mirrortac was keeping an eye on Mitac but was saving his energy for the moment. He glanced up at the dragon and noticed what appeared to be a blue jewel on its forehead … but then it blinked. Mirrortac's raised a brow. He looked away from the dragon for a few moments to scan the hall, searching out the throne where Yidu should be seated. Why had he not said a word? Why had he not been standing at the Master Werdstone, gloating over his prize dragon as it sought to kill them all?

Mirrortac gestured for Treetam to come to him as Ezof again chose to taunt the dragon with more stinging beams. He whispered in her ear then sent her after Mitac to climb up to the ceiling. Mirrortac stepped out in plain view of the dragon. 'Here I am you stupid lizard,' he goaded. The dragon abruptly halted its attentions on Ezof and turned towards the elder erfin in recognition.

'That be right, lizard. You know me do you naught?'

The blue gem on its forehead blinked again as the monster licked its nose and grinned crazily at him.

'You sent this furball to Thenigmas where I be lost my mind. But here I be. Come and get me.'

A wisp of incomprehension floated across the depths of its eyes before the anger returned like a tsunami wiping all away before it. The monster leapt up with one sweep of its wings until its body crashed into the ceiling, sending a rain of sharp crystal shards all around. The great dragon lifted its head and spasmed in great gulps of air. Ezof cried out in pain as he withdrew a sharp piece of serrated crystal out of his shoulder. The dragon was testing its wings now, creating a swirling wind that ruffled their fur. Treetam was half way up the far wall while Mitac clung desperately to a cluster that was threatening to dislodge. Mirrortac withdrew to the relative safety of a nearby column, as did Ezof, but the dragon was really intimidated now.

Giant wings crashed into columns and walls as the dragon drew in its breath. Mirrortac saw cracks appear in the column as it began to yield to the might of the creature. 'Hurry Treetam,' he whispered to himself.

The whole palace quaked as the dragon roared long and hard, releasing a fireball that shot out at the column like a projectile. The flames crashed into the stone with a thud, blasting the column in half and sending its crushing weight falling towards the elder erfin. Ezof tried to cry out but his shouts were lost in the thunder of crashing columns and the roar of the dragon's full rage. At that moment, Treetam reached Mitac and gave him the message.

Mitac screamed. 'Yiiiiidu!'

The dragon checked in its rage and shifted its head, seeking out the source of the scream.

Mitac screamed again. 'Yiiiiiduuuu!'

The dragon's head lifted and angled back to spy the erfin now dangling upside down from the ceiling. Its blue third eye winked up in surprise.

It was just a moment ... a micro-moment of fear that reflected in the monster's eyes as it noticed, too late, that a sharp beam of light was aimed right at the centre of its third eye. The beam struck true, splintering the tiny pupil that wobbled within a tiny sea of blue iris. It was the weak spot.

The dragon trembled and became divided. Its pieces tumbled down in a rain of white feathers, beaks and dangling legs. And with the dead chuffs came the man – the demi-god who was Yidu – plunging to the floor with a flop. He was not dead, but his third eye was now disabled, his magic lost. He lay prostrate amid the bodies of his chuffs, groaning with despair.

Ezof trudged through the mess of chuff bodies towards Yidu as three hyfnuks appeared from a side hall. They ran up to the where Yidu lay as Ameece entered behind. 'Take him to the chamber and lock him in there,' she commanded as she rushed towards the litter of columns on the far side of the hall. Her guardian Evarngar emerged to regard the man as Daghva, Iyaji and Karn grabbed him and started dragging him across the floor. Evarngar sighed and shook his shaggy head but said nothing.

'Mama!' chorused Mitac and Treetam as they clambered down the wall.

'It is truly you mama?' Ezof queried, standing hesitant as Ameece walked past him.

'Yeah, my child-fins ... but where is my Mirrortac?' She searched the debris before spotting a dark furry leg beneath a column. 'Oh, my heart ... please be alive!'

The triplets all drew in a breath as their eyes fell on the form under the column. 'Oh dada!' Treetam shouted, holding back tears as she raced to Ameece's side.

A low moan issued out from under the column as the two females fussed, pulling at the debris and the column with all their strength. Ezof and Mitac soon joined in, along with Evarngar who shifted some of the heavier chunks of stone out of the way. 'Be careful! The stone will fall,' Ameece warned. Soon the other hyfnuks had returned and rushed to their aid, clearing the remaining debris, and lifting the main column piece off the elder erfin. Mirrortac winced as he moved from his side onto his back. Ameece leant down and nuzzled him. 'My child-fins have returned you from the Netherworld. Yidu is defeated ... he be no longer Sky-master of Yidrogh.'

The elder erfin's green eyes rested on the face of his beloved. He gave a crooked grin and searched the depths of her eyes for the she-erfin who was Yenic. 'I see you.'

Yidu's crystal palace was now a shambles. There were pieces of crystal all over the floors; columns lay at odd angles, broken and shattered, while parts of the walls and ceilings had holes torn out of them. Yidu was locked in a small chamber off one of the halls with Karn and Iyaji keeping guard. They could all hear him taunting them in their minds, warning them they will pay for violating the great Skyemaster. But nobody took any notice, even Evarngar, who now realised he was just a flesh and blood being like the rest of them. Much of the magical construct of Skye was gradually disintegrating, allowing them to roam without fear. Mirrortac and Ameece, along with the triplets, traversed the former plain of fire separating Skye from Wergaen without recourse to the Tordwin, as the plain had cooled sufficiently to make for safe walking.

Mirrortac limped up the stairs to the castle; its forlorn walls crumbling with each moment. The sun of Luma traveled much quicker now across the sky as time began to equalise. The turrets lurched at an odd angle, with tattered flags and disintegrating webs. Ameece was by his side as they again beheld the gate, with its portcullis rusted and broken. The five negotiated the metal obstacle with ease then moved into the central tower and up to the turret room where they had originally located Oashu. There in the floor it had been reinstated, but there was no challenge in removing it, as its edges were bordered all around with cracks.

Mirrortac lifted the stone out of its place and gave it to Ezof to hold. 'This be the first stone … Oashu,' he said, as the triplets beheld its rounded oval form. The stone was lustreless, yet its enigmatic design seemed to generate a great energy.

The troupe returned to the palace, which had been swept clean of debris, and the bodies of the chuffs thrown out over the cliffs. Wa-ku had beamed Darm into the palace, enabling them to connect it to Oashu. The curved edge of the second stone folded neatly into place on one side of Oashu, leaving one curve bare for the final stone. Wa-ku called them through the Werdstone, where they all saw his face again, magically broadcast into the depths of the huge stone sitting on its pedestal.

'I must take my brother with me to my people. There is no need to seek the final stone as Yidu no longer has power to enslave anyone anymore,' Wa-ku said.

Mirrortac glanced down at all the white fur which was now rapidly replacing the darker hue, then back at the Werdstone. 'Yea, the danger be gone for now.'

The image nodded, flinging his golden locks back. 'Bring my brother to the Werdstone. He must go before the high justice.' His face took on a stern expression.

Mirrortac motioned to the hyfnuks who marched back into a side hall and returned with Yidu who now seemed to be growing older before their eyes. When he saw his brother, Yidu snarled, struggling vainly against the strength of three hyfnuks.

'You think this is over Wa-ku … traitor! This is far from over!'

Wa-ku lifted an eyebrow. 'And what are you going to do, brother? I'm taking you away to the high justice. You can declare your case there. Then I will show them the evidence of your dark plans to enslave three planets. How you abused the Three Stones of Destiny and the wisdom of the Ancients for your own gain.'

Yidu lifted his head and pouted. 'You have forgotten, haven't you? You forgot about my great-great uncle who is sworn to return. He will smash the high justice … the fools! Then we will reign again … as supreme gods!'

Wa-ku chuckled. 'That old story. You are totally out of your mind, Yidu. You are finished. This is the reality.'

Yidu was about to speak again when Wa-ku operated some device in the cosmo-ship, creating a beam around the man who instantly vanished from their sight. They could hear Yidu now beyond the screen image on the cosmo-ship, still rambling about his great-great uncle.

Wa-ku winked at them and waved as his image left the Werdstone.

Mirrortac turned to Ameece. 'Rainbow of my heart. We have so much to discuss.'

EPILOGUE – NERTHULE

A ship wallowed in the waves as a crane lifted a submersible craft out of the sea the Nerthulians called by a name that translated to 'Middle Earth'. A man yelled out instructions as the submersible craft was swung back on board after its exploration to the seabed below. The submersible had metal arms and claws that were now attached to an oblong silver container covered in barnacles and a growth of marine algae and corals. Once settled on deck, the submersible opened, and two men stepped out, grinning from ear to ear. They were chattering with animated faces, eager to inspect their find.

Some of the stronger men on deck grabbed some sharp metal tools and began chipping away at the top of the silver box. Marine sludge, shells and other matter sloughed off the box, quickly revealing what was fast becoming an ornate silver sarcophagus. The men sweated over the box, searching out the gaps in the lid before chipping away the last impediments. The sarcophagus revealed itself to the warm rays of the sun for the first time in several thousand years. Its clear silver surface reflected brightly while men and women milled around it, fussing over it and recording its image with magical alien devices.

Then the moment came to lift off the lid. Five men heaved the heavy top and slid it to one side, revealing an interior that prompted gasps and wide eyes, and much chattering and snapping of images. As expected, inside there was a body of a man, but all anyone could see was an outline, as it was cocooned inside a translucent crystalline structure that had a smooth surface. It was as though the man had been placed in ice, only it was not ice. The group could see that he was perfectly preserved although he had been dead for many thousands of years. The head man instructed them to replace the lid, which was duly performed after another round of snapping and animated talk.

They noticed that the sarcophagus was no longer silver but changing hue, lightening. A woman jumped and retracted her hand from where it had been resting on the sarcophagus. She licked her fingers, indicating that she had been burnt. A medicine man came out with some cream in a pliable tube and spread it over her hand.

Others were snapping images of the colour change and stroking their chins in thought at this phenomenon. In minutes the sarcophagus had turned a bright gold, much to the delight of the researchers who wondered at what it all meant. Then the lid flew off and landed nearby, nearly injuring a man who was standing there.

Faces became grim but intrigued as the figure of a man rose up out of the sarcophagus and came to stand upright in front of the astounded crew. The man wore a long golden robe. He was tall with two shining blue eyes and a third golden eye in the centre of his forehead. On his head was a crown of gold with a circle of gold clasped above it. He did not smile but seemed to look through them as he scanned the ship, the sea and the surging aquamarine waters all around them. Everyone stood motionless for some time before some gathered their senses and began snapping images of the stranger who had returned from the dead. The head researcher tried questioning the man but received no answer. Instead, the man turned back towards the sarcophagus, placed his hand inside and promptly vanished into thin air.

Although the Nerthulians had become used to the art of illusion, this trick threw them into a heated debate over who this person was and had someone played a joke on them by planting this sarcophagus in the sea. Some marveled at the prospect of this being a god or some such person, while others dismissed it as an elaborate illusion. The believers argued that the sarcophagus could not have been planted there as it had marine encrustations, and nobody was known to survive so long to be almost randomly discovered amid the ruins of a city that had been submerged for thousands of years, and only recently come to light after an undersea earthquake pushed up the previously hidden structures. The cynics countered with a theory that another boat may have followed their expedition and gone down with the false sarcophagus just before the submersible surveyed that area. 'But where is the boat then?' argued a believer.

The argument continued as one of the men peered in the now empty sarcophagus. Eyebrows rose above spectacles on a face lined with wrinkles. Grey eyes perused the one object left behind – a roughly triangular shaped stone with a curious design. And inscribed at the head of the sarcophagus interior was the Egyptian symbol for the sun god, Ra.

ABOUT THE AUTHOR

Paul is a freelance editor, author and former journalist living in Mackay, on the central Queensland coast of Australia. He has had numerous articles published in newspapers and magazines, published three fantasy novels, had his stage play performed, and his poetry published in anthologies. He has produced two more books in this series – *The Wizard's Sword* and *The Gold Sarcophagus*.